CLERICAL ERRⱰR

More Than a Minor Mistake

By

Brian R. Dill

authorHOUSE™

1663 Liberty Drive, Suite 200
Bloomington, Indiana 47403
(800) 839-8640
www.AuthorHouse.com

© *2005 Brian R. Dill. All Rights Reserved.*

No part of this book may be reproduced, stored in a retrieval system, or transmitted by any means without the written permission of the author.

First published by AuthorHouse 01/13/05

ISBN: 1-4208-1107-X (sc)

Printed in the United States of America
Bloomington, Indiana

This book is printed on acid-free paper.

Acknowledgements

This novel was written over a period of ten years, under the trials of pain. It is therefore appropriate that I recognize the following individuals for assisting me in the completion of my work of fiction.

"Clerical Error" is dedicated to:

Rita, my beloved wife of forty years, ever encouraging me to complete this book, if for no other reason than personal satisfaction and enjoyment.

Doctor Thomas Norton, neurosurgeon and friend, who kept me alive by remarkable life and limb saving operations, so I could once again use the keyboard.

Doctor Larry Putnam, whose pain management skills offered me relief in dire circumstances,

My closest, childhood friend, Dennis Slind of Toronto, who was ever affirming about my work, as well as a ready editor, and, rightly or wrongly, one who convinced me this novel was worthy of publication.

For these people I give thanks to God, who has skilled me just enough to attempt publication, offered me ample opportunities for writing by virtue of my Pastoral Vocation, and drawn me to other people to deal with the issue of pain even as this book, slowly but surely, was being written.

Brian R. Dill, Pastor Emeritus

Chapter 1

The runaway heartbeats had continued for a full week. In thirty years of marriage, the Reverend Jerry Grant and his wife Jennifer had never felt such a wretched sense of foreboding as the present. There was no plausible reason for the gloom this day however. After all, they had every reason to hope for a benevolent meeting with the IRS agent who summoned them. A virtuous couple, they would easily validate the generous charitable contribution claim which Jenny had posted while preparing the previous year's 1040. Their tax history, as well as the church's official documentation now in hand, was surely adequate — or so they assumed. Still, some kind of foreboding clawed at the very soul of Jerry, a sensation quite foreign to him; and to a far lesser degree, such was true for his stunning wife, his soul mate and sweetheart since high school. In one short week that cloud of doom had grown more ominous, ever darker.

So one short block from Tucson's Federal building, the Reverend Grant found a tidy little parking niche shaded by a Palo Verde, Arizona's designated state tree. He backed in, deftly parking his trusty compact. Stepping out, he slammed shut his car door in frustration mode. Then, walking to the other side, he gently reached for Jenny's hand as she exited.

Jerry had striven to be as perfect a man and husband as possible. Few others ever worked harder than he did in aspiring to a goal so lofty. The years had presented opportunities to teach him godly issues like kindness and contentment and righteousness as life's dearest and most rewarding attributes. Fear and anger were rare flaws in his disposition. Now, with his stunning spouse of 30 years in hand, he led the trek, walking briskly toward their mutual destination. In one brief week this revered icon of true manhood had experienced a rapid decay in the fiber of his being — since the day of that <u>wretched</u> letter! Jerry never cursed out loud, but when necessary, let it all hang out in his mind.

Why such terror, such amplified horror, vexed the soul of this "maestro" of faith and integrity was mystifying to Jerry himself and terrified Jenny. With grievous dismay she had watched this cancer claw away at her husband's being — body, mind and soul, changing him into a veritable grinch. His abiding smile no longer adorned his face on a daily basis. His words had often become caustic, so far removed from the genteel parson of many years.

Jenny was aware of his sense of foreboding, but hardly to its full degree. The admired pastor just knew, somehow and in some way, that something was wrong with the present picture. You just don't get called into an IRS office for one small entry! His countenance, pale and anguished, now betrayed the beast within the soul of a once joyful and vigorous man.

This day however, Jerry and Jenny were wilting, pounding the hot pavement, avoiding any and all discussion about their pending interrogation by the IRS. Small potatoes given the subject matter! Still, this matter of normally little consequence was at the root of Jerry's transformation. The unspoken tension made it hotter. Their silences did little to bond or console them in this real or imagined crisis. Soon they reached the newest trademark of downtown Tucson, a stately, modernistic towering octagon building which housed all things Federal, from courts to INS and IRS and many other branches of government's upper echelon which filtered down to the lives of desert citizens. Downtown was not exactly a renewal project, but a tidy maze of buildings most of which were government related.

The command post of the Internal Revenue service was prominently located on the 6th floor of this Federal facility, one swarming with humanity. The office number in fact reflected what many believed to be a satanic symbol — Suite 666. Masses walked the hallways seeking directions to the various courts or offices, bumping into one another while pondering their personal concerns and worries.

Much the same would be expected in the IRS office. But as this married couple of 30 years entered the Suite, a deafening silence and solitude mystified them. One always pictured such an infamous locale as a snake pit, crawling with anxious persons and defensive taxpayers, a nail-biter's haven. Yet here they were all alone, save for a single woman sitting behind her oversized receptionist's desk. The office furnishing consisted of a vinyl corner couch beside which was a magazine rack filled with Income Tax pamphlets and forms. The lighting was incomplete, overhead fluorescent racks not yet fully filled with the appropriate tubes. Of those that were installed, a couple flickered with annoying regularity. It was a scene hardly befitting a prestigious government agency as this.

Yet the true issue behind the scenes was still to be revealed. By the same token, the small and modest nature of such a Federal office betrayed its stated purpose. The task of auditing tax forms surely mandated more than one or two apparently small offices down the hallway of this singular tiny office. As such, Jerry Grant grew more dismayed, certain now that he was not there for a line item review of his tax form.

The couple had dressed for the occasion. Casual but very tidy clothing adorned them. Jerry was seldom one to wear a tie and Arizona men virtually had relegated them to the dark ages. Nor would he do so for this occasion; but as he was dressed, it did professionalize his presence and detract from his nervousness. Jenny wanted to hold hands, but Jerry kept pulling away and looking out the window. He wished now that he could be cooling down somewhere near Windy Point, a monument to nature's carving about milepost 16 up the Mt. Lemmon highway. This is where people stopped to see their city spread out over the light green adornment of the desert and the fine sand. There was life in the desert; plant and animal life. From up on high it was a stunning vista.

Behind her appointed desk the lone receptionist sat face down with eyes up over her glasses. She reminded Jerry of a disgruntled school marm he had once endured. Barely visible save for the hair bun, she elevated her neck and, with little ado, pointed to the sole corner sofa where the couple was obviously to be seated. 'Course they set their minds on a lengthy wait, even though they were quite alone. Whoever heard of an on-time appointment with any agency? Doctors and dentists had no monopoly on wait time.

Yet, and quite immediately, the receptionist broke the silence by informing them, "Mister Clinton will be right with you." There was no eye contact as she spoke, but she was right about the timing. As though out of nowhere a short and thin man appeared around a hallway corner. He was loud to be sure, but hardly obtrusive. "Reverend Grant, I presume?" "I'm Andrew Clinton." The auditor did not offer a handshake. Jerry noticed it was still well before 10 AM. It seemed unusual to have an appointment start ahead of time, let alone close to the designated hour.

"Yes sir, I'm Jerry Grant. And this is Jenny."

"Please join me in my office," Clinton invited, pointing down the corridor. "Quickly now."

Jerry looked at Jenny and offered his hand. "Come on honey. Let's go and talk with the gentleman." Jenny began to stand, reaching for Jerry's extended hand.

Andrew Clinton interrupted with a snappy remark. "Reverend Grant. I've been instructed to meet with you in private. Your wife will have to wait here." His voice was now somewhat gruff. He was, to be sure, in quite a hurry.

"But we file a joint return," Jerry protested; now slowly shuffling toward the auditor while pointing back to his spouse. "She has every right to be in on the audit." Of course he was technically correct, but the remark only aggravated his own tormented spirit regarding the nature of the visit. He had developed some strange feelings about the true purpose of this meeting, but knew not their origins.

Becoming impatient, Clinton advised, "I'm aware of your status," now gazing at Jenny. "But I just need to see your husband alone."

"It's okay, Hon," Jerry assured her. "Give me the receipts. I'll see the man and be out in a minute." That response caught the attention of the auditor. Andrew Clinton rolled his eyes when Jerry made that pledge, as though to indicate this was no short order appointment.

"But Jerry", Jenny now whispered loudly enough to be heard by Clinton yet politely enough to avoid confrontation, "We do have a right to be audited together. This is a community property state."

Clinton became confrontational, answering in his gruff and now staccato voice, "This - is - not - an - audit! If you read the letter you know it's a line item review and not a general audit. So what's the big deal?"

Jenny acceded to Jerry's prompting as he whispered, "stop the bantering." But she needed one more lick, quietly pleading and avoiding eye contact with Clinton, "Jerry, anytime anything is reviewed it's an audit. This man isn't going by the rules." She was firm in her contention. Now Jerry perceived that his wife had some ominous feeling in her mind, just as he did. It could not be rightly identified. Just a tight gut reaction. Still, Jenny Grant was hardly as apprehensive as her normally collected husband. If ever there was a positive and courteous man it was this tall, stately churchman who, next to auditor Clinton, towered like a lineman football player beside a puny TV announcer.

Clinton cut in yet again! Scowling at Jenny he cursed in a louder tone, "Listen lady, this is only a review of your charitable contributions claim. I've been ordered by my superiors to see your husband alone. I don't make the rules lady, but by all that's right I'm going to do what I get paid to do. Follow them!" He began his trek back to the office.

"Hey, friend," Jerry affirmed, "with all due respect I'll have no person — IRS included — talk to my wife like that. I'm the one who wanted her present, okay? Please watch what you say to her and how you say it." He was firm, and a dead calm ensued. There was no apology offered.

"After you Reverend Grant," the man ordered. He placed a sarcastic emphasis on the "Reverend" part.

Jerry looked compassionately at Jenny, tears now adorning her flushed face. He moved back to her chair, took her gently by the shoulders and admonished, "Let's just do what the man wants, love. You sit tight and remember this; I <u>will</u> be right out." He kissed her moistened cheek and wiped the tears with his hand. With that she relented, and, after a warm embrace, the two parted. Jerry sported a doomsday look, but then returned to where Clinton was standing, now tapping his toes as if disgusted with the delay.

"In here" snorted the aggravated auditor. The slam of the door jolted Jenny in the waiting room. How could she possibly relax? This whole matter just wasn't going down the way it was supposed to.

Jerry and the auditor disappeared into a small office. It was rather dilapidated and uncomfortably small. He deemed it an interrogation cell more than an office. His mind was begging for answers. "Why were he and Jenny the only people there? Why the brash outburst when Jenny requested her inclusion?" But, regaining his composure, Jerry entered the office all the way with a now confident stride, albeit a put-on, and sat where visitors would obviously be seated.

"Please, have a chair, Reverend Grant," Clinton motioned in a now more subdued tone, albeit after the fact. Whatever burr had been under his saddle now seemed extracted. "Coffee, coke, iced tea, water?" he asked — now politely.

"Yes thanks. "A cold coke if you have it. I take my caffeine chilled." Jerry had long practiced the notion that honey attracted more bees than vinegar. Experience had taught him the rewards of kindness, remembering the proverb, "A soft answer turns away wrath."

"Perhaps we can get on with this, Mister Clinton," he suggested politely. Jerry was feigning a calm attitude.

The stage was set. Each combatant exuded confidence, and in their pre-interview chit-chat, were posturing their tones like two boxers feeling each other out in the early rounds. With that unspoken event, Clinton placed on the desk what was obviously the tax return in question. Jerry scanned it.

"Do you have the receipts to verify your charitable contributions claim?" Clinton asked.

"I do," came the affirmation." It's from our church recording secretary and it tallies with our claim."

"Presumptuous man I see," the auditor retorted. That's for me to determine." His brow was wrinkled. There was no eye contact. Clinton stood, staring at the form for what seemed an eternity. Then he cleared his throat to speak. "This doesn't add up by my arithmetic." His glance was still downward; his voice a bit stammering with the opening remarks.

"There seems to be a discrepancy, Reverend Grant. You claim a church gift deduction of $30,700. Your receipts tally to $3070.00. Can you explain the differential?"

Jerry was taken aback! Shaking his head in dissent, he spoke directly, but softly now. "Sir, I did not claim thirty thousand dollars. If you'll look at the form again, I'm sure you'll see that."

With a simple nod, Andrew Clinton agreed to look again. He sought the line item a second time. Turning the paper for Jerry to review he spoke, "Here it is, Reverend. 'Charitable contributions, House of Worship, $30,700.'"

Reverend Grant snatched the form unhindered by his auditor and mystified at what he saw. But there it was, in vivid black and white. $30,700. "Mister Clinton," Jerry said, still soft-spoken, "The day we got your letter we checked our form and it matched what our receipts totaled. We claimed $3070, not $30,700. My gosh, that would be most of my annual salary."

"Maybe it's on your form at home," came the response. "But not on this one which you submitted to us. This, dear Reverend, is the legal, signed, form by which we ascertain correctness or error or, or — fraud."

Jerry paused a moment, confused, but still calculating. "Your form is a copy of the original we have at the house. Our return says exactly what I told you it says," he professed.

"So I suppose you conveniently didn't bring it with you?"

"Of course not sir." Jerry was still speaking softly. "Your instructions were for us to bring documentation of our charitable donations. So that's what we did. We brought the form our recording church secretary fills out."

"Reverend Grant," Clinton continued, "You can see for yourself they don't match! You got a deal going with this recording secretary? Or more than a deal?" That was a low blow at which Jerry could have become explosive. He chose to ignore the taunt!

"I can't believe that's possible," he added. The rest of the form is based on that claim, and it all adds up." It seemed the room was closing in on Jerry. He was most bewildered. "I think I know what might have happened, Mister Clinton."

"Just what might that be Oh Reverend one?" Now Jerry felt angered! Yet he seemed unsure of what to say next.

Jerry began, "Maybe Jenny," — he started over, "Maybe I simply misplaced the decimal or accidentally added a zero. So it came out looking like $30,700 instead of $3070. It's quite possible I did that and didn't even notice." Jerry didn't really believe himself. He was buying time to think this whole thing through. A pause ensued and Jerry continued, "You can't really believe I'd claim a deduction almost the exact equivalent of my annual salary, can you?"

"It's amazing what people will try to get away with," Clinton asserted. "But what matters is the form we got. This — this what we got here — is the original. That's for the record."

Jerry now felt the finger of accusation more intensely. He needed to know if his feeling was right. "I am deeply offended by your implication. I am neither a cheat nor a thief."

"Reverend, this is no implication."

Here it came! The auditor's eyes rose to meet Jerry's. "Do you know the penalty for intentional tax fraud in this country?" he inquired.

"There's no intentional tax fraud and you know it," Jerry insisted, firmly slamming the tax form onto the table top. "There might be a simple mistake, but even that is highly unlikely. I'd be out of my mind to try pulling a stunt like that."

Jerry's gut was even tighter now. This was not about a tax deduction. He sensed it. He felt the piercing glow of Clinton's gaze. A Goliath called the IRS was wielding a mighty weapon over Jerry Grant's head. For what, he knew not! Round one was going in favor of the opposition.

Considering the accusation once more Jerry then stood up erect and demanded, "Okay, what's the real issue at hand? What's really up, because it sure is not a tax matter? I want my wife to know the answer. Get her in here!"

"That won't be possible," Clinton advised. "Mrs. Grant has been driven home by one of our people."

Now Jerry was beyond containment. "What the heck for," he bellowed. "You people are taking a few too many liberties for my liking - and hang your authority. You are a servant, not a master, sir!"

"Tsk, tsk," Clinton cautioned, shaking his index finger like a Marine drill sergeant. "Such an outburst from a man of the cloth. I thought you people were supposed to be soft and gentle?"

"A simple matter of justifiable anger," Jerry snapped back. "You accuse me of being a cheat; you take my wife away, against her will. What in God's name did you tell her was happening?"

"Just that the interview process had run into a few snags. Oh, she's feisty all right. Put up a real fuss about going home." Jerry stood very tall!

"Mister Clinton, hurt me and I can turn the other cheek. Hurt somebody I love, and God help you because no one else on earth ever will."

Jerry sat back down, no less angered about it all. He felt a need to back off for a minute - to take stock of his emotions. Seldom had this man of temperance experienced such anger in his life as he now felt! He sensed again, this time more strongly, that something awesome, perhaps terrifying, was in the air; and he wasn't convinced it had anything to do with income tax. Knowing it was a chancy thing to say, but that it needed saying, Jerry asked, "What is it you really want from me?"

The reply was rapid: "A confession of tax evasion.

That's all!" Then it continued with barely a pause: "Well, there is another option," he heard the auditor say. "We could report this as a simple clerical error - no pun intended on your profession, Rev. Grant. But not a bad pun if I do say."

Jerry raised his eyebrows, as if eliciting more information. "Another option! Like what?" he muttered.

"Wait right here a minute," Clinton barked. "There's somebody else who wants to see you. For the record, I was just here to help you understand the issue is not at all about taxes sir. I didn't especially appreciate the job I was ordered to do!" Auditor Clinton left the room with a slam-bang of the door and Jerry was alone. "Now what," he thought. "The top IRS brass in the Treasury Department?"

The thought echoed in his mind, "This is not about taxes! Someone has intentionally altered the form? That was blatantly evident. Graphic experts could do almost anything they wanted. Clinton had mentioned another option! "What kind" Jerry pondered.

Amidst the stuff of the day, a low, rumbling voice interrupted his disturbing thoughts. Jerry dared raise his head to see who or what was now entering the office.

Chapter 2

"Reverend Grant, my name is Carl Blackwell." A big, strong man with dark slicked black hair 50's style was now hovering over him. He extended a welcome handshake but Jerry ignored him, a mistake he immediately regretted. He was still living by the sword so to speak. Jerry himself was well built, in stature measuring six-feet, four-inches. Yet his new adversary stood slightly taller. A cigarette, now half ashes, was trailing pungent smoke from the side of his mouth where it dangled. As he began talking he sounded like a car salesman, smooth tongue to match his hair. "Understand you're upset by the little matter at hand"?

"Little matter?" snickered Jerry. "Why should I be upset over this little matter?"

Blackwell began to explain. "Let me…."

"Upset," Jerry interrupted. "I'm accused of fraud, my wife is whisked away, and I'm asked to make a confession?"

This was hardly the Jerry Grant everyone admired. Far from it! It was a Mr. Hyde that no one knew. Not even Jerry!

He had spent his entire life building within himself time-honored virtues, yet his vicarious emotion allowed him to understand those to whom he pastored and those with whom he had other relationships in life. Jerry wanted people to feel good when they talked to him. He made an effort toward pleasantry in every situation, a manner to instill and invite confidence both in his church membership and in the other relationships of life. Those who spoke to him knew he was listening with his heart. Such a ready ear was much needed in a society which had evolved into singularity and isolationism — the "I'll do it my way" syndrome of modern America. He held forth the need for courtesy, individual responsibility and "going the extra mile" without concern for reward or recognition.

As such, the good Reverend had evolved into a reputed confidante and father confessor among his flock and within his community. Jerry Grant loved human beings, all the more so in their times of trial but no less in their times of joy. His interest in the lives of others was genuine, not a mere convenient facade that came with the territory. It did not matter whether people had ever set foot in a house of worship. Jerry's vocation was guiding as a pastor, the word for shepherd.

From the pulpit he preached to people, but never did he preach at them. But now the chips were down, and to walk the way he talked was becoming a tug of war with his Mr. Hyde. The good guy was losing, both verbally and in body language.

It was in that anger mode Jerry continued: "Nooooo — why should I be upset? Course I'm upset," he professed.

"Whoa man, there is a simple solution to all of this," Blackwell advised. "I've heard it," Jerry retorted. "Confess to fraud."

With a hint of veracity in his voice Blackwell then suggested, "No, not at all. We can write this whole matter off as a clerical error if you wish."

"I don't find that pun amusing," Jerry interrupted! "Your associate had the same idea. So if it's an alternative, then why not just do it. I didn't do anything wrong and you know I didn't." Jerry squinted his eyes as if to emphasize his point. "Can't you see how easy it would be for a decimal point to be misplaced one way or the other? As you say, it's a simple clerical error! Happens all the time, right? Why do you people want to make it into a Federal case?"

Jerry was still digging for the real purpose of his visit there. He knew now with even greater conviction that this meeting was not a matter of taxes.

Blackwell nodded his assent. "I can see your point, Reverend Grant. I can even believe it. Problem is, I still have to present you with a serious alternative; a way to make sure it'll go on record as a clerical error. Call it an option if you will, it's up to you."

"What might that option be," Jerry asked, preparing himself for the next shock wave.

"If you will agree to make a goodwill trip on behalf of the United States government, this whole thing will be shelved as a clerical error."

The silence was deafening. Finally, Jerry broke through it. "A trip? On behalf of the US government? I'm not even a citizen." He leaned forward, body language begging for more information with his eyes immovably focused on this new man.

"Oh, we know that," Blackwell chuckled. "That's why we chose you. Hey man, we know everything about you! We know you're an athlete; a biker, a hiker. We know you're clean as a whistle, morally. We know you can fly a two engine prop plane. We know you're a superb biker!! Oh, guess I said that! Name it and we know it."

"So what's with all this nonsense?"

Blackwell didn't respond. He just waited for Jerry to make the next move.

"Did you ever think to come and ask me," Jerry continued.

"Not that simple."

I'm all ears," Jerry prompted.

"You're a personal friend of a Richard Green, aren't you?"

"Rick Green - from Calgary? Yes, Rick was a member of my church there, and a personal friend as well. What's he got to do with anything here?" Jerry feigned a stretch, but in actuality he was readying himself for the next counterpunch.

"Richard Green is a member of the Canadian Parliament, is he not?"

"Yes, but…"

Blackwell kept talking, head down and deep in thought as he continued. "Richard Green is a respected member of a special division of Environment Canada? He serves on the national water and power commission, doesn't he?"

"That's not something I know about. And I'm not really sure I want to talk any more. Am I free to leave or not?"

Nothing was said, so the answer was clear. Jerry sat back down as if to clam up. Clam up he did, so Blackwell did the chattering. "Oh indeed, Mister Green is all those things," Blackwell affirmed. "And very knowledgeable about certain matters of dire importance to us."

Jerry squinted and asked, "How do you know all this, and what does it have to do with my tax problems?"

"It's my job to know," came an aggressive response. "Can I be straight with you, Reverend?"

"Lord, what a refreshing prospect. Do clue me in."

Now Jerry's curiosity was more dominant than his anxiety. He had a headache and a stomach ache, but he wouldn't let Carl Blackwell know it.

"Reverend Grant, I am not with the IRS. I'm a special field operative with the Central Intelligence Agency. Our government needs some vital information from the Canadian leaders. Your friend Richard Green can give us that kind of info." Blackwell sounded almost sincere.

"So, ask him," Jerry suggested.

"Can't! Lot's of history down the wash on this thing. We have to get the information some other way."

Jerry froze with fear. He felt a flush come over him.

"Are you asking me to do something clandestine, to pump a friend for secret information — and then tell you people what he said? You're crazy."

"You're catching on," Blackwell nodded, "but it's not clandestine. You're here as a landed immigrant and we're asking you a favor on behalf of the country you chose to live and work in."

"Not clandestine! Then what would you call it?"

"I'd say it's a matter of survival. It's - well - a matter of urgent national concern." Blackwell paused to light up another coffin nail. Those Yankee cigarettes had always been repugnant to Jerry. He waived his hands to show his displeasure, pushing the smoke around. Blackwell ignored it.

"Carry on, Mister Blackwell. I thought we were getting on the straight and narrow."

Out of the blue Blackwell let go a loud fart. Without hesitation Jerry thanked him for clearing up the odor of smoke. But Blackwell continued: "We would like you to take a vacation and visit your friend in Calgary." He flicked the ashes on the floor, and took another drag. "Parliament is in summer recess, so he's home now. Go visit him and find out a few things for us."

"How do I explain my sudden urge to visit him? What about Jenny? Does she get to come along?"

"That's two questions, dear sir." As for the latter, no! Jenny stays here. She serves as collateral for your return with the information we want."

"Would you tell me already what information you want? You said you'd lay the cards out face up. So call or fold."

Blackwell took the cigarette out of his mouth and pointed a shaking finger at Jerry. "Look, alien! I'll tell you what I want when I want to. So shut up and listen to me. We want you to visit Richard Green in Calgary, okay? Am I going too fast? And everything will be on a need-to-know basis."

Jerry began tapping his fingers on the table, more to bug Blackwell than out of nervousness. It was a defiant mood.

We want you to ask Richard Green about NAWAP. That's spelled N-A-W-A-P."

"What is that?" Jerry queried.

"It's an acronym for North American Water and Power. Richard Green serves on the committee which oversees the fresh water supply of the Canadian Northwest and Western mountain regions. NAWAP was a project initiated, oh, back in the mid 70's, I guess. Canada, Mexico and the U.S. were researching the fresh water question on a continental basis. All the governments agreed it was more a continental problem than a national one."

Jerry broke in, "so if you're working together, what's the problem?"

Well," Blackwell tapped his ashes on the floor again, "the Canucks pulled out; dropped the matter like a hot potato. Seems they accused us - Uncle Sam that is - of calling all the shots. It got to be quite a shouting match. Seems your people figured we were telling you how to manage your water supply. But now we have reason to believe that the issue has been resurrected - only just by the Canadians. And top secret at that. They're shutting us out of everything."

"Can't the U.S. do its own research? Spies, satellites?"

"Again, not so simple. Water resources are indeed a continental concern, not just a national one. Your home and native land is being pretty greedy."

"Why not just ask to be included?"

"Did! Turned us down flat!" Blackwell retorted angrily.

"Then why blackmail me. I have no say in the issue," Jerry protested. "Cause you're here - like the proverbial mountain. We want you to ask your friend if NAWAP has been resurrected. Born again in your jargon, preacher. We need to know if the fresh water supplies of Alberta and B.C. are being guarded militarily, or if they're being guarded at all."

"Like I said, can't your spy satellites pick that up?"

"Too many mountains with too many crevices!"

"What makes you think I can find out or that I'll even try?" Jerry was now engaged in a staring match with the agent.

"Because of the other option," he said matter-of-factly. "As for your first question, that's simple," Blackwell continued. "You can simply tell your friend the doctor ordered a week's rest. You know, nerves or something. Actually, your assignment is to be creative. We trust you can do that. So tell him you got bad nerves and were ordered to take a rest and get away from it all. Sounds simple, no?"

"You serious?" Jerry said. "I've never been troubled with bad nerves."

"Well then, be creative. Just say you needed a rest and you chose to spend some time in Calgary. Maybe a little golfing or skiing on the side at Banff. We know you do ski. Tell him you'd like to spend a few nights with him — to resurrect an old friendship. Get close to him. We know you were close to him when you lived there. These government people sometimes like to spout off about their pet projects, secret or not. Most of the time they spill more beans than they realize. So, just listen, and when you come back, tell us what you were told voluntarily. You might not even have to do that if we can record from his home. Like I said, be a little creative, Reverend."

Jerry glared back. "What if I just get up and walk right out of this whole mess, like right now? What if I tell you you're crazy and I won't be a part of a spying deal? What do you have in mind for me then? Deportation? I guess that's not a bad option at this point!"

"Then, dear Reverend, dear respected Reverend, if you refuse the Marshall outside the door will arrest you and confine you and take you to tax court. Believe me, you'll come out a loser. The good boys here at IRS are lending full support."

Jerry's heart was now stationed in his throat. He fought off the anxiety about to overwhelm him. The facts were simple. He was being blackmailed to do something for the CIA. No, make that something against his own country.

"Well, I guess the horror stories about you guys are all true. You're no different from any other country you like to condemn. You do the same things they do. You're going to get what you want and let decency take the hindmost? Here ends the sermon."

"That depends on one's perspective, Reverend." Blackwell was getting impatient. "We're thinking about our national interest — our people's interest. We need Canadian water to survive and the Canadians won't come to the table. We have to consider long range plans for our water supply. See, in fifteen years, our own water won't be good for nothin', what with the effluent and the radon gas and all the other junk. And you know the Colorado river project water sucks."

"So stop blowing off bombs in Nevada."

Blackwell didn't react to the comment. "So you see, it really does matter to our nation. We need Canadian water, and the Canadians won't strike an agreement, or even talk to us. We have options we don't really want to use."

"You really think I'll be the tattle tale? Sorry Blackwell. I'm a patriot in my own right too. You think you have a monopoly on national pride. Ha!

Get someone else. I'll take the tax fraud charge. And I'll win it: 'Cause I'm going to tell everything like it happened here this morning."

"I don't think you want to do that," Blackwell added. "We have the trump card. Your wife is in protective custody, at home mind you, but still in custody."

"So it's come down to more blackmail, has it? First my tax form, and now my wife. Now it's my wife or my country. Quite a choice."

Blackwell had no reply to the last statement. He glanced at his watch. "We have a plane to catch in ninety minutes. Conveniently we just happen to have a suitcase full of your clothes and personal effects. We have a wallet filled with cash and a Visa Card. We want you to have a good time and we'll pick up the tab. Virtually no limit on the credit card. Don't go crazy though. Agreed?"

Jerry turned his head and then turned up his nose in utter disgust.

"Hey, we're picking up the tab, my good man. You leave here on America West and get back a week from today. I'll be taking you to the airport and we'll share information en route. Then, it's life as usual. The whole tax case will be written off as, well, that you know by now."

"Clerical error," Jerry spoke deliberately. "Pretty massive clerical error that I ever moved here. Did you people get me here to start with?"

"Don't get philosophical on us now, brother!"

"Philosophy has nothing to do with it. I still have to answer to God."

"Oh, I see; a big martyr complex. A spiritual dilemma, is it now?"

Jerry didn't reply. "Well, you're good at handling things like that for other people, aren't you Reverend Grant? How's the saying go? 'Physician, heal thyself'"!

"Something like that," Jerry sighed.

"Okay then, let's make our move. And a week from today you can get on with your life. It'll be like nothing ever happened. Hell, we're sure not going to blow the whistle on you. That would be defeating our purpose."

"Yeah", Jerry said, resigning himself to it for the moment. I know you have all the bases covered."

Blackwell left the room, pledging to return in ten. Jerry was still pondering the nightmare, wondering if and when he would wake up. "God, don't let this be real: Please God". Five minutes passed by. Jerry recalled most vividly a day, one week ago, when all this began. June 30th. All was going as expected. Strangely, Jerry was in love with the desert heat. Most Tucsonans despised it and anticipated "sweater weather", especially so, Fall and early Spring. So till the Postal Service arrived, that had had been an ordinary day with an extraordinary outcome.

Chapter 3

Jerry began to contemplate another life, a life that happened before June 30th. He did it by considering the facts and noting them on a scratch pad—highlights of that fateful day. He began a step by step recounting of the former week, starting with the day the letter arrived. It had in fact begun as a normally great day.

The morning bike ride invigorated both Jerry and Jenny and now it was cool down time in the breakfast Lanai. A slush of cold orange juice – that special concoction of Jenny's making — would initiate the healthy breakfast as planned. After all, an early morning workout in the summer desert mandated a 6 AM beginning. By the end of the 75 minute ride it would be dangerously hot and even counter productive to carry on.

Suddenly, the tranquility of their respite was interrupted by the ring of the doorbell and a shouted inquiry . "Rev. Grant" the mailman hailed, "Got a letter that needs your signature. Certified mail."

Jerry rose to the occasion — literally. His stately frame topped by a dignified capping of snow white hair ambled, juice glass in hand, to the front door. "Hi Rob, what's up" he queried of their longtime postman?

"Who knows?" Rob responded. "Maybe it's your lucky day." Handing the signature pad to Jerry, Rob nodded for him to sign on the dotted line.

Certified mail was always a curious matter. And though no stranger to it, the Reverend Jerry Grant managed some mental gymnastics when asked to sign on this one. The mailman's forehead was raised and wrinkled, knowing of course the source of the letter and perhaps awaiting a visible reaction.

So while entertaining a flurry of thoughts about the envelope, Pastor Grant thanked the postman and engaged him in conversation. He was offered and accepted a glass of orange slush, making no bones about his thirst as he chugalugged it in one fell swoop. By addressing Rob on a first name basis Jerry was being consistent with his very nature of endearing people to himself. Nor would Jerry rush his verbal intercourse. That was why, for the most part, the distressed of his church felt at ease when they talked to him. Pastor Jerry called this aspect of his ministry a way to "happy up the world."

After the pleasantries of the morning, mailman Rob smiled, poured a second glass of slush down his gullet and retrieved the signature pad. He left for his appointed rounds on this typically hot summer day. Heading back to the breakfast nook, Jerry gazed inquisitively at this very official envelope.

"Whatcha got there honey?" his wife Jenny spoke while tending to her appointed rounds in the kitchen. She was a stickler for details in every endeavor and also primary home accountant through their years of marriage. Her money management skills were exceptional.

"Certified letter from — uh oh — from the IRS. I wonder what they want with us." Jerry felt a tiny flutter in his heart, strange for a man of such inner strength.

Though they were very honest souls, getting a memo from such an infamous source could briefly grab the guts of the Terminator.

Though not intensely worried, the unflappable Jerry Grant was mildly curious. His heart skipped a mini-beat once more, and Jerry wondered why even that would happen.

Jenny reached for the letter. "No, no my love. "It's my mail and I get to open it," Jerry hummed with a childish tempo. Tearing the end off the envelope, he slowly but deliberately sliced it open, smiling as though his ship had come in.

"Dear Mister Grant," he began to read aloud. "Please present yourself for an interview at the downtown office of the Internal Revenue Service on the Seventh day of July at 10 a.m. At that time you will be asked to document your charitable donations claim in the presence of Auditor Andrew Clinton. The documentation necessary is that for the last filing year. Please be advised that this is not a general audit, but a line-item review."

An official seal adorned the letter, and it carried an illegible signature above the typewritten name of Andrew Clinton. "Just another of life's little hassles" he advised.

"Say what?"

A small sigh oozed from Jerry's vocal chords. "Thank the Lord for the accountant I married," he quipped, giving Jenny a wink. His mate of three decades was not a certified accountant. But the annual 1040 due every April 15 was her baby. She was good at it, keeping sterling records of everything from business expenses to sales tax receipts. Jenny, in fact, sported a modest pride in that work, especially when a refund was anticipated. The Grant family believed firmly in the principle of "rendering unto Caesar what was Caesar's". Jerry Grant had the maturity to talk the talk and then go and walk the walk.

Tucson was a great big little city. Since their move from Calgary five years earlier, the Grants had been most impressed with the city's paradigm. It was a fortress of sorts, with expansion limits set by nature. Four mountain ranges guarded the Old Pueblo. To the South some twenty miles stood the Santa Ritas, boasting rights of a senior community called Green Valley. The West was privy to the city's namesake, the Tucson Mountains, albeit subdivisions had sprung up even further west of that range.

The eastern sector sported the Rincons, over which came the rising moon, inching its way, till, at the time of fullness it appeared as a brilliant, edible peach.

Then there stood the Santa Catalinas, 10,000 feet tall, proudly framing the city to the North. They housed plenteous cabins and homes, an entire village atop, radar and communication towers, and the southernmost ski resort in the United States. Half way up a small lake was stocked with little fishes for the weekend cottage fanatics. The trip up the Catalina's Mt. Lemmon was an adventure for tourists, going from desert floor to pines and forests in a single hour. The bonus was a drop in temperature by 30 or more degrees.

Arizona was a sweet home to the Grants. Canadian nationals, they had made the move after a ten year stint in Calgary, home of the famed "Stampede." Jerry had been a minister of high regard there as well, loved not only for his ready ear and easy way, but for his sincerity and devotion to God, family and country.

However, the lure of pastoring in a desert climate had proven too much to resist, especially given the harshness of their final Canadian winter. Even at that, it had been a difficult decision. His Calgary church had been so well organized, so devoted, and the membership constituted a wide cross-section of society, boasting people from labor, business and from all the professions. There were the rich and, equally comfortable in his parish, those who by fate or design were poor and even destitute. They all found a caring church and an available servant. Even an elected member of the Canadian government had been active in church matters when he wasn't in Ottawa. This respected politician had become a dear and personal friend to the Grants.

Voices were heard outside the office door, a quick link as it were, back to the present office timeout. When they faded his thinking time in the IRS office continued.

As landed immigrants they shared every constitutional right, except the right to vote and the right to serve on a jury. For those reasons alone they had often considered the coveted role of American citizenship. But, for the Grants, the second amendment to the American constitution proved a stumbling block of major proportions.

Exhausted by his Calgary church, the timing of the pastoral invitation to Arizona had been exquisite. Neither Jerry nor Jenny had ever harbored second thoughts about the change. When they left Canada the rule was, "no regrets." The work, the climate, the schools, the people — they all seemed so right if not divinely ordained. There were no major crises save Jerry's recurring headaches. It was a little too good, perhaps the reason Jerry was now dwelling on the IRS letter with awe, if not a tendency to fear. Their lifestyle proved a contented one and the Grants always prayed nothing would change it.

With the IRS matter still in hand and now more so in mind, Jenny went directly to the filing cabinet deftly to retrieve the tax return from the previous filing year.

"Charitable contributions — oh here we are. $3070," she affirmed. The donation receipts were stapled to the form, and she quickly re-calculated the total. $3070.

"No problem dear" she reported clinically. "The claim and the receipts match each other." Apart from ethical considerations, the Grants had additional incentive to be straight on their tax reporting each year. One of the many deportable offenses the immigration officer had listed at the original border crossing was tax fraud. A litany of a thousand others must had been read to them as well. With that in mind, any temptations to defraud Uncle Sam were quickly aborted. Keep the rules or get out. That was it. Well they knew how closely Immigration kept an eye open for any delinquent guests. Jerry rubbed his hands together to indicate the end of the matter. He felt yet a third skip of his heartbeat. Strange! He said nothing to Jenny, but when he looked at her to continue the conversation he saw her brow wrinkled. Perhaps she noted a squall in her husband's body language.

"Let's finish breakfast," he suggested.

"Wait, something isn't right," Jenny interrupted.

"Like what" came the casual retort?

"Like, why do we have to go to the office in person? I know that in single items like this corresponding by mail is usually SOP. Why not for us?"

Jerry smiled and held her by the shoulders, "Because these tax collectors love to confront people — put the fear of God into them."

"Cripes," Jenny confessed, shaking her head, "they already did that just by sending a letter. With their reputation I guess we better comply without second-guessing them." Her remarks betrayed a little trepidation on her part, or was is it anger at this inconvenience in life.

Jerry feigned a bold countenance and affirmed, "Let it go my love. I'll handle it." I'll take the receipt into the office like they asked, and it'll all be history. Don't be manufacturing a crisis. It's not like you." Jerry was right. Manufacturing a crisis was not his style nor that of his wife.

"Besides," Jerry continued, "we did do it all by the book, didn't we?"

With that she looked back at Jerry with a Teflon smile. "Well, she said, "I'm coming with you! After all, I did do the return. If I messed something up I want to be there and tell 'em I did the return and always do them."

"If you must, my beloved; if you must!"

"I must," she assured him.

"Don't you think I can handle this thing?"

"Sure you can handle it," she nodded. "But I still wonder what it's all about."

"It's about documenting our charitable claim, okay? Nothing more and nothing less."

"Okay," she consented. "I'm still gonna be there. Seems to me they're questioning our integrity, and I want to look 'em in the whites of their eyes," she blurted.

Cuddling up to Jerry, Jenny swung her arms around him. Her little squeezes were signs of better things to come. She was a terrific lover. Almost a zealot if you will. Lovemaking with her husband came not as a responsibility endured, but an overpowering gift. Enough of this absurd anticipation of future trouble. Jennifer had a better idea.

Out of the blue the sweetheart proclaimed, "I have to keep my lover content now, don't I?" Jenny stared at Jerry with an obvious enticement, the way only she could stare, eyes aglow with fiery anticipation. This was the pastor's day off, and by the tone of Jenny's voice the day was about to begin as only a good wife could help it begin it — with a lively romp in the sack.

Chapter 4

Jerry Grant was still reprising the events of the day his Certified Mail arrived when the office door swung open and the receptionist brought in a message. Jerry was startled because he was getting to the good part of his memories. "Agent Blackwell is coming in a sec" she informed him matter of factly! "He has a few more arrangements to make for you." What that meant was a mystery of course; what <u>arrangements?</u> Yet as important those <u>arrangements</u> might be, Jerry offered no visible reaction.

Shortly, Carl Blackwell burst into the room, clipboard in hand, a checklist so it appeared. "Okay, you're packed and we're ready. Let's head to the airport."

"Whoaaaa" Jerry protested. Who packed for me?"

"Jenny," Blackwell replied.

"How did you get her to do that?"

"Time shall out the truth."

"But if you took her against her will……..I don't understand!"

"You only need to know on a need to know basis. Not a bad alliteration for a homely agent like me, eh Rev?"

Jerry determined to wait on that issue. He had formulated a plan, mentally detailed, to force the hand of Carl Blackwell to allow him a conversation with Jenny. That was down the road a ways. But it would not be until he was on board the aircraft. To Blackwell it would come as a surprise — hopefully. "Sir," Jerry pledged, "I shall play it your way."

"That remains to be seen" was the retort. But it is the smart thing to do. We are not devils you know!"

Like it or not the seventh day of July was going to continue. Jerry sat erect, as though coming out of a trance. He only now noticed that when Blackwell reentered the room a couple of aides were with him, now standing one on each side of Jerry. As they helped him to his feet he asked, "Okay already; hands off. I'm not running anywhere."

The aides removed their tight grip, but still maintained a contact touch. Jerry thought of a bumper sticker he had once seen. "Was today really necessary?"

Such was this day. He knew he was en route to the airport, headed for Calgary, and against every principle he espoused the Reverend Jerry Grant was about to play traitor to his home and native land. He was a player in a drama he had not authored. of course, what about Jenny?

The two primary characters in this drama were seated in the back of a fancy limo. Any and all temptation for Jerry to panic and attempt heroic escape had subsided, and he now began to rationalize the irrational. A nightmare had suddenly been summoned from the land of fantasy to the world of reality. Cars and horns and train whistles and all that went into urban life were thrust back into his surrealistic world.

Jerry tried to be philosophical. Kipling reminded him, "If you can keep your head when all about you are losing theirs and blaming it on you…you'll be a man my son." It worked! Because suddenly it dawned on Jerry that this wasn't really a dilemma. Not if he believed his own preaching. It was an opportunity and a challenge. His practice was never to take the tough circumstances of life with undue seriousness. He believed from his faith perspective that life at its best and worst was a win-win situation. "Don't sweat the small stuff — rule number one. Everything is small stuff, especially in the hands of God - rule number two."

With that axiom, he had consoled his wife back in the office when she acted desperately. So Jerry determined to take things in stride, one step at a time. Jenny comes first!

What would be right and appropriate? He had no control over the actions of others, but he had full control over his reactions. This was a public aircraft he was about to board and that would play a part in his blueprint to call Jenny. Jerry could use to his own advantage the crowd on the plane, ending in an urgent need he had; the need to talk with Jenny. So the thought became the action. Jerry became Joe Sweet for a purpose.

"Would I be permitted a few questions, Mister Blackwell?" he asked politely and most serenely as they drove in quietude toward Tucson International.

"Go ahead, but I'll answer them only on a need-to-know basis," Blackwell grunted. That is how we work.

"These are need-to-know questions I assure you," Jerry added. "You want me to do a job for you, so there are some things I have to know."

"Fire away."

"What's happening to Jenny? Do I get to call her before I leave?" Jerry didn't raise his voice a single decibel — yet. It would however become an option.

"Your wife is in good hands. She has a female agent as a houseguest for the time you'll be away. And she will be monitored — Jenny that is."

"Can I call her now from the plane?"

"Nope." It was a rapid retort!

"Why not?"

"No time. You'll have to trust us that she's okay." Blackwell looked at Jerry in a nearly humane fashion. "She is okay, Reverend." He nodded affirmatively.

"Well, what about the people of my church? They're going to miss me if I just up and take off, aren't they?"

"All taken care of Reverend. Your Bishop has advised your church that you needed a week off for a friend's funeral back in Canada. The head deacon knows all about it."

"All about what's really happening" Jerry was quick to ask?

"No, all about the funeral. You and the Misses are at a funeral."

"What if one of the members goes to our home? They're going to find out Jenny's home."

"No problem, Reverend. Our female operative is your hired housekeeper for the week, okay?" Jenny will not be seen.

"It's still going to seem suspicious to my church people — me just up and leaving without telling any of the church leaders personally," Jerry argued.

"Bert's got it under control, so don't worry."

"Bert Benson, my head deacon? He's not one of your men, is he?"

Blackwell lit up a cigarette. "Yep — in a way," he squirmed. "Well, he knows there's an important government Mission taking place. He doesn't work for us as such. But he is being extremely patriotic and cooperative."

"Does he know I'm in on this espionage?" Jerry asked.

Blackwell sneered at Jerry. "Use that word once more and I'll be tempted to flatten your face," he asserted. "This is a mission, not blackmail.

"What word are you worried about? Blackmail?" Jerry teased. "That's what it is, so if you want to flatten my face, be my guest. But then I'll have to explain my flat face to Richard Green."

"Bert Benson knows you're a key figure in an important mission, okay? Or do you have some other smart-ass remark?"

Jerry was not about to be intimidated. He knew now they really needed him. What he did not know was how this mission would play out if he had to create the drama so to speak!

Blackwell had done a great selling job on the details.

"Guess even the most trusted church folk have a bit of Judas in them," he said, looking right at Blackwell.

That's all it took. Blackwell turned and grabbed Jerry by the necktie. "Listen foreigner, this man is looking out for his country."

"And I'm betraying mine", Jerry confessed, slapping Blackwell's hand away from his necktie. Uncharacteristically, Jerry hoped the day would come when he might get Blackwell into a boxing ring or on a dark street. "I've got to fight off those horrible thoughts," he admonished himself. Maybe it was time to change the subject and to act as if he was interested in the mission. Mission — the word conjured up hypocrisy. And the last thing he wanted to do was to endanger Jenny. Blackwell seemed the kind of guy who would take it out on her too. His threats were not idle chatter. But Jerry was not quite finished. He would somehow make contact with Jenny.

Chapter 5

"Would you please tell me more about what I'm supposed to find out? I really need a review briefing Mr. Agent!" Jerry taunted. Carl took it to heart however, angry at the request nonetheless. He too was a tired man, and perhaps fighting a somewhat tattered conscience by virtue of Jerry's feisty interrogation.

With clenched teeth he began to spell it out. Looking Jerry straight in the eye he prompted, "First, we want you, dear parson, to bring us a report. Does the Canadian government have any kind of military presence guarding the fresh-water lakes and rivers of Alberta and B.C.? Or any system of surveillance at all? Second, has NAWAP been put on the front burner? Third, what kind of plans does Canada have for sharing the water supply with us? You got all that or am I going too fast for you? I told you this thing would unfold bit by bit; so be patient."

"So I get this information by pumping Rick Green for it?"

"You're learning."

"What if he won't tell me? What if he gets, well, suspicious of my fishing around?" I mean, that's what I'll be doing, right"?

"That's your problem, Reverend. I hate to flatter you but there is an ingenuity inside you which is one of the reasons you were chosen. Bring us back the information and your life will be back to normal in short order. Tape it, whatever! Those little recorders are very hideable."

"I hardly think so," Jerry countered. "I'm going to spy on my native land and you think I can just put that behind me like a used toy and resume a — a normal life?"

"Frankly Bud, I don't give a dang whether you can or cannot live with it," Blackwell cursed. "Do the stupid job or live with the options."

"Oh yes — tax court and Jenny. You'd really hurt them if I spilled the beans to Richard Green? Of course you would."

"We'll sure know if you do," Blackwell promised. "We'll be listening to everything you're saying. Got a bug in every part of his house. Now look what you made me tell you? Okay, so you know! But we can't bug every place he goes."

"Then what do you need me for."

"To get him to tell it out loud, what do you think? With one of these mini tape recorders, and a good memory, we'll get it all together."

"Will any harm come to my friend?"

"Stupid question! No, you got my word on that."

"What makes you think I won't choke and spill the beans?"

"Well, if you do tell him the plan, he's going to have to inform the Prime Minister, no?"

"That'd be his duty."

"And if he does, our people in Ottawa will find out in short order, I promise you that."

Jerry shook his head in disbelief.

"Just remember, we have the collateral."

"Yeah, Jenny!"

Jerry glared at Blackwell. "Touch her and I'll haunt you all the way to hell and back. You can count on that you tic-turd!" This was way out of character for Jerry, but then everything in his life had virtually changed so one more bad mouthing won't make God any madder.

Carl Blackwell turned to Jerry, patted his shoulder and said in a uniquely pleasing way, "Reverend Grant, do your job and you haven't got a worry." That's the faith and trust of the United States of America. It's my word as well."

"Just how far would you really go in hurting my wife?"

"Far as necessary. It's nothing to us if anyone has to be eliminated for the good of the country."

Jerry was stunned. "You are just contradicting what you finished saying two seconds ago." Silence prevailed! He had no problem believing what Blackwell was telling him. They had everything too well planned — from the "clerical error" to the hostages to the plane trip. All the turf was covered. Whether his family lived or died or were whisked away to some God forsaken place —all rested on Jerry's shoulders. That was the given!

Resourcefulness, ah! Such would be the weapons of his warfare from this very moment.

Blackwell, sensing that Jerry had finally submitted and ultimately acknowledged the enormity of his mission — and the responsibility he knew he bore, turned straight toward him and, smiling, gave him the finger. He was a man of many faces. Maybe that's what his type of work did to him, or perhaps it was his character untrained for such deception. Central Intelligence Agent meant a lot of things that Jerry would yet discover.

"That's all the questions I have," Jerry assured him. Yet he was still deeply troubled. Should he effect the plan to speak with Jennifer? Could he still consider this an opportunity and a challenge? That philosophy was getting harder to swallow. Could he live up to his swan song that he shouldn't sweat the small stuff and, that in the long run, everything was small stuff? That was something only God could know.

Whatever the future held, Jerry was sure of one thing. He wouldn't go down without a fight. To be sure, it would be necessary to make the trip, bring back the information, and feign that it was all over and forgotten. If anything was to be revealed to the

Canadian authorities, it would have to be done after his return trip, and at a time when he could safely hide away his family. Such plans could not be made at the moment, however. His assignment must first be completed. Or at least it could be made to appear that way.

"Everybody out," Blackwell commanded. As Jerry exited the limousine Blackwell advised him to follow. The others flanked Jerry, with Blackwell at the head. Moving directly past security, they went to gate 27. A lot of people were waiting for that flight. They led Jerry past the departure gate and directly into the aircraft. He was shown a seat, right up front in first class.

"You've got your ticket straight thru," Blackwell told him. "Don't deplane at Phoenix or Vegas. When you get to Calgary, get a cab to the Balmoral Hotel and register with our Visa card. Stay there overnight and then call Green tomorrow morning."

"What if he's not home?" Jerry questioned.

"He's home. He was instructed to stay there till tomorrow. He's expecting a call from the Prime Minister. Not that he'll get one."

"How did you work that one out?"

"Our people can do most anything." Blackwell sat next to Jerry to discern any last minute details. "Got your mission straight?" he asked. "Enough questions!"

"No," Jerry retorted defiantly. The people were now in the general boarding process, and Jerry was going to take advantage of that.

"What the dickens you mean no? How many times do I have to repeat it?"

"No more if you let me call Jenny. I got a loud voice Mr. Agent. The people on this plane will put up quite a fuss if I act like a loony." Plan "A" was starting.

"No time for a call."

"Then take me to tax court, 'cause I'm about to make quite a scene with all these people moving around here. I'm not going anywhere till I talk to Jenny." Jerry stood up to prove his point.

"Don't cause a disturbance now, you idiot," Blackwell urged in a half-shout. Blackwell was now the nervous kid on the block.

"Why not?" Jerry asked. "My life's been plenty disturbed." Jerry had a feeling he was going to win this round.

"Out of my way, tough guy" he told Blackwell, pushing at him as he began to move to the aisle. The two goons closed in on him, but with the passengers boarding Jerry was confident they wouldn't do anything rash. So he began to holler. His plan was now fully activated.

"Hey everybody, I'm being…." Blackwell clamped his hand over Jerry's mouth. "Okay, okay." He glanced at one of the men assisting him and ordered, "Get a phone hookup in the cockpit with Mrs. Grant for cripes sake. Hurry it up."

Jerry smiled in triumph and sat down, waiting a call to the cockpit. It was not long in coming.

"In here Mister Grant," the pilot summoned. "We have orders to give you secrecy in your conversation. So we'll leave. Press the button to talk, and let go to listen."

"Jenny, Jenny is that you?" he asked.

"It's me, Jerry. Where are you?"

"How much've you been told hon?"

"I'm so proud of you Jerry," she affirmed.

"What do you mean proud of me?" he asked.

"They told me you were going on an important mission that would benefit Canada and the US. And what you're doing will make you an important person."

"Did they tell you what I was doing?"

"No, they said it was in my best interests not to know - and that it was too secretive anyway. They said you were the only man for the job and that both governments had picked you. Jerry, I love you. I know you're not at liberty to discuss it with me, but good luck in whatever it is."

"What about the way they treated you at the office?"

"Oh, after you went in with Mister Clinton, they brought in this nice lady to tell me about it. She showed me her I.D. from the State Department, so I wasn't upset hon. Jerry, I'm just so proud of you. I packed your stuff as they probably told you."

Jerry was stunned. What a snow job they had done on Jenny. "Well," he thought, "maybe this is in her best interests."

Jenny continued, "This lady is staying with me to protect me from all the newsmen and cover for me. She's going to be taking all the calls and answering the door as if she's my housekeeper. The people at church aren't supposed to know I'm here. We're supposed to be at a funeral in Canada."

Jerry was silenced. The snow job was getting deeper and deeper.

"Jerry, are you still there?" Jenny asked.

"I'm still here, love. I'm ah - glad you know all the facts; or at least, as much as they feel they can tell you.

Now, I'll be gone for a week; tell you all about it when I get home. Love you honey."

"Love you too Jerry. Bye."

Jerry stepped back outside the cockpit and headed back to his seat. Glaring at Blackwell he muttered, "I can't believe you guys. What liars."

"We're doing the right thing in telling her what we told her and you know it."

"Mister Blackwell," Jerry asked, "have you ever darkened the doorway of a church?"

"What's that got to do with anything," Blackwell snarled.

"Just the lying! I mean one after the other after the other."

"Goes with the turf."

"No, seriously, did you ever go to church. Do you consider yourself a Christian man?"

"Yes, I do consider myself a Christian man," Blackwell said proudly.

"How do you reconcile all the— guess I can't use certain words here - all that deception in your line of work? Doesn't it ever make you feel like a hypocrite?"

"Not at all," he answered, "It's all for God and country."

"That's King and country," Jerry corrected him.

"Naw, God and country. When you do things for your country, it's like you're doing them for God, right?"

"Whatever."

"Okay, you're going to be taking off now, Reverend. A week from today it'll all be over and done. Do the job and we guarantee the IRS will never bother you again. Not ever!

"Humph," Jerry assented sarcastically.

"Got your credit card and cash, Reverend?"

Jerry nodded in the affirmative and Blackwell deplaned, with his two aides trailing.

The masses had filled the plane now. Stepping toward his seat, a stewardess inquired if he wanted a drink. Jerry shook his head to indicate no. Normally, he never drank. Not that he had a moral objection to it. The stuff just didn't appeal to him.

"Oh come on sir, you look tired. Why not try one?"

So Jerry accepted; more to please the stewardess than anything. "I'll have a double Canadian Club with water, please."

"One C.C. with water. Right." she answered.

"Maybe my last chance to do something for my country, he said." Jerry guzzled the drink for effect. And affect him it did. Before the plane had taxied to the end of the runway, Jerry was out like a light. He was tired, maybe drugged a little. But at least the Reverend Grant couldn't make a fuss now. And for what lay ahead, the rest, however achieved, would be a welcome refresher for his body, mind and spirit.

Chapter 6

That the plane ride should be a rough one came as no surprise to Jerry. The day had been equally unpleasant and he didn't expect anything to change. The hot desert updrafts always tested the metal of the passengers and the flight crews, to say nothing of the antiquated 737's. It was also purported that the dust devils which danced on the desert floor could often rise to 12,000 feet, the very cruising altitude which the aircraft flew during the 22 minutes between Tucson and Phoenix. Nor would landing in Phoenix for a pit stop be a delight. The hot air wind shear generally made for white knuckle landings in the summer months.

Yet through all the turbulence, Jerry was in a twilight zone, not capable of full concentration. Maybe he had been given a sedative in his drink. No, not maybe, of course he had. The flight attendant had virtually shoved the drink at him. That much he remembered. But try as he might he could not clear the cobwebs. There were dreams. Time and again he relived the office experience. He thought about Jenny. His mind was a beehive of activity but it could not remain posted to a single agenda.

———————————

Then with an involuntary mental synapse, his thinking geared forward to the start of the present day. He was doing a jigsaw puzzle of the past week by an analysis of every detail from the mailman's delivery to Auditor Clinton's "Follow me."

Why such detail? Was it a defensive maneuver of the mind? Or a calculated way of assessing his status? Was everything in his life flashing through his mind, as is said about those about to die? A premonition perhaps, that his old life was about to go the way of the world, ashes to ashes?

Still his mind did a rewind to this very morning, July 7th; a few hours in the immediate past. The weather was typically desert — a high of 105 was forecast, with a chance of evening monsoons. That was par. That the IRS interview was but a few hours off didn't dominate the conversation just yet.

As for Jerry, he had long since tried, without success, to place the IRS issue on the back burner of his talking agenda, but could not duplicate the feat in his mind. His inner strength was mostly characterized by his casual but take-charge manner. A lean man, he was strong of spirit and equally strong of body. Athletics had been the joy of his youth. Even now, at age forty-nine, Jerry kept his body fit as a teen.

The week had been hard. And with more stress ahead, it was agreed to begin the day with a morning workout. Jerry fine-tuned the twenty-one speed bikes, and they set out in tandem for their bike ride. Old Spanish Trail was a special place for them. Established by the county a few years prior, the bicycle path had proven a place of refuge from the harsher world.

The path bordered a gargantuan cactus stand. The trail terminated at a National Forest monument where the saguaros stood tall and proud as true sentinels of the desert never sleeping or yawning. Their arms were stately positioned as if directing tourists to stop and envy them. Ambitious cyclists could take an additional eight mile drive around the one way loop. It was a scenic route with the added dimension of a challenging two mile climb. Jerry called it "make me or break me hill." Those desiring a closer communion with nature would use the loop drive as the final reward of their workout. Cacti were only part of the scenery. There were also rabbits - millions of them in the spring. Lizards bolted across the roadway in hoards. If one were lucky, snakes, coyote, deer and Javelina could be spotted. Javelinas are the wild pigs of the desert. Though nocturnal creatures, they might well be spotted by the early morning rider. Such were the sights that made cycling there such a spiritual hiatus. The smell was a bonus, especially after a night's rainfall. One could benefit both from the euphoria of hard physical exertion and the spiritual freedom of the desert dawn, sights, sounds and smell included. What capped it off so beautifully was the Rincon mountain range, a purple backdrop to the lush green desert.

The Grants would often begin their day in such a fashion. Nice thing was their home was only a few yards from the start of the path. Cycling was a hobby of recent discovery to them. Make that an addiction! Each year, some three hundred superb biking days were coughed up by the Sonoran desert. Jerry had been the first to succumb to the craze, and Jenny followed in his path, literally and figuratively. They were equally committed to the regimen and proficient in the tricks of the trade. As with all who ride the two-wheelers, both had endured their share of spills, but with no serious injury. Custom was, when they took a spill on the bike, they made sure no one was privy to their clumsiness. Only then would they worry about injury.

Jerry preferred the aft position. It gave Jenny a chance to set the pace and offered him the obvious pleasure of trailing a beautiful body. He would frequently give commentary on the scenery and he didn't have in mind the desert handiwork. Jenny was gorgeous, but never sought to accentuate her beauty by artificial means. Somehow, she had retained the charm and figure of her youth. Mothering children and serving as wife hadn't taken their toll. She was, well, beautiful! And if ever there were a loving couple, it was the double J's; Jerry and Jenny Grant. Nor were either of them hesitant to express their affection verbally or physically.

How proud was Jerry to have a wife so sexual, yet so faithful and caring to the man of her dreams. The two had been high school sweethearts, and many a man longed for the kind of wife Jenny Grant was to her chosen mate.

Following an inspiring workout, they reluctantly agreed to continue the day. That was the sad part of the sport. It always had to end. For Jerry, it was especially sad. He felt capable of major rides — like cross state and the like. Perhaps a local marathon for charitable causes. Maybe someday he would get the chance. He was certain he could meet the challenge. Such possibilities as this filled his mind as he shaved and showered for Uncle Sam.

"Sir! Wake up, sir," he heard someone mutter. It was the flight attendant. His brief but sweet memory of the soul was ended. Yet it had proved a respite. Somewhat!

"What's going on?" Jerry muttered.

"We're on our final approach to Calgary International airport. Would you place your seat in the upright position," she instructed with an attendant's customary politeness.

"Calgary", Jerry said. "You mean we're already in Calgary?"

Jerry obliged her. He knew now he had been sedated. But perhaps that sedation had kindled the early morning memory — the candy before the dentist.

But now it hit him and hit him hard. The mission that is! With a surge of adrenaline, Jerry regained his faculties. "Lord, I guess it's real" he contemplated.

People lined up for customs always seemed unruly and ill at ease. Some had good cause. They would attempt to bring contraband into the country, or at least, more goodies than the law permitted. Canadian customs had a reputation for languor. It was one step at a time and one person at a time, save for couples traveling together. There was a yellow line a few feet from the immigration booth, with instructions to wait there until called forward. Jerry was near the front because of his first class place on board. "Next," a voice summoned.

Jerry stepped forward to the customs booth and was greeted by a young lady with a pleasant smile.

"Purpose of your visit sir," she asked?

"Uh", Jerry was caught off guard.

"What's the reason for your visit to Canada?" she repeated?

"Personal"!

"Could you be a bit more specific sir?" Noting the pallor in Jerry's countenance she queried, "You okay Mister?"

"Ah — yeah, sure," Jerry replied. He paused briefly. "Just a little air sick I guess. Yes, ma'am, I'm here to visit a friend — just a short vacation."

"And how long do you expect to stay in Canada?"

"One week."

Jerry was fighting off the temptation to blow the whistle here and now, but given the advantage

Blackwell had, the idea was promptly preempted by the perceived consequences.

"Is this all the luggage you have?"

"Yes ma'am, this is it."

She handed him a card and asked him to proceed to the next line.

Jerry moved on and handed the card to the gentleman manning the next post. From there he was motioned directly through which meant there would be no baggage inspection. That was always a chore and a bit intimidating as well. He had never been subject to search going either way, a matter attributable either to the luck of the draw or to his clean cut appearance. One in twenty would be checked, as well as anyone who appeared nervous or suspicious. With one more hurdle behind him he proceeded hastily to find a direct phone line to his hotel. That however, would prove unnecessary.

"Over here, Reverend Grant," a voice called out.

Jerry saw a man with a chauffeur's hat waving at him. He approached him with some apprehension. How in the world did he know his name?

"Who might you be please" Jerry requested?

"Yes sir! I'm the van driver from the Balmoral Hotel. I believe you'll be staying with us for a while?" Jerry followed him to the van. He wasn't accustomed to such gracious hospitality as this. Blackwell's idea no doubt. Maybe this man wasn't just a van driver: probably hired to keep an eye out on Jerry. "Shake it off already" he tried to admonish himself. Not everyone works for the CIA." He was in Canada now and reasonably confident that Canada was running her own show.

The way to the lodge would be short and swift. Van drivers like cabbies, always did too much talking. Recognizing his position however, Jerry realized he had to act as normal as possible. So much was at stake, not the least of which was his whole future. So like the Jerry of yesterday, he took part in the conversation, discarding the confusion still riding roughshod in his mind.

"How far to the hotel?" Jerry queried.

"Fifteen or twenty. Right in the heart of the city. All four lanes though, right to downtown."

Jerry asked, by the way, how did you know my name?"

"Well," the driver pondered, "they told me a preacher was coming in. I seen you in the suit an' figured you must be the preacher. Slow night, so I was just waiting at the airport anyway."

Jerry nodded, acknowledging the explanation. He didn't buy it though. The remainder of the trip was the normal chitchat: weather, sports, and a few other trivial matters. In short order the van pulled off the expressway and entered the driveway of a posh hotel. "Here she be sir — the Balmoral lodge. Hope you have a good stay in our hotel."

Offering the driver the customary tip, Jerry ambled to the registration desk. Quickly he was escorted by a bellboy to his room on the fourteenth floor. And after tipping the bellboy as well he turned on the light. It was 9 PM, and not yet dark outside. The room was fit for a king. King size bed; a large sitting area situated beside a bay window, overlooking the sprawling cow town. Jerry sat, elbows propped on the window ledge. "Calgary, Good old Calgary."

Then he became pensive. Perhaps more than that — nostalgic. He was remembering the early years in Calgary when the kids were young. On special days, the family would go to Happy Valley to ski the little mini- slopes - and ride the toboggan. If they had two or three days together, it would be a trip to Banff. In the summer they would camp, and in the winter they would rent a cabin and sit around the fireplace, playing games, fooling around and laughing as only a loving family can laugh.

God, they had been happy. 'Course the kids always had to haul the portable TV along, even though the reception in the mountain areas was terrible. Had they missed Yogi Bear they most likely would have felt robbed and damaged for life. How proud he and Jenny were of his son and daughter. Mind you, they were seldom in touch by virtue of their vocation. They had become church related missionaries and teachers with a broad spectrum of duties, and being associated with CUSO (Canadian University Services Overseas) they had made their way to the upper echelon of supervision while still being, as one might say, field operatives. Their communication was now via cell phone, if of course they weren't buried in the Andes or hemmed in by giant jungles. From time to time E-mail became possible simply because they managed to reach a place of 20th century technology.

Kenton and Kerry, now 23 and 21 respectively, turned out to be very good human beings — really good. They were good in every phase of their lives – now, and especially so in their vocational decisions. Both had gone through the trials of youth. Still they had seen so much need in the world by looking at their father and mother and how they ministered. Mom and Dad were role models and that's how it was suppose to be.

Both kids had grown so quickly from teens and developed an unusually close rapport between siblings with all their little spats. Strangely too, both decided virtually in tandem to prepare for this work of helpers to the world and take that compassion to remote parts of the world after language training, some paramedic training, cultural studies and enrollment with CUSO. They had also learned both in Calgary and in Tucson, all the resources available to bring the needs of life in loving fashion to those who were living in squalor and filth with the hopelessness. That followed.

So, at present, it was a true blessing they were not reachable or the CIA would have them as collateral too. They could be in the slums of Hong Kong or in the highlands of Lima. At any rate they were due for leave and a return home later in the Fall. But for now, their childhood antics were making Jerry's heart smile, a good catharsis for the moment at hand. Kenton was always running and falling and getting hurt when they skied or tobogganed and Kerry couldn't get enough sports.

He chuckled to himself. But Jerry and Jenny never minded their children's' ways. Too quickly they would outgrow their youth. So family trips were frequent. As husband and wife they had private and intimate matters to discuss on those trips. The kids didn't always want mom and dad baby sitting their childhood play.

Ah — those times at Banff — especially in the winter cabins; they had proven the most memorable for them. It was a setting created for lovers. And lovers they were.

Spontaneously, Jerry began to cry. He wasn't here to think of the past. He was here to betray a friend and a country. And for the good of those he loved, he had better get on with it. Looking in his notebook, Jerry rustled up the phone number of Richard Green. He dialed and waited. It rang once, then twice....

"Green residence," a voice answered. "May I help you?"

"Yes ma'am," Jerry answered back. "This is Jerry Grant. I'm a friend of Richard Green and I wonder if I could speak with him."

"One moment please" she said. A moment went by and a voice came on," Jerry Grant - is that really you?"

"It's me, Rick. Alive and well."

"What in the world, old buddy. You planning on moving back here? What are you doing in town?"

It passed through Jerry's mind that Richard Green assumed he was in town. He could, after all, have been calling long distance. The thought passed quickly.

"Well, I just came up for a week of R and R," he said.

"Jenny with you of course?" he assumed.

"No, just me, myself and I. All three personalities."

Rich Green seemed astonished and there was a pause….."Gosh, that's a first for you guys, isn't it?"

"Yeah, I guess so.

Fact is, Rick, I had been feeling run down so I was ordered to take a rest. Decided to spend some time on the golf course and up in the hills."

"Where ya at?"

"Balmoral lodge - downtown. Quite a view of the city."

"Fair deal," Richard replied. "That's a great hotel and I'm glad you picked something classy. You deserve it, old buddy."

"So how's Betty?" Jerry inquired. Another pause ensued………

"Jerry, I'm a little embarrassed. Betty and I separated last year and got a divorce just after Christmas."

Jerry couldn't believe it. It didn't fit Rick's character - or Betty's for that matter.

"I am really sorry to hear that, Rick. If you want to get together and talk about it, I'd be happy to lend you my ears,"

"Thanks anyway Jerry. But it's over and done. I'd just as soon put it all behind me."

"Your choice Rick. Reason I'm calling is that I wouldn't mind getting together once or twice while I'm here; maybe some golfing and swimming. Whatever."

"What do you mean once in a while," Rick asked. "Why don't you be my guest at my estate?"

"Gosh, I can't impose on you Rick." Jerry was hoping Rick would pursue and insist. His mission- not that he had chosen it - was to garner the trust on his friend and then — well, do his job via misplaced trust.

"No imposition. Heck, I got the house and plenty of room. Fixed it all up in the last couple years in fact."

"Well, if you think you want the trouble."

"No trouble Jerry. You can use the Mazda. Do what you want. And when you decide we'll do the golf course or take a ride to Banff. I'm off for the summer and hadn't put any other plans together. How about if I pick you up tomorrow about ninish — brunch on me?"

"Sure. Why not?" Jerry consented. Beats a hotel anyway!

Then it hit him again - a gut-wrenching truth. He was about to take advantage of a friend's hospitality only to betray that same friend's hospitality and love.

"It's settled then," Rick suggested. "See you in the morning Jerry. Rest easy."

The phone clicked, and Jerry rubbed his head with the phone receiver. He hurried into the bedroom, took a hot shower, and lay awake till morning. This was not a night to rest easily. It was a night to plan.

Sunrise took its time to brighten the longest night Jerry ever endured. He could never remember experiencing insomnia. At least, not like this. Having readied himself for his reunion the phone rang on schedule.

"It's me Jerry."

Richard Green was in the lobby. "Want me to come up and help me with the luggage?"

"No it's okay Rick. I'm ready and on my way down. See you in a minute."

Jerry grabbed his garment bag and slowly headed for the elevator. True to his friend's word, when the door opened to the lobby Richard Green was standing there. Jerry embraced him and Rick reciprocated. Again Jerry felt like a fraud. These had always been friends willing to show their affection, as could Jerry with anyone he cared for and befriended.

The duo went to the desk to check out, and, after setting his bag in the lobby, the two friends went to the coffee shop for brunch. They talked about everything that happened in the past two years - save the divorce. Nary was a word mentioned about it. And Jerry was troubled by it.

"Well, let's head out to the old estate," Rick motioned. He paid the tab and led Jerry to the waiting limo. It was a benefit all MPs got; both at home and in Ottawa each had a limousine, mainly for personal security. Nor was it an unpleasant experience to ride in. Smooth and classy.

"Only way to travel" Rick surmised. "Excellent chauffeur too."

Jerry knew that Rick was accustomed to the good life. But he also knew that he handled it very well. Richard Green was a respected MP, and a proven Christian man whose character never belied his creed. Save for the thick skins government officials developed, he was sincere and a devout friend of Jerry and Jenny Grant. And a model for everybody at the church he attended.

Arriving at the estate where Jerry had spent significant time during his prior Calgary ministry the two men walked to the house. Leading him to an expansive guest room, Rick suggested, "I've got a reservation at the country club for 1:00 PM Jerry. Hop into some shorts and we'll head out. Sound okay? Oh, and I have some clubs for you."

"You've gone to a lot of trouble for me" Jerry observed. "Thank you."

Rick left the room and Jerry looked around in awe: A king-size bed with canopy; spa; giant bath; remote TV. "Boy, would the spa would feel good now," he thought! "But there'd be no time for that."

The last thing he wanted to do was golf. Nor did he want to pump his friend for the information Blackwell had demanded. But with the CIA holding the trump card, there was no option. Jerry would have to play out his hand. And if the opportunity presented itself on the golf course, he wouldn't pass it by. Not that he was anxious to begin his assignment. Yet his family was more important than some national secrets. And Jerry was a family man. But no matter how he rationalized his pending plans and activities, Jerry kept hearing a little voice. "Judas! Judas!"

That name would ring constantly in the mind of this man whose faithfulness to every person and every cause had been notable and respectable for so many years of pastoral service. Unlike the Biblical Judas though, Jerry harbored the faith that in some way, this byway in his life would lead to a pleasing resolution. Apart from that hope, fanciful as it might seem, he might as well do as Judas had done. <u>"Judas went out and hanged himself."</u>

Chapter 7

To some degree breakfast with a morning fix of joe cleared the cobwebs. Jerry was facing a moment of truth. Because sadly, the dawn also signaled the start of the facade — man to man. Jerry was pondering ideas whereby he could spare the true friendship with Rick and, maybe, Canada's right to decide the future of her water supply – the finest on earth; not to mention the first contemporary conflict of any proportion between the two nations who shared the longest, and virtually unguarded border on earth. If he was the man he had chosen to become, he would make it happen — at this point, an effort to no avail. For his inability to change the direction of this whole matter, Jerry got down on himself. But he would not cease the internal conflict his soul demanded he face nor stop the fight for right in the chambers of his heart. Would he cave in to the pressure or start now to renew his true character?

The initial conversation centered on Jerry's supposed need to get away; to take solo flight from work and family. That Richard Green didn't question this story was one less matter needing added fabrication. Jerry manufactured a few contemporary issues; they were norm for the now generation — stress, depression, mid-life crisis. It was most disturbing for him to endorse this somewhat nonsensical stuff, so he called it, but his confirmed assignment for Jenny's safety was to be creative. He also wanted to ease into the mission without trying to get a revealing jump start in prying out the information Blackwell demanded; it was nerve racking!

En route to the golf course Jerry steered the topic to the changes in Richard and himself. "Guess we're graying up a little bit" he observed. And Rick, no offense, but you do look thin and gray! Anything buggin' you old friend?"

Rick retorted, "Receding hairlines go with the aging old buddy." He seemed to evade the issue with that single reply. "Lots of changes you'll be seeing here." On the way to the golf course Jerry tried to observe the massive evolution, but his concentration was still "the mission."

The western backdrop to the city of Calgary was like a Norman Rockwell painting. The ground sloped up into colorful foothills, the foothills into high hills, and then — the crowning backdrop of Calgary: the grandiose Cascade and Rocky Mountain Ranges, standing 15,000 feet high some 100 kilometers to the West, beautifully misted by distance and dust. But in this magnificent setting, Jerry again, with all sincerity, asked Rick what was troubling him, repeating his sincere observation that he looked thin and drawn. Rick would again steer the talking away from himself.

The trip to the golf course passed all too quickly. Now at the clubhouse attention was, of course, to checking in and getting a start time. As for the mission — dare not forget the mission!

One thought plagued Jerry with persistence. There had to be a way of sparing the deception. There must be, and if there were a god in heaven he would drop it down into the hands of Jerry Grant. Jerry needed an inspiration he could and would pursue.

Apparently Richard Green, Member of Parliament, could just walk in and be assured a tee time within thirty minutes, a perk for serving King and country. This course was among the finest in Canada, the greens and fairways being treated to plenteous rain and spring snow flow. The first tee was but a few steps behind the clubhouse, and it was there that Rick invited Jerry to put down his club bag and step to the tee. For the sake of exercise they had forsaken an electric cart. There at the first tee a trusting and trusted friend named Richard Green made Jerry an offer, "You have the honors my dear friend and Pastor."

All Jerry needed was to hear a heartfelt profession like that. His body felt spastic. He knew his reputation because he knew himself, and now he was forced to be what he had never been: A hypocritcal liar. Jerry addressed the ball and swung. He shafted the initial drive and hooked it into a faraway bush.

"A little rusty old friend?" Rick snickered. "Maybe you forgot to get down on your knees this morning and ask the Almighty for a good game, eh!"

The Reverend forced a smile. He'd better start with concentrating on the game at hand or Rick just might consider something amiss and start asking more probing questions about his sudden trip to Calgary. It was in Jerry's mind that, being such a trusting man, Rick just accepted the simple explanation he gave.

"Hey friend, that was a freebie; try again," Richard told him. "Let's write that one off as a practice swing." Jerry teed off once more, and this time lined a long, low, straight and pro like drive down the center of the fairway. For a fleeting moment he was reminded of those days when he had actually played consistently well. That was years ago.

Rick followed with an equally good drive, his ball landing within three yards of Jerry's drive. The two men tarried along the course making small talk as they walked toward their driven golf balls, strangely enough, one beside the other. This visual aid reminded Jerry about the former closeness their friendship once meant. "Fluke" he thought.

"How's the old government game going?" Jerry asked.

"The political game? Pretty good. Got a nifty appointment last year about the end of November."

"Hey, what's that — if it's my business?"

"To a chairmanship. Not Minister but executive chairman to the Minister of Environment Canada — Department of the Interior. Actually it's a special branch which deals with conservation of water and all that stuff."

Jerry sensed an opening. "Go for it," he thought. "But be careful."

"So tell me more," Jerry suggested. "Like how does this thing play itself out day by day?" Should he have jumped so quickly on the issue? He hoped he hadn't messed up with a sudden zeal. But it would be so noted.

"Well, what's with the immediate interest in my political life? You used to tell me it was all out of your league."

Jerry had feared just that response, but his own response came with a newfound spontaneity.

Best way to forget about oneself is to learn a lot about others." That was an axiom Jerry often used in his counseling ministry. It was one that kept him as sane and upbeat as he was, save for the present moment.

"Great, great," Rick assured him. "Life's going great all things considered." Jerry noticed that Rick was especially attentive to his surroundings, always on the lookout, moving his head in one direction, then another, as if expecting to see someone or something. Jerry gave it little thought at the moment. After all, politicians knew anybody and everybody. Jerry would be surprised if Rick didn't run into a dozen or more people he knew. There just wasn't much privacy to be found in his lifestyle. That must account for Richard's looking to and fro. Yet the glances were more than occasional. More than furtive!

Now it came to mind, Jerry's that is, rather than hearing of Rick's political exploits out here it would be far superior to get into detail back at the mansion where there were, as Blackwell inferred, listening devices. Perhaps he had video cameras beaming a satellite description of the men, the room and picking up the sound. That way Jerry wouldn't have to try and remember all the details Rick might offer in the course of the game, details he might forget to report when he got back home. "Forget the work stuff" Jerry proposed. "We'll get into that or maybe we won't, what the heck. This is a do or die golf game Rick! For the world championship."

Rick was pleased, and for the first time gave an honest smile. He assented to the idea and both men put heart and soul into the pleasure before them. The game went on and Rick surged into the lead. Jerry was an athlete — but only a fair golfer. Still, he would consistently break ninety in years past. He enjoyed the walking and talking more than the swinging and looking for lost balls. There was however, a lingering demon – the "mission" — and a heavy heart that came with the territory. More than anything, he anticipated an opportunity to learn, right now, more about Rick's little secrets. It was becoming an obsession and Jerry recognized it as such. Given the high stakes, he resolved to stop being so critical of himself and await the return to Rick's hideaway mansion.

At the end of the game, sitting in the clubhouse, Jerry rehearsed in his mind, "I'm going for it as planned. Jenny is my wife and my life." To that end, he set his sights on a casual attitude but a reasonably quick return home.

Fashionable and expensive, the 19th hole sported a sauna, a pool, a bar and a giant screen TV. "Let's get some O.J.," Jerry suggested. "This one's on me."

"Sounds good," Rick assured him. "But would you mind if we beat a trail back to the house then?"

Jerry perked up! "What a godsend that remark was" he thought. Yet he noted there was a growing and well defined edginess in Rick's voice — a sure and discernible nervous tone. Rick once again gazed around the lounge, sliding downward in the leather chair as if hiding his face. He seemed to take note of every person who walked in. Then he drank his juice like there was no tomorrow and urged Jerry, "Let's go hit the spa and the pool at my place. Not feeling really great old friend. I think it's just too humid."

Jerry jumped at the offer. "Me too, I'm wiped," he feigned, remembering again that Richard Green's home would be the best place to get information, and Blackwell or someone else would be listening and recording. That made it more urgent for Jerry to use tact, to act with due interest on the issue without engendering suspicion about his motives.

On the way Rick offered a choice; a quiet conversation in a relaxing spa or on the front balcony upstairs. Either way, maybe he could get what he needed without forcing the issue. Rick seemed a little jumpy when Jerry tried to broach the subject earlier. Then again, that was in the middle of a golf game.

The trip home was quick and easy. Too quick! Avoiding the heavy traffic and taking the back routes also proved a more scenic drive. They had used the Mazda sports car, and Jerry was driving. Rick had insisted so Jerry would be used to it for the rest of the week. Besides, there were 3 more cars in the driveway plus the limousine.

They arrived at the house, entered and quickly changed attire, melting with groans into the spa.

"Aah", Rick uttered, as if he had been struck with a dose of paradise. "So how's it going down in Tucson old friend?"

"Pretty good. I guess you know that the people in this town always have a special place in my heart though?"

"I know Jerr. Shucks, if we hadn't laid so much work on you maybe we could have had you stay another ten years."

"No, that's not it. It's not that the people lay the work on you. You just need to do what needs doing. I mean, who can plan the time they're going to die or get sick or have marriage troubles?"

"Yeah - marriage troubles, "Rick continued. "Well, the fact is Jerry, that Betty and I broke up over my job?"

"Like how - you were gone too much?"

"No! I had talked to Betty about some pretty important things and she blabbered them all over the place. I was told to shut her up somehow or lose my post. But that was arranged for me; getting her to be quiet that is. There are people who can pull that off. They set me up to have an affair, Jerry. Like a fool I took the bite, and it ended up Betty dumped me. She never knew she spilled any beans about some supposedly sensitive issue. God I loved her." Rick cried!

"That's awful. Who did all that?"

"The boys in Environment Canada. The Senior Minister of the Interior mostly. I am considering resigning. And they won't let me."

"What could be so all fired important that your wife couldn't pass it on," Jerry asked.

"The whole issue of NAWAP," Rick answered.

NAWAP! A familiar topic from the Tucson office. Jerry had his grandest opening now. At least, so he thought. But was Rick really inviting him to dig a little deeper. After all, how could he expect him to know what NAWAP was?

"Well, what you want to tell me you can Rick. What you can't, I respect and understand. But NAWAP - that's a new one on me."

"I know I can trust you Jerry. Can I tell you something about NAWAP in utmost and very extreme confidence?"

"You know me, Rick. It's your choice." Jerry was getting ready for the whole scheme now. Then, with an inner urging, Jerry stopped the play acting! His conscience led him to a reasonable option. His moral strength took forefront.

———————

Jerry stepped out of the spa, went to a table with a writing pad and scratched out a note. But before doing so he touched his lips, zipped them and wrote a notice as dead silence engulfed the room. Rick took it and read:

"Rick, trust me. Don't say a word. This is big-time stuff I'm going to tell you but it has to be in a place where we might be seen but not heard. It involves you and me and your work. And Jenny and God know what else."

Rick looked astonished. He began to talk in response to the note, but Jerry lipped to him — "shhh!" Then he proposed in normal voice, "can we go take a quick walk in the garden? I haven't seen your famous flower beds yet. Then we'll come back in and carry on our elite conversation." With that, Jerry again put his finger to his lips, summoning Rick to hush up. He grabbed Rick's hand and whispered, "Follow me outside and be quiet. I'll tell you in a minute"!

Rick looked even more quizzical, but with wrinkled forehead, followed his friend's lead and went out to the garden as Jerry made small talk. There in that garden, amidst the fine flower beds for which Richard Green was famous, Jerry told it all. He looked around at the garden to make it appear, should someone be watching visibly, that he was talking about roses and petunias and other beds of entrancing flower mixes. In a rapid speech of evocation he told everything as he had reenacted it in his mind, not letting Rick get a word in; always forcing him to listen and trust him. Every detail was relayed. From the letter, to the interview to the plane ride to the snow job done on Jenny, and now, to the real purpose of his visit and the deception he was supposed to carry out. Silence followed. They stared at one another and shook their heads, dismayed. Both grew silent.

Now the issue at hand was the outcome of the truth; perhaps Jenny's life. Did he jeopardize that and his own?

"Not at all" he concluded. Ambling back to the house Jerry strongly suggested that as they discussed the issues of Rick's work, Rick should fabricate totally <u>false</u> information.

Though still stunned, Rick nodded his head in the affirmative. Jerry hugged his friend and said softly, still outside in the garden grove, "trust me — give me wrong answers when we get back inside. I know this is the right thing to do — lay the facts out for you like I did. Rick, I could not go on! I care too much about you."

"I'll do my best" Rick retorted. "But boy, what a shocking story. Thanks for coming clean brother Jerry. I am not a good actor I must admit though."

"Not a good actor! Gees, you're a politician. Of course you're a good actor" Jerry smiled. "Let's get back inside. We've done what we can in five minutes. Now it's drama time."

"For the record" Rick cut in, "I want to resurrect NAWAP, but I'll tell you the opposite of what the truth is. You sure you want that?" And Jerry nodded in the affirmative.

Chapter 8

The stage was set. In that beautiful garden, no "bugs" discernable, Jerry had confessed his true purpose and Rick, not yet understanding all things, agreed to respond to each question with an answer opposite to the fact of the matter. Perhaps, with Jerry's confession and Rick's response, the friendship was salvaged and Jerry's heart felt more at ease. Jerry led them in a prayer and both reentered the spa area.

"So where were we?" Jerry prompted Rick as they stepped back into the Jacuzzi, refreshments in hand. Jerry was ready to go! "Great flower garden my friend. You are amazing! Now, you got my interest up on this water thing so tell me what you can trust me with."

"Oh I was mentioning this water thing we had going in Environment Canada, and my appointment to oversee it. We had a tripartite group going with the U.S. and Mexico back in the 60's — called it NAWAP. Not important what it means. It had to do with the only fresh water supply left - ours here in Canada. Anyway, Canada pulled out of it. We knew the Yanks were manipulating us."

"How?"

"They said they were interested in our well being. But they weren't. They wanted the great northern trench to be diverted and flushed through the Great Lakes or other rivers to clean up the aquifer around the U.S."

"And what's the great northern trench," Jerry inquired.

"That just means the waters that run together across northern BC and Alberta and then flow east or west at the continental divide and south via mountain trenches. The Yanks really believed diversion could be done with some digging and trenching and strategic blasting and all that stuff. We knew this would deplete our fresh water supply sooner or later. We knew they'd end up taking over the whole Master Plan. So we told them to take a hike." That part was true! Good enough to let out what would now follow; the antithesis.

Jerry said nothing, waiting for more information. After a short pause, Rick continued. "Anyway, we brought the plan into effect on our own for our own use and even saved a little for your home to the south. That's why I got the post; to work on the preservation of our own water supply."

"Well, you're the man for the job," Jerry assured him.

"But now that we have some plans, it seems every move I make is being watched or criticized. If things aren't done perfectly — like the - ah —defense part — I catch it from the really big boys."

"Defense part?" Jerry queried. "What defense part?"

"A perfect response" Jerry thought to himself. Very real?"

"Oh, I got stuck with working to defend the water supply. The great, great Canadian military is under my direction for this project specifically. I'm supposed to call on them if I need their help. Now I'm being criticized for not being aggressive enough."

"How aggressive are you supposed to be?

"They want me to make a war of it — and I am to set up troops along the major waterways. We have set up a military watch in the important areas of the fresh water supply."

"What are the Canadian leaders afraid of — your own government I mean?"

"The Yanks. They actually think the Yanks are going to bring in troops and siphon water to the Western U.S. Can you imagine anything so stupid in this age of diplomacy?"

"Does sound a little far fetched" Jerry acclaimed loudly.

Rick continued, "far fetched. We've been buddies with the Americans forever. They can handle their own water problems. Heck, they nearly have it down pat how to do the desalination of the bloody oceans. They don't need our water."

"And you don't see eye to eye with the others in Ottawa?"

"Nope. But I have to do it! They all want a Maginot line type system set up. Like digging in and posting armed troops around a waterfall. The fact is we already have enough to ensure the safety of the water supply."

"Like what's enough?"

"Like troops on the watch, and a fleet of 30 helicopters for borderline searching; air reconnaissance; and armed, modern helicopters with guns and a lot of missiles. Got thirty of them on duty every day, in parts of the West. I have a major budget to keep these troops and choppers looking out for imaginary Americans coming to steal our water. They'd need a bucket brigade or an entire army! Sorry Jerry, I don't know, but something is rotten in the state of Denmark."

Jerry nodded at Rick, signifying he was doing a great job in spitting out all the wrong information as had been agreed. He was also certain the CIA was hanging on every word, as spoken from the Calgary Spa room, way back in Tucson. They were in a house full of bugs.

"So what do they do all the time; the choppers?"

"Fly around at low level and monitor - well - look out for any unusual activity. Far as I'm concerned, it's a waste. Heck, who could ever divert enough water to make a difference to us anyway?"

"What would you consider unusual activity?" Jerry began to see a little further into the mind of Carl Blackwell now. How far would he go? He was, after all, a patriotic zealot in the worst sense. At least, he was to Jerry's way of thinking!

"That's the point. I'm not even sure how to define unusual activity. But it seems to me thirty high tech choppers keeping an eye out for water thieves is, well, dumb! We're not at war with anybody. Nor will we ever be at war over water of all things."

Jerry knew differently. "Yeah, seems a little strange," he admitted.

"I've tried to convince the members of the committee that's plenty of defenses. Good Lord, I can't believe we're defending water."

"Is that all the defense there is then?"

"Yeh, and there's more with agents spying on the activities of the U.S. military. We're covered man. Guaranteed, if the Yanks knew all this — and it's unlikely they ever will — they'll think twice about robbing water."

"True" replied Jerry, feigning a smile. "Canada's safe from foreign water thieves! What an absurd commodity to consider stealing anyway?"

"So that's the whole ball of wax. I'm the head of the committee and I get the last word in recommendations to the P.M. Some of our idiots really believe our water needs defending. Stupid - like the Americans had and still have their communist bogey man; well, we have our water bogey man — Americans."

"Could some of your bosses have information you don't know about?" Jerry asked?

"Nope. I'm the head honcho in the department. If they do have input, I'm supposed to know. They're all nuts. I know good and well that what we're doing is too much. Like I said, we can't afford that kind of reconnaissance by choppers day after day. That's not even the point. We don't need it. Hey, you will keep this under your hat friend, won't you? Heck, sure you will. Why would I ask a dear friend like you that I could trust with my soul?"

Jerry nodded his assent. He had already accomplished his mission, so he thought. What Rick told him was exactly what Blackwell wanted to know. Maybe it wasn't such a big deal after all. Rick was so convincing that Jerry virtually believed it. For the American government to know what Canada is doing in guarding her water wasn't all that unreasonable a request. Surely they wouldn't go in and take it. Just from an engineering standpoint, that would be impossible. Who's going to come and steal water? A big bucket brigade of conscientious Americans as Rick had scoffed about.

Jerry snickered to himself. The whole matter seemed way out of proportion. Why all the mystery and intrigue in the Tucson office? Well, maybe the CIA just had to act in secrecy to uphold its reputation.

Given the lies, Jerry had no idea if Blackwell would buy the story. At least Jerry had his conscience back, which would let him sleep and remain Rick's friend forever. The two embraced and Rick whispered, "Jerry, thanks for the truth. I didn't think it was actually going to happen. I could kick their balls off for recruiting a friend like you and taking Jenny hostage just to find out what I told you." Rick scratched a note: "Jerry, we have no water guards at all. So let's pray everything goes your way now and I'll get the information you brought me to the P.M." A few tears ensued, and Jerry loudly thanked Rick for telling him about his life and Canada's current status regarding water safeguarding, such as it was. That was what he wanted Blackwell to hear in whatever way they were now eavesdropping!

The drama went well. Rick played a great game and Jerry felt he had the right responses. Both smiled and in the midst of a more spirited moment, the chimes from the front doorbell broke their train of thought.

"Sorry friend, it's the maid's day off," Rick reported as he got up out of the Jacuzzi. "I'll just be a minute, Jerr. Help yourself to a cold drink. Lots of coke for you abstainers" he joked. He knew Jerry didn't like alcohol, simply a matter of taste.

Jerry settled back to get the jet stream on his neck. Then he caved in to his craving for his single addiction — apart from his wife. He got up for a cold coke and opened the can. He was looking for some ice and a glass. It was a rare time of peace. Forget the mission; enjoy the setting.

In the blink of an eye the peace was shattered. A dreadful boom — bang — boom was heard coming from the area of the front door. It was like a mini-bomb. "Gas explosion," Jerry pondered? He began running through the house and hollering, "Rick, Rick, are you okay? What happened?"

A second bang-boom-bang thundered through the house. Everything stopped, a virtual freeze-frame. The world was in slow motion. Jerry stopped in his mental tracks. First there was noise, now a thundering silence. "Rick, where are you?" He was quite a distance from the front door, now standing outside on the Jacuzzi patio.

The front door slammed shut. Jerry heard it and scampered through the house and down the hallway. As he rounded the corner to the main entrance he saw his dear friend. Richard Green was lying in a pool of blood— dead! He had no face left at all! The noises had been gunshots. Rick was torn apart. Jerry took a quick check for Rick's pulse but his friend indeed was no longer part of the present world.

"Rick, oh my God, Rick what's happening?" He embraced the lifeless body and cried buckets of despair and grief. This was horrific. Richard Green had been shot. He was dead — and he was dead beyond a doubt. Body parts had been blown away. Was Jerry responsible for the outcome of those mistruths? That groveled in his mind. Maybe the truth would have saved his life, not a fabrication. "God, what have I done? Good God Almighty," Jerry prayed. "What on earth is going down" he hollered, kneeling over Richard's lifeless body.

His heart was going a mile a minute, pounding right out of his chest. What to do? He ran to the front door and, against his better instincts, quickly opened it. What if the perpetrator had been there waiting. There was no one visible. But at the end of the long driveway he saw an official looking car steal silently away, tires not even screeching; like, well, all in a day's work. Jerry tried to glance at the license, but couldn't make it

out except for one large word. It looked like "GOV'T."
But then he may have wanted to see that word.

"Which government", he asked himself. He
remembered the edginess Rick had displayed at the
golf course, and his desire to make a beeline home.
Did he have enemies he feared? Was the Government
vehicle an American one? A Canadian one?

No matter. Right now it had no importance. But
what would come next in this ungodly drama?

There was little doubt about this question. Bolting
back to the Jacuzzi room he snatched his clothes and
put them on, ensuring that his wallet was in the pocket.
Under no circumstances should Jerry be found at the
scene of the crime. Then he remembered the keys to
the Mazda. He had placed them on the table beside the
Jacuzzi. Hastily snatching them he made a dash for
the driveway, glanced furtively to scc if anyone was
looking, and peeled out. Thank goodness the house was
an estate isolated from public scrutiny. He could at least
get away without anyone seeing him and contemplate
the future on the move. Nor was he about to inform the
authorities till he had some time to sort things out.

His mind was oriented to the fate of his family —
Jenny and the kids who hopefully were not hostages
against their knowledge. If it was the Canucks who had
done the deed then the question was why! And surely
they'd find a scapegoat. If the CIA did it, they'd do the
same. Fact was, Jerry didn't know quite what to do. By
instinct he headed for Highway 1, the Trans-Canada
ribbon of gray, and set his auto pilot sights on Banff

down the road. How would he keep tabs on who knew what? Or should he?

"The radio! I've got to listen to the radio." Jerry fumbled with the dial till something clear came in. It was a country and western station. He slapped it as if to force it to speak. "Come on, somebody, say something already." But the news of this murder would not be quick to hit the airwaves. This was political stuff. And how long would it take to find Rick's body anyway.

The town of Banff lay 110 kilometers west of Calgary. Jerry pressed the pedal, then backed off. He dare not be stopped for speeding in a vehicle owned by a murdered man. So he stayed under 100 kph - well under. He was not yet in control of his emotions, but he settled on a game plan. Find a little motel and hole up for the night. He pressed on. The sign on the highway read," Banff, 5 km." Jerry pushed a little harder on the gas and pulled up to a small motel beside the highway, then turned around, heading further into town. Visibility was not what he now wanted. Being a recluse was the only option. He remembered the little side road that used to direct his family to the cabin near Banff. "Why not," he asked himself. "God, I hope I can get it," he muttered to himself. There it was, just down the road. Newly painted, but still the same little log house which had provided the Grant family with some of their most precious family moments. Jerry slowed down and parked casually by the registration office. He entered the building and asked for cabin 10. That was toward the back of the complex, bordering a forest of pine trees. If necessary he could take flight into the woods. Within seconds all these observations were ensconced in Jerry's mind.

The clerk broke the momentary silence. "Guess we can accommodate you, sir. Cabin 10 is available tonight."

Pulling out his credit card, Jerry offered it to the man at the desk. Then he drew it back. "That would be a dumb thing to do. Pay by credit card," he thought. He looked in the cash pocket of the wallet. Blackwell had been right. It was well stacked with Canadian money. He paid the man and was escorted to the cabin. But on the way the motel clerk suggested an imprint of Jerry's Visa Card would be appropriate and customary to cover additional expenses that might be incurred. Jerry accommodated the request.

"By the way," the manager said, "we have satellite TV now. Enjoy your stay." At the moment Jerry thought little of TV, but Satellite TV usually meant access to CNN; and CNN was the most up to date news organization in the world. Jerry saw the clerk back outside, closed and locked the door, and instinctively turned on the tube. It was nearly 6:00 PM. Maybe he'd hear something. He sat on the edge of the bed, eyes and ears attuned to the set.

Not that he was ready for the top news item. Time passed. Finally this news bulletin: "Calgary police have reported the shooting death of Richard Green, Member of Parliament for Calgary West. Mister Green was found brutally murdered at his home. According to authorities the only lead is one given by the regular maid, Evelyn Martin, who reported that a Jerry Grant had phoned the night before seeking an old time friend of Mr. Green. She said she remembers Mister Green talking of meeting him at the Balmoral hotel. It is not known if Mister Grant had knowledge of the death, but he is being sought for questioning. Stay tuned for further information as it becomes available."

What a quandary. Somebody would certainly remember him as a pastor in Calgary two years earlier. Then they'd give a description to the police. At least Jerry had one thing in his favor. Through all the confusion, he had the foresight to register as William Walters, not quite as suspicious as Bill Smith. Even with the credit card imprint the facade had not been recognized. Not a very creative name, but a cover nonetheless. That was the good news. The bad news was that Jerry Grant was now a wanted man. How he got that way was still a mystery that stunned his senses.

The Reverend Jerry Grant was a fugitive, a fugitive far away from home. He had vowed someday to get even with Blackwell. But right now, he wished that Blackwell were there to answer some questions. If torture were necessary Jerry would be quick to use it. The cleric was transforming from a genteel, kindly man to a vindictive, vengeful character ready to kill.

"Why did Rick have to die? Why couldn't it have been me", he prayed. Was there even going to be a future for a man who, till now, had an astonishingly, well crafted life? Could Jerry Grant keep on living? Did he even want to?

Chapter 9

There is nothing more pathetic—nor perhaps more human—than to see a fully righteous man filled, with every gracious quality, down and out with a heart filled by demons. There was anger, dismay, worry, guilt and the whole kit 'n' caboodle. Samson had his hair trimmed, and now he lay face down on the bed emptied of tears and a void in his heart. Choices, circumstances, events of other men are choosing; such were the matters that brought down the mighty warrior of graciousness. If ever he needed a booster shot it was now. He bowed his head, and through the tears, this man of inner strength blurted and spurted his heartaches and burdens to "Whatever God be listening!" In due time a serenity wafted into his troubled soul. "What are my options?" he prayed and pondered. One by one the possibilities were discarded. He could turn himself in on the condition that he be given a chance to explain everything from the start. But would anyone believe it? Not only that, but would it endanger Jenny? He could attempt to reach home by whatever mode, and hope to find Blackwell in a sympathetic mood. He did have the information, after all. But would Blackwell be amenable to such a quick return. The schedule had been spelled out in precise terms. One week from the day he left, he was to return. Would a hastened return incite Blackwell to make good on the promise of a tax evasion charge? Or hurting Jenny?

So Jerry's recovery had it's beginning in the quietude of meditation and reason. He considered the possibilities and charted a course. He would try to reach home, inform Jenny, and then locate Carl Blackwell through whatever means. Such became the game plan. Deep inside him he affirmed that innocence found its own respite. "Sure," he questioned, "try telling that to Jesus."

Peering out the cabin window Jerry saw a lighted phone booth at the end of the darkened street. He needed to call Jenny — collect. But he couldn't be sure her guardian angel, as she had been led to believe the agent with her was, would permit a conversation. Yet there was no other way; no other idea came to mind. He ambled outside the cabin toward the phone, whistling along the way to simulate normality. Jerry dialed the operator who answered on the first ring.

"Yes operator," he began. "Please give me a collect call to Jenny Grant. Area code is 607 and the number is 555-7887. The call is from Jerry."

"Last name please," the operator requested.

"Oh, I'm her hubby. She'll accept the call with the name Jerry," he assured her. She agreed to the terms. Jerry heard the number being dialed. To his surprise and delight, Jenny was quick to answer. "Hello" she answered in a polite manner.

"Collect call for a Jenny Grant from Jerry," the operator said. "Will you accept the charges?"

"Yes, yes of course operator."

"Go ahead," she urged.

"Jerry, is that really you? What's up hon?"

"Plenty, Jenny." There was a pause. "Listen - what's that funny clicking noise on the phone? How come you answered? Thought sure I'd get your lady guard".

"Don't know", Jenny responded. "It's been giving us some trouble since you left. I got to the phone 'cause the agent's drunk and asleep. She's always dozing off and she's supposed to take the calls. She sure is doing a good job protecting me though. But she is a drunk! Actually I sometimes feel more like I'm under house arrest. Jerry, what's really happening? I'm told nothing. Are things different than I was informed?"

"Okay listen carefully. Jenny, there is a glitch!"

"Are you hurt, Jerry?" she queried anxiously?"?

"No, but I have to get home. I can't give you details over the phone, but I'm coming home tomorrow. I'll fill you in then. Jenny, we've really got ourselves into the middle of a major — operation I guess you might call it."

"Will everything be okay then?"

"Heck ya! We just accomplished things you were told in a rapid fire manner. But I moved away from the game plan a bit and they might be a bit p.o.'d at me for that. Just need a favor from you."

"What is it?"

"I have to get home and here's what I want you to do. Phone America West and make a reservation for me for tomorrow's morning flight from Calgary to Tucson. Whatever you do Jenny, don't put it on a credit card. I have enough cash to pick it up in the morning here at the Calgary airport."

"What's going on, Jerry? This sounds awful."

Jerry had no desire to keep Jenny worrying. "Jenny, it's not that big a deal, really. I'll fill you in when I get home. Don't get all uptight now. Do what I say honey, please. And do it now when I hang up. Jenny, one more thing. Be sure to meet me at the airport if possible."

"If I can Jerry, but lush here will be watching my moves to the doors. They changed the locks and I have to beg for a key to go out and get the paper."

"Huh!"

"There's a lady here with me, remember. I'm not supposed to be at home. I'm at a funeral with you in Calgary."

Jerry recalled the plan. "Oh, right. But really, she's looking out for your welfare" Jerry feigned.

"Listen, I will really try. I don't know for sure hon. She has been letting me out on occasion, but just at night to get some fresh air. And, like I said, sometimes to get the paper."

"Okay, then don't push it. Make the reservation under the name - oh - Gary Carter. Yeah - Gary Carter. By the way, is your guardian angel listening to you talk?"

"No, she's quite stoned. Really is quite a lush. Wait a minute — isn't there going to be a problem using a false name though Jerry? I mean they always ask for ID now."

"That's my problem, okay! Make the reservation now, and I'll take a cab from the airport when I arrive if you can't get there. I'm not sure if this call is being monitored or not. If they don't want me home we'll find out. And Jenny, if anything should go wrong — I love you so very much."

"Jerry," she began to sob, "what's going to go wrong?"

"No, not that it will. But I'll see you tomorrow. Love ya. Bye." Last thing Jerry wanted was for Jenny to panic.

Jerry was unsure of his plan "A", but could not consider a plan "B". He shuffled his way back to the cabin determined to get some rest, laid down on the bed, clothes and all. Then he sat back up. "My gosh, the Mazda. I can't drive the Mazda back to Calgary in broad daylight." He searched the phone book for a bus service. "Trailways." Thank God for that. Jerry gave a call from the room and asked about the schedule out of Banff. The ticket agent said there was a bus out of Banff at 6:15 a.m. That would put him into Calgary around 8:30, and he was certain the plane would leave about 10 a.m. That was cutting it close but was his only option. He set his computer watch alarm and, shivering with fatigue, crawled under the covers. There would be no sleep that night, save a few winks now and again.

"Beep, beep, beep." Morning! Jerry jumped to his feet and quickly cleaned up. He grabbed the keys to the Mazda, checked the wallet, and headed for downtown Banff.

"I better not park at the bus depot," he decided. He pulled into a space in front of a coffee shop, across the way from the depot and well behind a cluster of bushes. It dawned on him he hadn't eaten, and even with all the stress, Jerry now felt some pangs of hunger. There was more than enough time till the bus left, so he shoveled down a full breakfast and then some. After paying his bill he moseyed across the street to the Trailways station, toothpick dangling out of his mouth.

"One to Calgary," he asked. The agent gave him the ticket and, without raising his head, instructed him, "Bus leaves in ten minutes." This would be a difficult trip. Jerry didn't know if he would get out of Calgary or not. When boarding time arrived, Jerry got on the bus, and found his way to the back. He snuggled in a far corner, chilled by the morning mountain air. Banff was a beautiful spot, but right now, the only spot he wanted to be was home. Jenny needed to know everything and Jerry needed to tell somebody. I fact however he was reticent to give Jenny the details.

The miles passed slowly, but he was getting to his first destination. Calgary was in sight, and then it happened.

<u>Roadblock!</u> The bus slowed down and came to a halt.

"Looks like we have a roadblock," the driver radioed back. "Sit tight everybody. We'll be on our way shortly."

All Jerry needed was a roadblock. The bus crawled ahead to where the Royal Canadian Mounted Police had stationed their vehicles fully covering the roadway in both directions.

After the driver opened the door, an officer stepped in. "Morning George," the Mountie said glancing back into the bus.

"Morning Phil. What's up?" Obviously, the driver knew the policeman.

"We're looking for a new Mazda — fire-engine red. Seen anything on the road like that?"

"Nope, drove overnight mostly," he replied. "Can't tell the color of the cars in the dark."

"Okay George", the policeman motioned. "Go on in."

Jerry opened his eyes. For once he had done something right. Had he driven the Mazda back to Calgary, it would have been the proverbial curtains.

"Thank you Lord," he prayed in silence.

The bus pulled into its appointed spot. Jerry disembarked and deftly summoned a cab. He figured on about 90 minutes till the plane left. A taxi quickly arrived and Jerry hopped in.

"Airport please."

"Right on, sir," he answered. "The going's a little tough this time of day, but once we hit airport road it'll be fast. When's your plane leaving?"

"About tenish" I think. Jerry was right. They reached Terminal two at the airport and he got out, giving the cabby a generous bonus. As he entered the airport he noted the monitors with all the times on them. "America West: Las Vegas, Phoenix, and Tucson. 10:10 am." So far so good. The words of an optimist.

Jerry approached the counter, and was pleased there were few people in line. "Do you have a ticket here for Jerry — make that Gary Carter?" Friends call me Jerry."

The agent gave him a furtive glance, and then a second one. She punched up the computer and Jerry's ticket rolled out."

"Here it is. To Tucson, Mr. Carter, right?"

"Right." It all seemed too easy! But sometimes fate deals you a royal flush.

"That'll be $155, please." Jerry had only US currency left.

"Can I pay you in American dollars? That's all I have?"

"Oh sure. Our American cash fare is $119."

Jerry laid the money out, all in 20's, and got a buck change. Surprisingly, he still had some left. Blackwell had been rather generous in the expense account department.

"Here's your ticket sir. Can I see some picture ID please?"

Jerry whipped out his wallet, and, having removed the Driver's License held up the picture in front of the ticket clerk, making sure his thumb virtually covered the name at the bottom. She barely peeked at it, though Jerry sported a skuzzy two day beard.

"Thank you sir. Have a good flight. The custom and immigration pre-clearance is to your right."

"Dang, I forgot about that. Well, I can't run now. One more hurdle to go," he thought. Walking briskly to the immigration and customs area, Jerry stepped to the booth. Again there was no significant lineup.

"Where is your residence sir?" the agent asked.

"Tucson, Arizona," he answered, with a pleasant smile.

"How long have you been out of the country?"

"Two days."

"Citizenship?"

"Canadian."

"Do you have a work permit or a resident card?"

"Sure. I am a parish pastor in the finest city of America." Jerry dug into his wallet for his green card and turned it over. Then a thought struck him. The Immigration Officer had his ticket and Card and the name on the Card was plastered all over the news. Then too, the names on the respective documents were different. The best he could hope for was that the agent hadn't heard the news or ingested enough caffeine to be very alert.

Jerry handed the card to the officer. "Okay Mister Grant. Anything to declare?"

"Nothing sir. Canadian stuff's too expensive."

The officer nodded in assent to his observation and waved him through. Officially he was now on American soil, and, in spite of his citizenship, how glad he was. So far so good. Then again, maybe all that was a bit too easy! Right now there was no such thing as a sure bet. But the airport I.D. issue and the customs clearance was a little too — well, easily accomplished. "Blackwell!" That name rang in his mind.

America West was noted for its promptness. Nor would they disappoint anyone today. The taxi to the runway was right on time, and the flight a lot more favorable than the day he had arrived. Of course he still had to fly through the hot desert air en route to Tucson from Phoenix. But now Jerry was feeling more confident. As much as he despised Carl Blackwell, he felt a compulsion to see him as soon as possible. Blackwell was likely the only person who could explain what was happening. And the more he thought about it the more he believed Blackwell would be at the airport gate.

The airliner made its two scheduled pit stops, and then took off for Tucson. It was 1:00 PM and home was twenty minutes away. All the horror that happened was still so vivid. Nothing about it was foggy. Buckling up for the final approach Jerry began to consider his reactions. Things would never be the same of course. But he had to believe that what had happened could be put behind him — somehow—some way. If it couldn't, there was no hope for a reasonably content life. So while posturing his station in life, the craft landed with a gentle thump and taxied to the appropriate gate. Jerry chose not to rush the deplaning process. His wish was to move with the crowd and not stand out in any way. He saw no one observing him. Looking left and then right and then left again, Jerry kept moving down the corridor. He pulled out fifty cents to buy a paper — just another way of playing the casual game. Placing it under his arms he proceeded to the exit gate. His garment bag had remained in Banff, so his hands were free.

"What did that headline say?" Jerry asked himself. He remembered noting something in bold print. Bold print was usually reasonably big time news; most significant. Sometimes however it was just yellow journalism. He veered over to the side, hoisted the paper to eye level and read aloud. What he saw stunned his spirit and gave him a new lease on hatred.

"October Wargames planned for northern U.S." That was the headline. Below it read the article: "The US army and Airforce will be engaged in exercises in the northern states of Montana and Idaho later this year. The Pentagon affirms this is a routine matter and has no bearing on political hotspots around the globe."

Jerry's face turned flush. He lip-spoke his conclusion. "The mentality of the Canadian leadership had not been paranoid. Troops would be stationed in the upper states for a purpose: A military incursion onto Canadian soil with the purpose of manually trenching fresh water from a foreign source. This was grand theft of a natural resource. Resources — bombs, underground nukes, manpower by the thousands. Not unreasonable at all."

Jerry's power of reason had always been precise.

"My God," he muttered. "It's all true after all. The American military is going into Canada to take water by force." How — he wasn't really sure. But that they intended to do so was a more than an hypothesis; it was, to him, a factoid entrenched in Jerry's mind. Everything added up. The CIA had heard all the information from Rick, though Rick was fabricating the story. Or maybe he wasn't! Rick's house was well bugged. So when the information was verbally volunteered during their time in the spa it was recorded by the CIA which couldn't leave any loose ends. They had to eliminate Rick and set up Jerry as the guilty party. And as soon as they had the information about the choppers, they could act.

"October war games," He thought. "This is no game. This is war," This is really war; an invasion by the United States of America." Pensive and confused Jerry felt the touch of a hand on his shoulder. He turned to see what was happening. There was Carl Blackwell with his two sidekicks, breast pockets bulging with their official weapons. Blackwell smiled and said, "Welcome. We made it easy for you to get back here, friend."

Now the mild mannered Jerry Grant was not to be denied. Without thought or warning, and by pure instinct, Jerry leaned back, reeled forward, hauled off and belted Blackwell squarely in the kisser. And a good one at that. CIA Superstar was sporting a bloody nose, messy face and a prone position. "That's for everything, you slime. For me, Jenny and oh yes! Let me give you one to remember Richard Green by!

Blackwell's mates held back Jerry's arm. But not his mouth.

"You scumbag! You murdered my best friend." Blackwell was stunned all right, reeling from Jerry's right uppercut. The two guards now sensed Jerry's increasing loss of control. They grabbed him and pinned him to the floor. Jerry tried fighting his way loose but this time was well outmanned.

"Let him up," Blackwell said surprising everybody. "I'll give him that one for the great job he did." Jerry was taken aback by the reaction. Blackwell had obviously bought the drama enacted by Jerry and Rick. He even extended a hand to Jerry and offered to pull him up. Jerry shoved it aside and stood up, rubbing his knuckles, now smarting from the punch.

"I'm rather glad you made it, Reverend. Very, very enterprising."

"And now I'm a dead man, right."

"Not at all," Blackwell said convincingly. "You're a free man — under our conditions of course." His tone was nasal. No wonder since he was pinching his bleeding nostrils together.

"Why? Why bother to let me live." A small crowd had now assembled.

"Because you did the job we asked. You got the information, and we heard it all. Because your hands are tied. We still have the ace in the hole."

"My wife?"

"And your kids— yeh, we found them down in Lima! Oh, and your tax form."

"That's your collateral for life."

"That's the way it is for a lifetime."

"What's next then?"

"Nothing," Blackwell answered. "We're going to take you home, and, when we get there, we'll answer your questions. As far as we're allowed that is."

Jerry stared at the ceiling.

"Can I count on a quiet performance to your house?" Blackwell asked.

"Yes, you can. 'Course I'm assuming Jenny's unhurt."

"That she is" came a believable retort.

So Jerry decided to be Jerry Grant again. After all, he was about to see his beloved wife. He had his wife to embrace and a plan to formulate. His mission was now directed to his native land. In less than two months, he had to get some very urgent information to the Canadian government — and convince the leaders to believe him. Jerry had to be a good boy and pretend the matter was over and done with.

But even at that, he wasn't sure if he was going to be driven home or detoured to some dark alley and dumped as refuse which had outlived its value.

Chapter 10

They shared a warm and loving embrace. Neither spouse sported any qualms about showing affection publicly. Blackwell and the lady from the State Department stared dispassionately. Undismayed by their smirks, Jerry and Jenny were embracing and kissing with the passion of youth. Screw the onlookers. These two were sweethearts cherishing the moment.

Knowing their telephone conversation from Banff to Tucson had been monitored, Jerry was also delighted he had chosen to tell Jenny so little, save the fact there was a glitch. And now Jenny asked about it.

"Oh that!" Jerry glared at Blackwell before turning back to Jenny. "No, it's just that Mr. Blackwell here decided we accomplished in a day and a half what we might have taken so much longer to do. But you know

Jenny; I'm not supposed to share too many details with you given the nature of the mission except that it was about restoring water — ah — environmental issues on a more formal basis; like between Canada and the U.S. having their water talks on a more frequent basis."

This left open the possibility that Jenny may never need to know the most gruesome truth. That didn't mean Jerry wouldn't share it. He sensed a spirit of uncertain dismay and during a second but shorter embrace whispered, "Shh — later Jen."

As for their affectionate ways, it was part of their marriage style. They took this unity business with due regard, and there was never a doubt that their vows would be honored "till death us do part."

Blackwell had strongly urged Jerry to leave good enough alone, especially to "shut-up" about gruesome details. He had also made it amply clear that, until the military mission was finished, Jenny and Jerry would continue to live under extreme scrutiny. Their phone would be monitored; their daily activities observed, and travel outside the U.S. was a no-no until further notice. Such restrictions affirmed and confirmed the suspicions Jerry held about the plot being established, namely the forceful takeover of whatever water the U.S. wanted and needed. Iceland, together with Canada, shared a universal distinction of the best water sources on earth — drinkable water that is.

"We're going to be leaving you now," Blackwell said. "I want to remind you both that you're still away in Calgary so far as your church people are concerned." Jerry had asked about this in the car en route from the airport. In his own persuasive way, he had convinced Blackwell that early morning bike rides would cause no problems. The neighbors were some distance apart in the rugged desert terrain. He had even convinced agent Blackwell that it would be good therapy both to cycle on a regular basis and go for an evening drive that night under cover of darkness. "After all" he had reminded Blackwell, "you do want me to forget all about the matter, don't you? Get life back to normal? And you'll be watching!" They would be free to take up life as usual, save the knowledge of their movements and phone conversations being necessarily monitored for the sake of America's security; that of course meant a successful incursion mission into Canada's western water supply.

Blackwell had concurred. What Jerry suggested had indeed been part of his own original advice to his adversarial partner in crime. But Jerry was not about to forget the grotesque murder. Nor the plot! Not till justice was done for Rick's murder and the military plot revealed.

That the American State Department was involved was also a troubling prospect. It implied the mission had been given the green light from high up, possibly the White House itself. Jerry would draw no premature conclusions. He had but one resolve: get back to Canada surreptitiously before the War games began. That would take some intrigue and imaginative planning. What a shame he hadn't read of the military exercises prior to leaving Calgary. 'Course it may not have been news in Canada then. As a matter of fact, it would hardly be news to Canadians at all. What the American military did was customarily of no interest to Canadian citizens, and sometimes only passing interest to the Canadian political leadership.

His single dilemma in fulfilling his resolve of full disclosure was whether to include Jenny in planning an escapade to Canada, in the flesh of course. Would she be better off knowing as little as possible or just staying out of the picture? Did Jerry Grant truly want his wife to lay her future and security and life on the line, or should he go it solo? Besides, he recalled his wife had been told that his mission for the common good. For whatever reason Jenny had not yet required an explanation of all the intrigue! Time would tell if she had forgotten or was just awaiting opportunity. Or perhaps she had, by this time, sensed that matters things were not as she previously thought.

As for the present, this evening would feature a full moon. For Jerry and Jenny that meant a night on the patio, romancing and talking. Yet for a good hour it remained a silent night. On this unforgettable evening, neither one was sure how or where to begin. Jenny finally broke the awkward silence. She took Jerry by the hand, as if knowing he needed consolation of some sort, and spoke softly, "Want to talk about anything, hon?" Jenny asked.

"Sure, a topic of your choice." That was always Jerry's way of tossing the ball back into her court. He did enjoy meaningful conversation, and was ready to surrender his interests to hers. Vice versa was also the case. That usually made for an impasse and neither would opt to begin. After the past days where could they possibly start?" The issue at hand was what Jenny knew or did not know.

Feeling he had better steer the conversation away from the events of the immediate past, Jerry gave in and began to speak.

"Listen, babe, what say we do a morning ride around the loop?"

"If you feel up to it," she concurred.

"Sure! I need to pedal off some tension anyway. Sitting in airplanes always makes me tight. Usual time?"

"Usual time," she agreed, cozying up to him.

"But that means we're going to need a good night's rest. Want to hit the sack?" Jerry said smiling and with eyebrows lifted.

Jenny read his mind and was quick to react. She stretched out her hand to his, and he pulled himself up from the chair. Then, as was her way, she placed his hand on her breast and leaned against him. It was her signal she wanted to make love. Jerry hugged her and led her to the bedroom. He wasn't certain if the room was bugged or not. "If so, give 'em an earful" he thought. They had only been separated two days. But both knew the moments immediately ahead would be special. In matters of romance, they had that youthful desire. Soon, neither was thinking of anything else but the joy of the moment. And as the moon was part of the sky, Jerry and Jenny were part of one another. How they wished it could last forever.

When all was said and done, Jerry lay next to Jenny, joyful and contented, and gave thanks for the wife that was his and his alone. For the first time in several days, Jerry had the benefit of an undisturbed sleep.

At 5:45 a.m., he was wide awake, polishing the bikes and checking brakes and tires. Jenny was getting on her biking gear. Lord, did she look good in it. They wore the same colors, helmet and all. Turning on the radio to catch the morning news Jerry listened with half an ear as he greased the gears. It was approaching 6:00 a.m., and he hoped to catch the headlines of the day. What he heard brought back the memories of the past two days.

The announcer spoke matter-of-factly: "Military War games are being planned for the northern states of Montana and Idaho. It is estimated that some 100,000 troops will assemble for one of the largest such exercises in recent history. Spokesmen for the Armed Forces are calling these exercises routine. They will begin this October."

"Routine," Jerry thought. "100,000 troops, and that's routine." He wondered what the American public would think if they knew the facts? Or the world community? It struck him that if he could make the facts known, and he fully intended to do so, somehow and soon, such an effort might well terminate this plan. Make that aggression, not plan!

The radio continued with the local news. At the time, Jerry didn't know why, but one obscure item struck him as being important. He would file it away in his mind for future reference. The announcement came:

"On the local scene, officials are already preparing for the annual October hot air balloon festival. Thirty balloonists are expected to converge on Tucson for the annual event. With the hope for normal Southeast winds, leaders of the event believe it will provide opportunity for free flight to Phoenix. Balloonists will launch from the Sabino Canyon area, and the public is invited to come out to observe. Further details will be brought to your attention as the event draws closer."

Hmm! Jerry had never been up in a hot air balloon. But he knew a fellow clergyman, Gordon Woods, who actually owned one. Furthermore he would likely be involved in this year's event as he had been in the past. Come to think of it, Jerry had a standing invitation from him to join the ride, but always refused with a "thanks, but no thanks." The only phobia in Jerry's life was heights. Planes were one thing, but swinging baskets supported by hot air — uh, uh.

He might go and watch though. As a matter of fact, Jerry and Jenny had a bike route to Sabino Canyon which served as an alternative to the loop drive. And once there, a three mile challenging climb to the top was the real workout! They had never attended the festival, but maybe this year they could. They needed something to look forward to. Perhaps the two of them could go out there together. What a sight that would be, hot air balloons rising into the blue morning sky, sailing over the purple Catalina mountain range; albeit many weeks away. Jerry was attempting to put something into their lives that would get them back to some semblance of sanity.

But then, for some mysterious reason, he mused to himself, "Maybe I can sneak out of this city in a balloon basket with Gordon and once I get into Phoenix, slip onto an airliner to Canada." Then he chuckled it off as totally absurd. "Stupid," he mused. What a retarded idea!"

Chapter 11

Jerry had been away from home for two nights, yet a lifetime had passed. But unlike the quiet fog of Sandburg's poem, the change had hardly come on little cat's feet. It seemed more like an elephant stampede that had altered his destiny and changed the beauty and serenity his life had become in Tucson.

That night Jerry slept minutes at a time. He was quite emotionally stalled but could not be content with that mode of living. It is often said in adventure literature that the hunted becomes the hunter. Perhaps in reality he could find a way to reciprocate the deeds of Carl Blackwell et al. Perhaps the <u>haunted</u> could become the <u>haunter</u>, and, in some meaningful way, atone for decisions gone awry. Jerry was not a vengeful man. That was, in his conscience, the territory of

Almighty God. Justice of course was quite different from revenge, and Jerry lived with justice as one of his primary mottos.

At this point in time Jenny was mum and Jerry knew why?

He knew that she knew far more than what she had initially been told when he forged the phone call episode from the airplane cockpit. And she knew that he knew that she knew: It was a twisted version of the old Abbott and Costello dialogue "whose on first", albeit this one was unspoken.

The past would not go away. Jerry's nightmare was still primarily one of guilt. Did his admonition to Rick to fabricate the information backfire? Did Rick understand that his <u>story</u> was actually the truth, or close to it? And that he, Rick, was either going to be dragged into it or placed elsewhere in Environment Canada —- Department of the Interior. Maybe it was the Canadian government which had done the deed to Richard Green!

The following Sunday, eight days hence, Jerry would be back in the pulpit. As for home here and now, what was to be said? His conscience was a rat's nest of confusion. He lay awake hoping their morning cycling regimen would begin to arrest the gory and grotesque memories he now held and the recurring nightmares that the darkness harbored. That night Jenny was oft awakened by the sudden grunts he made, but in her faithfulness, while not fully understanding Jerry's recent living nightmare, she snuggled up when he was in distress. The unspoken may soon need to be verbalized. As for Jerry, he was ready for full disclosure at Jenny's request. No sooner!

"What day was it anyway" the Reverend thought? It was Saturday morning. While not reclusive by nature, the Grant's found their home's relative isolation on Old Spanish trail to be a boon in the present crisis. It was possible for them to enter and exit their driveway unbeknownst to their neighbors. Nor was it a special concern that during their biking they might encounter church friends. While they had made the acquaintance of many who shared their passion for cycling, such people were neither intimate friends nor church members. So should they meet an acquaintance the rule of the road with avid bikers was that you don't break up a good ride with a long time-out for socializing. It was a sport unto itself.

Even the lights in their home at night were barely visible to others from a few feet beyond their driveway. The spacious desert lots and trees like juniper, eucalyptus, olive and mesquite gave them a privacy they cherished. Other thick desert plants enhanced it. Still, their location afforded them the proximity of the city.

Time to hit the trail! Jerry was tired but willing. Jenny stepped out ready to go. They met the bike path at the driveway entrance and turned left toward Saguaro National Monument, the great forest of eastern Tucson. The ride there was a steady incline, though not very steep. For bikers it was a boon, since the return trip would take place after their difficult climb around the loop drive; a treat so to speak.

Jennifer was out front as usual, now setting a brisk pace; Jerry, though not admitting it, had a tough time keeping up. In spite of the supposed rest he had, the days past had taken their toll, not only emotionally but physically as well.

In short order they were at the entrance to the loop drive. There stood the monument office, housing a small museum and slide show about the desert. Outside the office was a mini-garden sporting every variety of plant to be found in this eastern portion of the Sonoran desert. At this time of day, bikers and joggers hogged the one way loop drive. Others in cars would come later in the day and, in air conditioned comfort, get a 20 minute view of this forest of saguaros, prickly pears, or as natives said, "Mickey mouse" cacti, Italian cypress, lightning burnt areas and the many other sights unique to the desert.

"Want to stop for a minute, dear," Jenny inquired, noting Jerry was puffing unusually hard. They were in front of the Monument fascia. There were benches for tired bikers and hikers, as well as shaded areas for those wishing to make this a pit stop. Commodes for urgent, time sensitive functions were set inside a clean outhouse with running water.

Jerry answered, "Naw, keep going. We can stop at the Vista." He was talking about Loma Verde Vista, a beautiful scenic spot made for tourists and photographers. It was four miles to that scenic lookout through the ups and downs of the desert forest. Being half-way up a steep hill, it also proved an excellent place to rest, take pictures or videos, and eat a bite while viewing a surrealistic scene. They continued to the Vista and pulled up together at the railing.

What a view! And this day they would be blessed to see waterfalls dripping down the many rocky slopes, unusual in the desert but customary after the kind of heavy rains they had experienced the previous nights. It gave the desert a pungent but not offensive odor. With the water flowing they saw and counted seven mule deer grazing at the pools.

"Chow time," Jerry advised. "Let's find some shade and have some cinnamon rolls and juice." It wasn't their custom to eat en route, but they had planned to stop and just spend some time in the middle of this desert handiwork. Jerry suggested they move away from the bikes and take off their helmets, straying off into the trees a short way. Jerry sensed they were being watched, and perhaps overheard by someone with one of those new parabolic mikes like they use at football games to let the TV audience hear the crunching of helmets and bones. They moved back, keeping their bikes in full view leaning against the railing that overlooked the hills and vales. But then came the inevitable. Jenny made her request. She folded her arms across her chest, walked a few feet from Jerry, then turned around like a speeding bullet and demanded, "Jerry, the time has come!"

"What?" Jerry knew what, but he wanted to be sure.

"Lay it all out for me Jerry. I am your wife and I love you. Something is rotten in the state of Arizona and you're into some very deep doo doo. We are not leaving here until I know what is really going on." Jennifer wanted to use a questionable word, but now it nearly slipped out. She was asking her beloved to put the cards on the table face up, and to hold nothing back at all. "Jerry, I'm all ears. And I love you with all my heart! What is happening?"

At one and the same time it was a surprise but not unexpected. Jerry's first reaction was relief, knowing that Jenny must have been boiling from the inside out, her mind and heart in turmoil over so many unknowns. This was the moment of truth, decisive to their futures as well as to the present. More importantly, their marriage had always been based on the absolute trust that each was telling the truth. Now the fulcrum of the truth was at Jerry's disposal. How he worded it and how much detail to include, especially about the messy murder in Calgary, presented a personal and present challenge. He had to be strong but forthright.

Jerry hung his head then raised it and took a deep drink of modestly cool water tinged with lemon. He nearly choked when Jennifer, a second time, so firmly and emotionally demanded what she had every right to demand. The saga began.

"Jennifer Jean Grant, I love you too! What I'm about to tell you is going to test your metal as it has my own. The past two days nothing has been as you were told. Course you obviously know that. So here it is." Jenny stood silent.

Jerry began with the fiasco in the office of the IRS, repeating virtually every word spoken after Carl Blackwell had entered. He confessed throwing a tantrum in the airplane in order to speak with Jenny by phone. He revealed the true nature of this mission, as his dear wife sat motionless soaking up all the details.

The most difficult part was addressing the grotesque murder of Richard Green. Jerry held nothing back, because Jenny had asked for it all. So when Jerry referred to the hole blown in Richard's chest, it was time for her to let it all out. And cry she did, sobbing unfettered into folded hands, uttering both a scream and a prayer. "Oh my God! Where do we go from here?" And at this point she began to pace, refusing an embrace from her loving husband. She needed to grieve and get angry. So Jerry let her, and then asked if he should wait till later to complete the escapade.

Jenny retorted, "There is nothing else to say. Murder is the bottom line. The rest I've pretty well pieced together." Nonetheless, Jerry quickly summarized his trip to Banff and the ease by which he was able to return to Tucson. "Everything was a setup" he ended! "And Jenny, I or we need to get word to the Canadian authorities. Somehow and sometime soon!"

"Are we in danger, Jerry?" She didn't sound terrified.

"No, not if we keep quiet and stay put," he said.

"But how can we do that? I mean, we've got to phone somebody. Or e-mail them? Not to mention a life to live."

"We can't use our e-mail or phones love. The e-mail runs through the phone line and we know they have the frequency of our cell phones. It's all bugged. Our house is bugged. How do you think they knew I was arriving in Tucson? And who knows for how long before the IRS letter came they had listened to our lives, private matters and all."

"But Jerry, a murder? And what about this business of a military takeover of Canadian water? Why?"

"It's too complicated to explain," Jerry offered. "But there'll come a time when I'll tell you more. Right now we have to get out of here and start playing the game of pretending like all is said and done."

"Got any ideas?"

"None that you'll like. But listen anyway." Jerry was about to toss out the idea of a hot air balloon escape from Tucson. And he was obliged to wing it since he had not thought out any details whatsoever. But this <u>stupid</u> idea suddenly became a plan, a possibility; maybe the beginning of a new chapter in the story of their lives. Now this <u>stupid</u> idea was going to be planted in the mind of a very intelligent but virtually shattered woman who was his life.

"Jenny, are you sure you want to hear my plan now? Hon, you've just been through a trial of fire and you want to hear it? It is pretty far out, but something that has a chance of working. Wanna wait?" In reality, Jerry needed more time to think it through than did Jenny.

"No! Now!"

"Okay Jenny, hear me out. And help me with the details. See, I'm making this up as I go. It all started with this item in the news about the hot air balloon festival we have in October."

"Go on!"

"Jenny, don't laugh till I'm done. Gordon Woods — you know — he pastors the community church down the way; well, he's got a hot air balloon he takes up every year at the festival. He's begged me time and time again to go up just for a tethered ride, let alone a free flight! And this year the festival won't be at Midvale Park but over at the Sabino Canyon area. If we could persuade Gordon Woods to take me along, and if the winds are right — hey, it'll be a free flight to Phoenix this year — and if he would get me to Phoenix without anyone knowing I'm in one of those balloons I could make a run for it by air to the Canadian border. I might catch a plane out of Phoenix and it would be an easy escape".

Jenny wrinkled her forehead, and dropped her chin to the ground. "Jerry, have you lost your mind? You can't stand the idea of going up in something like that! And how would we get to the Canyon anyway if we decided to try this stunt?"

"Okay, details! Let's try something like this on for size. We bike to the Canyon area. Carl Blackwell knows that's one of our semi-regular bike routes. He'd have no idea I'm trying to get out of town in a hot air balloon."

"So how would I do any good?" Jenny seemed a little more empathetic to the idea with her tone and body language.

"Here's how I see it hon. We ride to the Canyon, take our rest at the tram stop, then get back on our bikes, go down the first incline and out of sight. You head for the top. There's no way you can be seen going up the mountain. Then, at the first down slope, I get off, and from where Blackwell's watching he can't see me. You go to the top with the specs and watch the action close up."

"Go on."

"So okay Jenny, you're the decoy! You would stay at the Canyon top till later in the day, oh, noonish. Now picture this. After I get off at the first downhill — it's only a mile, I change into clothes that balloonists wear; in fact I get a special uniform for the ride. Then I crawl back up and casually go to Gord's balloon in whatever the heck the flight clothing is. Imagine Blackwell seeing you come out alone."

"Then what do I tell Blackwell when I return alone?"

"You could cover yourself by saying I took the back side of the hill down the road; you know, the one the men at the state pen had built. Or better yet, tell him I decided to stay up top for another half-hour because I was having a nap and you wanted to get back down and get some cool drinking Gatorade. So by the time Blackwell realized I was gone; I'm in the skyway to Canada. Three hours to Phoenix and a quick exit on any plane out of the country to Canada." There was silence. Jenny hmmm'd around a bit!

"So where do you go in Canada?"

"From wherever I land in Canada don't worry. I will get to the P.M. It is a long shot, but at the present, there seems no other way. And I'm not trying to be heroic. But knowing what I know, the CIA is going to be tailing us, especially me, and bugging all our calls and E-mails."

Jenny smiled, not insensitively, but with a new intrigue. "That's the greatest dumb idea I ever heard. What do you think will happen when it's discovered you're out of here?"

"Look dear, Blackwell will be watching us till the U.S. has done the deed or we've put a stop to it. He'll watch our every move, listen to every conversation. He researched our lives very well. So it won't be suspicious to him if we bike out there. He'll just follow us and hang out in the parking lot till we come back down from the ride to the top. Those fellows like to sit in cars with earphones and spy binoculars. I think they get off on it since the cold war is over. I'm really sure they'll stay at the tram station and wait for us to return from the Canyon ride at least down to the Tram station. When I don't come out, hopefully Blackwell takes a seizure! By that time I'll be in and out of Phoenix and on a plane to "Anywhere, Canada." But a lot depends on us being good boys and girls till the opportunity arrives."

Jenny was interested in details now, and kept on asking more pressing but urgent questions. "How can you be sure Gordon will let you go with him?"

"Heck, I've got a standing invitation hon. I'll phone him from the payphone back at the monument office after our ride."

"But if someone's tailing us now won't they be suspicious if you phone?"

"Nope.'Cause I'll pretend to use the cell phone here. Then I'll look at it the way people do when the battery dies at a bad time, shake it, and take out some change from my little emergency pouch cache to phone Gordon. And how about this — then I call the Kentucky Fried Chicken outfit. When he sees us pick up the chicken on the way home he'll think it was just a routine chicken call." Jerry sounded proud of his little deception.

"Jerry, I'm scared. This sounds awfully complicated. I don't want you up there in one of those balloons. What if something goes wrong?"

"What if the American military steals Canadian water by force?" Jerry countered. "What if more people like Rich Green are murdered? I mean, I don't even know if Betty is aware of what happened. Rick didn't say where she was; just divorced."

"I guess you're right. But isn't there an easier way — like phoning some official guy in Ottawa by payphone?"

"Well, that might work love. But I'll tell you this. I don't think anybody is going to believe a man who phones and says there's a plot for a military theft of our Canadian water, do you? Especially from a payphone to which I'll be traced if I try to get close to the top dogs in Ottawa."

"Maybe you're right on that score. Jerry, I'll do what you think is best. How can I help?"

"Pray a lot to start with. And oh yeah, one more thing. If I am discovered getting into the balloon and get followed to Phoenix, I'll have to plan another way to Canada. What I need is a routing of some secondary highways. Can you make me a map pretty soon? If worst comes to worst I'll steal a car."

"You want me to start a map already?"

"Jenny, I guarantee you this. Two months seems a long way off, but this is a serious issue. It is life or death, and it'll be on us before we blow our noses. If this is a viable plan we start arrangements like now. It gives us time to change details that could go wrong."

"I guess you're right, love. Sure, I'm the navigator."

Jenny was telling the truth. On all their car trips she was the lady with the map. And Jerry could never recall her making a goof when it came to automotive navigation.

"One more thing Jenny. When we talk around the house from now on, be sure that the radio or TV is on — and plenty loud. Whatever bugs are planted, if we have the cover of other noise, we can finalize our plans."

If you have any other ideas hon, tell me. I don't think the military is going to wait a long time. They'll have 10,000 troops up there. They're going to shoot down the helicopters on surveillance over the fresh water areas. At least, they think there are choppers and a big defense if they bought Rick's phony story. Boy, he did a great job just on my word!"

"How do you think they'll go after the water?" Jenny posed the question.

"I'm not really certain," Jerry admitted. "But with that many men, it wouldn't surprise me at all if they trenched it, or build an aqueduct from one the fast-flowing rivers down to a northern U.S.lake somewhere."

"Gad, that sounds like science fiction," Jenny replied, shaking her head.

"Richard Green thought that too, love. And he's not around to talk about it any more. I hate to trouble you with gory details, but that man was blown away. Don't know if there are enough pieces to pick up and bury."

Jenny nearly gagged. "I guess they're not kidding, are they?"

"I wish they were. I thought this whole thing was pretty far out too till Rick got shot. And when I saw the headline, I knew it was serious."

"But why?"

"Okay, let me fill you in on what's behind this all. The simple fact is that all the water down here is pure poison! Blackwell told me they had only fifteen years of drinkable water left. This country is desperate."

"Why won't Canada help them out," she asked.

"I don't quite know that," Jerry replied. "Maybe I can find out if I can get someone to listen to me."

"So who do you hope to talk to when you get to Canada," she inquired.

"The Prime Minister," he asserted. "I don't think anybody but the Prime Minister will listen to me."

"Why not?"

"Because it's too far out. I mean, look at the trouble you're having just believing it!"

Jerry and Jenny embraced. They hopped on their bikes and finished the ride. Then from the Monument office payphone area Jerry took out his cell phone to feign a call, knowing full well that phone was also bugged. He shook it to give whoever was watching the impression the cell phone was not working. "The moment of truth" he said to Jenny." Then he went to the payphone. He called Gordon Wood's number which he knew by memory and asked about the possibility of taking a ride at the time of the balloon festival. Gord was thrilled, and Jerry made overtures to get together at a later time for details. Next he called directory assistance, and for a 50 cent charge was given the number but also directly connected to the nearest KFC. The conversation was quick so as not to raise suspicions about making airline reservations which, of course, would keep him on the line for quite some time. He ordered the chicken. In short order, he hung up.

"What did Gordon say hon?"

"He was delighted," Jerry said with a devilish grin. "Said he was waiting for the day when he could test my faith. It's all set. We'll be meeting to work out further details." Let's just set our minds on what we were talking about. I know it seems a long way off but it'll be on us soon!"

"Okay hon, I'm with you."

As the couple mounted their bikes Jerry noticed a familiar face in a car parked near the entrance. It was a Blackwell "goon". Jerry was not reticent to call them that. He smiled at the shadow that wasn't concealing himself very well — and perhaps didn't intend to — and then waved with his middle index finger. Jenny slapped his hand and shamed him for doing that. But as they set out for home on their bikes Jerry looked back and summoned the agent to follow. That felt good. Very good! Once they got to the chicken joint, he knew the fellow in the car would be madder than the wet hen they were taking home to eat.

Chapter 12

To the surprise of both, only 90 minutes had passed since they first stopped at the Vista for a rest and formulated an outrageous plan to get Jerry out of Tucson. Though Jerry had not preplanned the details, they had come, as it seemed, by sheer inspiration. They closed in on home base after a pit-stop at the Colonel's joint. It was a quarter mile from there to the house; the bagged bucket of Fried Chicken wafted its enticing smell till both looked at each other, smiling, salivary glands hard at work.

It would be an early lunch since they really hadn't eaten anything much during their stop. Not often did they indulge in junk food, but this was an exception. Since it had been so long since their last visit to KFC they didn't wait to enter their home before the finger licking began. As Jerry observed the ever visible black vehicle now at the end of their driveway he waved a chicken leg at whoever was inside. It was a taunt. They were still being so closely guarded Jerry began to wonder if Blackwell's people were not somewhat suspicious about the Grants trying to do something with the information they had. The windows of that car were so heavily tinted the driver and sometimes companion were never discernable. 'Course a greasy face gave pause for a long, succulent tongue—touching French kiss. It was another taunt as well as a personal delight.

All in all, the ride to KFC and then home seemed to invigorate Jenny and Jerry. Perhaps they felt a little less helpless now that they had initialized some kind of plan, wild as it seemed, to get Jerry into Canada. And indeed, the need for some intervention had become more pressing after the revelation Jerry set forth. Their lives had a new sense of urgency, a new purpose if you will — forestall or prevent two historically friendly nations, whose border was virtually unguarded for 4,000 miles coast to coast, from warring over H2O.

Dinner was soon finished. All the skin had been eaten. "That was a great chicken pig out" Jenny quipped.

"And that was a great oxymoron" retorted her husband.

Both of them normally drank cold water with or after a meal. This time however, while doing so, a thought struck Jerry with a question he had not yet considered. "Why" he muttered in Jenny's hearing range: "Why would Canada be so stingy with the overabundance of clear and delicious water in ample supply flowing forcefully from the great northern trench? Water is life! Life is something you share!" He recalled Jenny asking this similar question at the Vista but gave it no deep consideration till now. And it bothered him. "Did God mess up and not make enough?"

That concept would plague him in the future much more than it ever had in the past. Jerry went back to plan "A". "One more thing Jenny, we've got to document all this stuff; like make a dozen or so diskettes on the computer or do a videotape. Point is we need to outline everything we know and keep it for safeguard.

Jenny was quick to respond. "Jerr, couldn't we send whatever we do to the newspapers or TV stations? Or do you think we might be able to get this stuff to the government of Canada?"

"Oh, I think not—-at least not the latter" he concluded. "It just has to be in person face to face with someone high up in the government ranks. And you know if I bring up the name of Richard Green someone is bound to listen. But I like your idea of sending copies to newspapers and TV stations. Then again, what if they read them and start coming around to get some more information? That could make Carl Blackwell really angry. Jenny, I want nothing to happen to you—in fact, I want nothing to happen to me either."

"So when do we start?" Jenny queried.

"I think we should start ASAP —Sunday after church! Now I'm talking really detailed stuff. I need your wording skills on that since all the details will need to be fully included. We make a dozen copies of the diskette and put them in a safe place. I don't think a videotape would work because our mail is being checked out. We can always smuggle a diskette in an envelope and mail it if that's what we plan to do. But if we e-mail it we'll be screwed. We're monitored because we use the phone line. Dang, I knew I should have gone with that other kind of modem!

"I get the idea Jerry. If push comes to shove, we tell the CIA the diskettes or tapes have been sent all over the U.S. and Canada; to papers, TV stations, and political leaders and friends. That may save our lives; it's our own little extortion game."

"So be it" hon."

"And if I understand you, plan "B" will be for me to mark secondary highway routes for you in the event you need to bolt out on wheels. I think we have something that is worth our best efforts." Jenny didn't believe it was safe, but in trying to renew some hope for their lives and the situation that the U.S. was trying to get water for the American southwest in a hostile fashion provided something akin to a future.

It was time for a shower, and as was often the case, Jerry and Jenny grinned at each other knowing they were going to have some good clean fun. She would soap him down, stressing the thighs and biceps, and especially so the tight buns that turned her into his own pleasing Geisha. She admired his strong body, muscular but not muscle bound. He was a long way from needing Viagra. Fully lathered, Jerry took the sponge and the body lotion and, in turn, lathered up his lover. Once fully smoothed with vanilla soaping they would meld into the unity of body, mind and spirit which they avowed on their wedding day. The final consummation of their love would come forth in the God-given pleasure of sexual climax.

Time passed by and Jerry began considering his status at work. How would he be received on Sunday? Would the people be aware of accusations made against Jerry in Canada? Sunday morning would tell the story. So it was. Arriving at church an hour before morning service began he was warmly greeted by ushers and deacons that helped him prepare for the morning worship. Bert Benson was the name of his most reliable helper. He embraced Jerry, then told him he had been sorely missed and bid him the consolation of the members regarding the death of a dear friend in Canada. Then he said something that turned Jerry into a paleface. "Did you know that we had a visitor from the U.S. government last week after service was over? He told the church about your involvement in assisting the American leaders in getting cooperation from Canadian authorities on our water crisis here after the funeral in Calgary. Boy, he was most commending of your efforts. So as a Yankee let me thank you as well. We're proud to have you as our preacher – Canadian notwithstanding, eh!" Jerry despised that "eh" business but let the church people have a little fun with it anyway. They didn't know the expression was more common in Michigan than most of Canada. And if he was in a bad mood or a little testy, he'd some times reply with that little factoid. Especially so if the taunter was from Michigan. In Tucson, a lot of winter visitors came from that state, but mostly from somewhere in the Chicago area.

"Ah", Jerry paused, "Well, I just put the American authorities in touch with the proper department people in Canada. I know some who work with environmental issues. No big deal!"

"You always were too modest" Bert retorted.

"I guess the universe is unfolding as it should. I do hope I can do more good in the future." 'Course Jerry was contemplating his newest venture. "They want me to go up to Canada again in a couple months" he added. "So however I can help I will Bert. With the church's blessing of course?"

Just before service began, Jenny walked into the office and straightened out her husband's clerical garb. It always did take her final touch to get ready to go into the sanctuary. But now would come the test of their emotions as they entered the sanctuary. Any doubts were soon put to rest as the people in church all rose and applauded Jenny's entrance, followed of course by Jerry. Jerry responded with a quick thank you" and invited the congregation to get back to worship. "My God" the Reverend thought, "if they only knew the truth of the matter."

Pastor Grant continued the course of ministry as he would do until such time when their plan of action would be activated with the opportunities afforded by virtue of the hot air balloon festival. That was two months away—-not really all that long. But long enough to watch the news and surf the net and try to get a handle on the War Games that had earlier been headlined the day he arrived home from Calgary.

After the service ended Jerry and Jenny stood together at the exit to the sanctuary and bid the people thanks for their warm reception back and the time to go back to Calgary and tend to the human need at a dear friend's funeral. They went out for brunch, returned home, and talked about the issues they would have to document and discuss. There were two. First, the computer account which they would co-author; and second, the return of their children, Kenton and Kerry, for a Fall Furlough from their exhausting missions of mercy. That was to happen about the end of October. By then, Jerry trusted, he would have accomplished his mission of getting to his homeland in the hopes of salvaging a long standing healthy relationship between two nations in which he had a personal interest; and possibly in averting an armed conflict between Canada and the United States over the sharing of water resources.

He had hopes that if successful, his escapade would result in no harm to Jennifer. Of course he had not forgotten his determinate objective to provide the Canadian Law Enforcement people with the truth about the assassination of his dear friend.

There was just so much on the agenda, and even more on the back burner of the unknown! Thank God he had enough faith remaining to believe the proverb,

"O Lord, my times are in Your hands." Somehow, in some way, everything at church was normal and that would work in Jerry's favor. For when he would request time out in October for a restful <u>vacation</u> he would have to maintain this outstanding Pastor-Parish relationship. As for the rest of the summer and till the end of September, there were plans to make. And for them to work or have any chance of working he would have to regain his former status as a revered icon in the ministry of bringing consolation to saddened hearts and offering advice to the forlorn. The St. Francis prayer said it something like this, "For it is in giving that we receive."

Chapter 13

Normally a post church nap was in order. Today would be an exception. The issue of documenting all that had happened would begin in earnest. It was precise, a virtual verbatim. Jenny typed while Jerry dictated, but Jenny's aptitude for writing was also part of the procedure. Not one iota was left out of place with intent. After a week the document was ready on hard drive. It was given the name "rawsmage", a muddle of the letters in War Games. Twelve diskettes and another dozen CDs carried copies of the document as they worked deeply into the night. Then the hard drive was placed into the recycle bin and permanently deleted. The diskettes were not labeled but filed by color code.

July was drawing to a close. Thankfully the kids had no information about the burdens heavy on their parents' hearts. Jerry and Jenny both knew that their children could well become collateral for the United States when they came back home for Furlough. They were sorely missed, yet as gracious as their life's calling was it left an empty nest with few contacts possible about their work or well being.

Such was the price of tendering your life to the cause of others. Oh, Mom and Dad would get a few e-mails when Kenton or Kerry found themselves in civilization, but they had not taken cell phones at the time they moved on to their outposts.

Summer moved onward, Jerry constantly reminded Jennifer that their normal conversation should be geared to the volume control on the radio or television. For as much as they despised loud TV or radio those devices were now covering for their talks. Many of their planning times--little details—took place on the patio or during biking. One evening when Jerry was not away counseling or at meetings they put together a formal oath at the beginning of each diskette. It was to affirm the truth of that which followed.

According to the latest reports, the military presence in the northwest had not yet begun and the matter was not yet a newsworthy headline. So they lived their lives day by day in the hopes that it had just been a fleeting headline. Still, Richard Green was dead and that could not go unattended. This was grimly outlined in their story. It took high priority.

The 15th day of August became monumental to the Grants. Papers and TV reports began to speak about the gathering troops from all areas of the military for War

Games or some Military Exercises. And it was always noted that the spacious but challenging mountain areas of Montana and Idaho were host to these exercises. At one particular presidential press conference on August 25th, the question of their purpose was posed by a reporter, that is, why such large contingents of military personnel were involved. The CEO of America shrugged it off as a Pentagon matter. Commanders in Chief of the U.S. military, day by day issues were not the president's domain. He pleaded blissful ignorance except to say that in a terrorist world nothing could be left to chance.

Jerry noted something unique about the reports as time moved on. Reporters then began to editorialize the real purpose of such a large contingent of military forces. Such reporters were unable to obtain any answer except standard procedure. At least this made him feel as if the media were trying to ride herd on the military. This as some perceived had become the ultimate purpose of the American press. It seemed that reporters and announcers viewed their task not only as reporting news, but creating news. Nothing new in the arena of yellow journalism.

Jerry and Jenny were eating breakfast on a late August morning when the phone rang. By coincidence it was Gordon Woods. To his friends he was known as Gordo, a kindly, pious but outgoing parish pastor. Gordo wanted to set up a luncheon for a talk about the balloon ride. That little matter was nearly forgotten by Jerry but a date was established and their meeting came to fruition. Of course Gordon was curious about Jerry's sudden impulse to take a ride -— not just a tethered one in a wicker basket either. Jerry responded by saying he had lived his life too cautiously and now it was time to smell the roses and ride the rapids of the wild rivers.

All things considered, the authorities had cleared the way for 15 balloons to sail skyward toward Phoenix and attempt a landing in an open area just to the west of the city. The conditions had to be as such: No winds over 15 mph at liftoff and a 200 foot tether cord in the basket for help on the final portion of the descent and landing. The temperature of the day played a part in planning as well. The ride must begin early because in this sport there had to be a 125 degree differential from the outside air to the air being pumped into the balloon filler. This was the safety standard set by the Dep't. of Transportation in consultation with the National Meteorological Society. Jerry took notes of the types of sporting garb needed and even assessed the risks which Gordon felt obliged to ascertain. Fair enough!

Jerry told Pastor Woods that the day of the ride he and Jenny would be meeting them at the balloon site assigned to Gordon. It would not be difficult to locate. That balloon was one of the more famous of those regularly taking part in the festival. Some had pink elephants and others were equally creative, Gordon Woods touched the patriotic hearts of the people in Tucson with his extra big and colorful American flag design, and the name at the top made Jerry a little bit uneasy: "The Stars and Stripes forever." This symbol of love for America would be used by Jerry Grant to scramble a plot he now knew was for real; the trenching of Canadian waterways down to the USA with the best equipment available.

August became September and the members of Jerry's church put on a massive celebration to mark the occasion of their pastor's birthday which fell on the 27th day of September. During the catered meal in the Parish Hall a familiar but undesirable figure was spotted in the food line. When his plate was loaded he came to the head table to greet Jerry and Jenny on this great occasion. Carl Blackwell sat down and, for a few minutes, thanked Jerry for getting his life back to normal. Of course the discomfort this caused in the hearts of the Grants was indescribable.

Bert Benson noticed Carl's presence. He had been the one to address the congregation after service on the Sunday Jerry was away. So Deacon Benson and Agent Carl Blackwell had a little chat of their own. Thankfully, the visit would not be long. Nevertheless, when it came time to bid goodbye Blackwell had a quiet hint as they shook hands like longtime friends. "Hang in there Reverend. We need to make sure you're on the straight and narrow because we do understand what you've been through."

Jerry whispered back, smiling and feigning a hearty handshake, "I'll haunt you all the way to hell you killer! Count on it. I am not done with you yet." Carl Blackwell was pker faced. He left. But Jenny poked Jerry in the ribs and chastised him, "That was a dumb thing to do. We want him away from us not shadowing us. You should have known better Jerry." And she was right. Jerry Grant had just raised the suspicion level of the despised agent to a level he never intended. "Brain fart! Sorry hon."

On the way home from the party Jenny again brought up the subject of her husband's idiotic mistake. "Gees" he said, "how many times can I say I'm sorry? You have not been through what I've been through or you would have congratulated me or clapped or something Jenny."

"I have Jerry; for God's sake I am your wife and what you've been through I've been through. Now are you still bent on getting the job done or are you giving it all up?"

"No, I'm with it. That's why I'm so mad at that demon Blackwell. He's messing with my head."

"Is he going to win" Jenny asked calmly?

"No, not as long as I have you to keep me in line. And I really mean that Jenny. So let's move on and remember the serious nature of what is happening. We'll check out the news at 10 and see if CNN has any updates." And indeed they did. It was news time and strangely coincidental that, with Blackwell having showed up unannounced at the birthday gathering, a television interview was taking place between a White House correspondent and the Secretary of defense. The issue being discussed was the War Games. The question being bantered about added fuel to the embers of angry fire in Jerry's soul.

Said the correspondent to the secretary, "Has there ever been such a large movement of troops and high tech equipment in the history of the military before? I mean, my gosh Mr. Secretary, tanks, helicopters, hand-held missile launchers—Idaho? Why that choice of terrain?"

"Do you ever want another 9-11?" Jerry was stunned.

"No sir, but with all due respect the people we're likely to engage in conflict are Aramaic, are they not? If we have War Gamers or Military exercises this extensive, should it not be done in the open desert?"

"Well you could argue that; but look at Afghanistan – lots of those desert areas have mountain ranges as well. Can't be too prepared." Jerry and Jenny looked at each other with a "that was a run-around answer" gaze!

"So for how long will the troops be deployed?"

"Who knows" said the Secretary. "And what difference does it really make?"

The interviewer was stuck for a reply. She paused and stated, "Okay, time out for a few commercial announcements. We'll be right back with the Secretary of Defense." At that point, Jerry and Jenny turned off the TV and went to bed. They had enough of the deception they were hearing.

Chapter 14

It wasn't that their children couldn't handle the whole truth. But why plant the seed of concern in their hearts with some special communiqué? So a decision was made to leave them one and only one floppy disk with their story ensconced upon it. Marked as "Childhood memories of Kenton and Kerry," by Jerry and Jennifer Grant, it contained all the sorry happenings of recent weeks. Whether Jerry or Jenny would be around or alive after the attempt to escape could not be ascertained.

They made a notation of it in their will, added as a codicil. Far away as the children now were, it would be just a few weeks till their team arrived home. There was no way to accurately anticipate the future. The heart is surely a lonely hunter, and Jerry's heart was full of prayers that all would go as he hoped and that nothing in their lives would substantially change. He only hoped for a meeting of the minds between the officials of both countries. Such was his purpose, not to forget Lady Justice who needed to be summoned for investigation into the murder of Richard Green.

Other questions remained open-ended! Would Carl Blackwell spirit Jenny away and subject her to the third degree if Jerry made it to Canada? They could only pray that Jennifer would be left alone, and that if the CIA did conclude that Jerry had escaped, they would concentrate not on Jenny, but on locating Jerry. Then, if Jenny did make it home after the bike ride, her personal safety needed to be neatly designed. Jerry was about to offer a suggestion when Jenny embraced him and said,

"Jerry, leave that part to me. Lord knows if I have to hide away I'll find a way to do it. Let's go with what we have, okay sweet thing?"

If there was a God in heaven at all, He could make it turn out all okay. Jerry believed that everything worked for good when planned in good faith and placed into the hands of God. He had back his faith, his hope and a newly found sense of purpose in life.

―――――――――――

It was Friday night. Tomorrow was D-Day! Jerry and Jenny went out to eat and then returned home for a quiet evening on the Lanai now enclosed with the small retractable mini-ceiling Jerry had built to combat the cooler evenings of Fall and Winter. There was also a heater hooked to the gas line; it was built to look like a small fireplace and threw adequate heat as needed. The plans for the morrow were again discussed and it appeared every contingency was covered.

Jerry also had Jenny's map of the western and northern states, detailing secondary roads. It would be used only if he could not safely get out of Phoenix by plane. Then, in the midst of their discussion, the phone rang. "Jerry, this is Gordon Woods."

Jerry's heart leapt to his throat. Should Gordon say the wrong thing Blackwell would be on the Grants doorstep in a minute.

"Hi Gordon. Listen old pal, I'm all set for tomorrow's bike ride to Sabino." Jerry was hoping to say the right things for both Gordon's benefit and to avoid suspicions that Blackwell might consider worthy of examining. One thing he could not do was to let Gordon get a word in about the balloon ride.

"Do you know what time we head out?" Gordon asked.

"Yep, 7 a.m., "Jerry replied.

"Okay," Gordon answered, "and pray for good winds. By the way, did you ever get around to the sports shop and find some warmer garb?" That statement did no harm!

"Trust me Gordo; I am more set than ever before." Jerry was now stumbling for words. What else would Gordon address?

"By the way, you talked about wind conditions. I always pray for good winds," Jerry said. "Nothing worse than riding a speed bike against the wind, especially if it's cold."

"Did you think to pack a parachute?" Gordon chuckled.

"Dang" Jerry thought. "What do I say?" He felt intimidated. He wasn't sure what kind of a comeback he needed now. All he could do was try, and hope that Blackwell was too out of touch to add up what Gordon was saying.

"Naw," Jerry affirmed. "If I fall over the edge I fall over the edge." It was Jerry's hope that Blackwell would take this to mean the edge of the cliff on the last half-mile up the canyon. Or if Blackwell himself wasn't listening, that his appointed eavesdropper would interpret it as such.

"Okay, Gordon responded. Glad you're coming with us. We plan on having a great time."

"I'm sure we will," Jerry choked, quickly hanging up the phone.

"You look pale, hon," Jenny observed. "Did we blow it?"

"Won't know that till tomorrow, love. But I don't think so. I just hope whoever was listening can't read between the lines."

"Well, we have a whole night to pray about it," Jenny affirmed.

That their phone was indeed monitored was evident by the tiny but evident clicking noises, the same kind Jerry had heard when he called Jenny from Calgary. Those little clicks had proven a plague to the bugging experts even in the modern era. Jerry just hoped there would be no more calls from Gordon. And especially so no visits from Blackwell or his people.

The lovers sat in harmony on the patio swing, holding hands and swinging to and fro. This night was made both for contemplation as well as star gazing. Only now was the enormity of their plan beginning to sink in. Only now was the urgency of their task becoming evident.

So with the planning behind them, there was no use in fretting. Strangers in a foreign land, these two ordinary people were trying, against all odds, to terminate a military plot put together over what must have been a long period of time. There were the CIA, the IRS, the State Department and the United States military. Yet Jerry and Jenny had the gall to believe they could impact the course of events between Canada and the United States, two nations long linked in friendship.

"Remember what Prime Minister Trudeau said once?" Jerry asked.

"What was that?"

"When you sleep next to an elephant, you know it if he rolls over in bed."

Jerry was referring to a fact the Canadian people learned to live with. The American government went a long way in forever determining Canada's destiny. Canada was not an entity to herself. She was interdependent upon the United States of America — militarily, socially and economically. Yet in the midst of such interdependence, both the American people and the Canadian people were blissfully ignorant of what was about to terminate hundreds of years of friendship; an armed incursion into Western Canada. But if Jerry could get to those whom Richard Green had termed "paranoid," and present them with what had transpired perhaps he would be believed. And perhaps, even the Prime Minister would feel moved to hear his case.

"Want to talk about anything love?" Jerry asked.

"I'm scared Jerry."

"Yeah, me too," he confessed, holding her tightly.

"Do we need to go over the plans again?" she asked.

"Nope. We've done what we can. What works, works. What doesn't is out of our hands."

The night would not allow them to sleep in peace. Under normal stress, they both slept well. But this was far beyond the norm.

Jerry dozed, but with each wink of sleep came recurring nightmares about Richard Green's murder. He relived the boom of the gun, the escape to Banff, the roadblock on the highway back to Calgary, and the anxiety he had felt at U.S. Customs. He felt a surge of adrenaline as he saw himself belting Blackwell in the face. The headlines kept jumping into his mind, "Military exercises in the Northwest. War games. One hundred thousand troops." This night blessed them with no peace. Romantic encounters would have to wait. It would be a night for emotional gearing, and for more praying than he had ever done before.

Saturday, the twelfth day of October, was perfect. Jerry and Jenny prepared for departure. Cyclists were not permitted in the canyon after 9:00 a.m. Leaving at 6:00 a.m. by bike, they set the auto-pilot for Sabino Canyon. Since their destination was a half-hour ride away, they had thirty minutes to say their farewells, and still time enough for Jerry to change clothing and climb the hill back to the top of the canyon.

"Got your wallet and maps?" Jenny inquired.

"Check."

"Credit card?"

"Check."

"It's not the one Blackwell gave you, is it?"

"No chance," Jerry responded. "They probably took away the line of credit by now anyway. Boy would I love to charge all this up to the American military."

Jerry was in his cycling garb. The rest of the stuff was in his backpack. They felt a slight breeze from the southeast. Jerry took a deep breath and sighed, "Maybe it's going to work. The wind's beginning from the right direction anyway."

"Are you ready hon?" Jenny sighed.

"Ready" Jerry affirmed. With that, they began their trip.

There was no bike path as such to the canyon area. Most roadways had one side of the street strip-painted to designate the right side as a bike path. This had become common practice in Tucson, given the popular nature of the sport. There wouldn't be much talking along the way. They were resolute in their plan. Granted, it was a plan of faith with a lot of variables.

Still, it was something. By this time they not only felt compelled, but obsessed with their mission. In effect it was the possible prevention of a conflict between two nations who, throughout history, had shared four-thousand miles of unguarded border. Would a supreme effort on the part of one couple or one man prevent this possible conflict? Only time would tell.

"There they be," Jerry observed as they neared the canyon. The entrance was jammed with cars, but on their bikes they were able to shinny by and head down the stretch toward the first hill. It would be a mile from where the balloons were ascending, and Jerry would have to hike back, hoping of course that Blackwell or his watchdogs wouldn't spot him. Actually, Jerry liked to call the watchdogs "goons" but Jenny restrained him. They coasted down the hill, now hidden from the entrance area, and brought their bikes to a rapid stop. Then walking down to the creek, they sat down for some final moments.

"I guess it's time," Jerry suggested.

"I know hon. Are you sure you want to go through with this?"

"No, not really," Jerry confessed. "But do we have a choice?"

"No choice. Just thought maybe I'd wake up from a dream. It seems more unreal now than when we were making it up."

"It's real. I saw them following us," Jerry admitted.

"Where?"

"Just as we turned into the parking lot. Same car and driver that was sitting out at Saguaro Monument that day we started all this stuff. Oh, it's real all right."

Jerry stood up, lifting Jenny with him, and after a warm embrace and loving kiss, bid her farewell. "I love you, Jenny. Big time! I'll be back. Stay safe, whatever you have to do. God is with you, love."

"I'm a big girl," she sobbed. "I love you too. Be careful."

Jerry changed into his soaring outfit and ascended the hill on foot. Rather than climb the roadway, he traversed the rugged terrain of the hillside. At the top, he stood and looked for Gordon Wood's hot air balloon. There it was not more than a quarter-mile from where he was standing. This was, unmistakably Gordon's craft. It stood tall and true to its name's sake. Ironically it was called "Stars and Stripes," a living monument to the American flag. And Jerry was about to entrust himself to the symbol of a country which, for all practical purposes, had shattered his life.

Jerry approached the balloon. "Good to see you Gordon." He extended his hand to Gordon and climbed aboard.

"Glad you could come, Jerry," Gordon affirmed. "We're about ready to head out. Ground crew is ready and waiting to lift us off and follow us to the great metropolis up north."

"What's the flight plan?" Jerry asked, hoping for the best.

"Well," Gordon continued," it looked for a while like we'd just be tethered but we just got the okay to

head to Phoenix. I hear we are projected to land a little
to the west of the city in about three hours or less."

Jerry's heart jumped for joy. The plan was working,
at least initially. Gordon turned the flame on high burn.
The noise was thunderous. As the hot air filled the
balloon, it began to stand erect. And then "The Stars
and Stripes" left the ground. The ground crew released
the tether and Gordon pulled it aboard. The three people
– Gordo and his wife Sally—together with Jerry Grant,
were now at the mercy of the wind.

Jerry looked below. He saw Jenny waving furiously,
still below in the canyon. At the entrance to the parking
lot, he spotted the now-familiar black limo. There was
no way he could be seen now, especially given the
countless other balloons that were filling the skies. As
far as Blackwell's man was concerned, he and Jenny
were still in the canyon. And that is precisely what they
had hoped for.

Up and away climbed the "Stars and Stripes",
ever higher. Before his eyes, Jerry saw a panorama he
couldn't ever see from an airplane. The desert spread
out like a sheet of tan and green. He had never realized
how brilliant was that desert floor; how luminous
the green which adorned it. There was no fear in this
experience, only awe. How sad it wasn't but a pleasure
cruise. Though the basket in which he stood was
bobbing and weaving Jerry was looking only at the
vista beneath.

There it was! His city spread out as if to greet him,
and, in one fell swoop, he saw his house, his church,
his bike-path, and the bordering mountains. Glancing

down, he took one last look for Jenny, hoping to get in one more wave. She had begun walking the bike and seemed to be going back up the hill! "Why?" Jerry pondered. "Strange!" Okay, it didn't really matter. Perhaps she wanted to sneak a peek at the balloons from a better point of view. He was free and, at least for now, on his way to right a terrible wrong. Above there was nothing but a clear blue ceiling, like the open palm of God's hand with the Lord Himself providing the glowing promise of divine oversight. Thoughts of a preacher, no doubt! Ahead lay an uncluttered skyway toward the city that rose from the dust of the ashes. Phoenix!

Now Jerry hoped that the there would be a Resurrection for himself, his family and their future.

Chapter 15

"In the unlikely event of a water evacuation, swim!" Gordon was doing his best to assure Jerry of his confidence and competence. He was humorist of the group, and, as Jerry knew by now, the soldier of fortune. Hot air ballooning wasn't exactly a sport everyone could get into - or wanted to. Setting aside the expense, there was considerable risk involved. Still, if anyone in the group would participate in something this far out, it would be Gordon. A man of free spirit he nevertheless took both his work and his play with all seriousness. He was living proof of the veracity of the proverb, "Whatever task lies at hand, do it with all your might."

Jerry did not experience any of the fear he anticipated from the height of the craft or his lack of enclosure therein.

"So tell me, Jerry, what made you decide to take me up on my offer?" he asked. I've been after you for five years?

"Well, to tell the truth Gord, some of us are just too conservative most of our lives. Thought I told you that when we met to make plans?"

"Yeh, but you — a conservative! Naw! Matter of fact, I had a feeling you'd be up here with me someday. Sally even said so."

"How is the love of your life?" Jerry asked.

"Doing great, aren't you sweetheart?" She arranged for the landing crew in Phoenix. They're on the way now. They got us in their sights all the time like the guardian angels."

"You know," Jerry continued, "I never did figure out how you land these things."

"Well," Gordon grinned slyly, "count on me. You land them the way they dance at a nudist colony - very carefully." Both men chuckled at that one.

"Believe me, I am counting on you," Jerry confessed.

"What we do is to begin our descent in accord with the wind. They'll color a patch of territory at the landing sight and we'll start descent a few miles out. With a little luck, we can drop the tether close to the touchdown site and the crew will haul us down and stabilize the basket when we touch."

"Ever miss your target?"

"Oh yeah! Big time once. Back at the Albuquerque fiesta we got a wind gust a hundred feet above ground and touched down two miles away. Look Jerry, just trust me. We'll get you down upright, okay. Besides, you're a pilot. As the saying goes, 'any landing you walk away from is designated a good landing.'"

"You're the only pilot I have," Jerry answered. "I wouldn't be up here if I didn't trust you. 'Course, we do have a pretty reliable co-pilot, don't we?"

The balloon armada was something to behold. He felt he was part of the old classic, "Around the world in 80 days." The other balloons were beside, above and below them. Variety made the display so attractive. Shape, size, color: Very creative colors at that. They were red, yellow, deep blue and multicolored. This season's fiesta even featured that famous pink elephant balloon from Canada.

The colored adornments had risen nearly upright, then, at the wind's beckon call, navigated over and around the northwest corner of the Santa Catalina mountain range. Now, at whatever altitude they were, Jerry could see for what seemed like a thousand miles. Winds had intensified, and their pace was brisk and smooth. What amazed him were the warmth and the clarity of the upper atmosphere. They could already see the town of Florence and the city of Casa Grande, and they had been in the air slightly more than an hour. The constant hum of the burners, as they blew hot air upward, became less of a distraction and more a part and parcel of the activity. For a brief time, Jerry was actually able to enjoy life; "up, up and away in my beautiful balloon" he hummed softly.

The basket in which they stood was waist high. Gordon had taken along some coffee and goodies. The ground was passing rapidly beneath them, and the minutes seemed but seconds. Two hours down the way they indulged themselves. Time was moving swiftly, more swiftly than Jerry wanted it to, and his ultimate mission soon began to dominate his thinking.

"There she sits," Gordon pointed. "See that patch marked out with red border. That's the landing spot."

"Jerry looked down and saw it. Scores of vehicles were there together with the landing crews, awaiting the arrival of the group.

"How do you know which is your crew?" he asked Gordon.

"Well, when we get a bit further down, there's a van with a big red "X" marked on the roof. That's ours. Every balloon has a designated letter or single indicator."

They began descending, the burners sending up less and less hot air as they did. Silently Jerry recognized that Gord was well equipped to do what he was doing so well.

"Stand back and enjoy yourself," Gordon smiled. "This is the part I like." The "Stars and Stripes" was sailing. It was less than four hours since they began. Stronger winds had prevailed, but winds still true to the appropriate destination. Jerry had informed Gordon he wouldn't be traveling back to Tucson with them in their van. A friend was to meet him at the landing site in Phoenix and the two would have lunch together and talk some business before he would be driven back to Tucson in the early evening. At least, this is what he led Gordon to believe. He would assist Gordon in packing the balloon into the trailer hitched to the van. Then Gordon and his crew would head back and Jerry could await the arrival of his friend. In reality, he would, of course, take a cab to the airport and make his run for Canada. At least he was in Phoenix, and, given the hour, Blackwell couldn't possibly know he had even left Tucson.

As the ground rose to meet them it became obvious that all calculations had been more than close. They were precise. Spotting the van first, Jerry exclaimed in rookie excitement, "There it is Gord."

"Good eye, pal," Gordon commended. Then came a rapid descent, more so than Jerry expected, and he clung to the basket side in preparation for a white-knuckle landing. The balloon had hovered somewhat beyond the van but low enough for Gordon to drop tether. Grasping it firmly, the ground crew began the struggle to assist in a soft landing. The gang tugged away and, before long, the two clergymen and one wife were only a few feet above the ground. It was an exciting part of the flight. Finally, touch down. Softly and gently, the crew edged the "Stars and Stripes" downward to ground contact. Gordon grasped Jerry in victory. "Great job," he told his crew. "Very classy."

Jerry was down in Phoenix, and phase one had worked like a charm. As the warm air oozed from the balloon, the "Stars and Stripes" began to dissolve. This spaceship which stood so tall and firm a moment ago now crumbled to earth like an exhausted creature. And within minutes, the crew was preparing it for packing. Gordon had the trailer beside the van, but not hitched up. Talking about the flight as the crew readied the balloon for its rest, Gordon asked Jerry, "What did you think?"

"What can I say?" Jerry confessed. "Nothing short of spectacular."

"Go ahead and sit in the van Jerry. It's getting darn hot and the air conditioning is running," Gordon advised him. "We'll take care of packing this thing."

"Why don't you let me help," Jerry requested.

"Oh, let's just say we've done this before."

Jerry moseyed over to the van, and climbed in the passenger side. The cool of the air conditioning was welcome indeed. "It must be a hundred degrees already, and this was still October," Jerry thought. "Gosh, it's still before noon." When they had left Tucson, the differential of the outside air and the inside air easily achieved the 125 degrees F. differential for ascent to begin. 'Course, higher up, the air was cooler, especially so at this time of the year. He hadn't realized how warm it really was back on earth however till they began to stabilize the craft.

Leaning back on the headrest Jerry sighed. It was unconscious preparation for phase two. Then, with a start, his worst fear was realized. "No, he thought; no way!" A familiar looking limo, black in color, was coming down the road. Jerry slithered down to eye level, peering out the window as the limo passed by.

Blackwell was in the back and his two agents were in the front. They hadn't spotted him, but it wouldn't take long. Exiting the car, they walked toward Gordon.

Jerry's mind began to whirl as he considered his options. Almost instinctively, he slipped out of the van to the vacated limo. Blackwell had his backside to him and Jerry seized the opportunity. He reached into the passenger side of the limo and grabbed the keys. Then, running back to the van, he jumped behind the wheel and peeled rubber down the grid road. There was no other way. Now it was going to be Wiley Coyote and the Roadrunner!

Peering through the mirror, Jerry saw Blackwell running after him, then stopping and raising his hands in disgust. He had bought a little time. Knowing Blackwell all too well, he was quite ready for a hot pursuit. Jerry knew the CIA could and would impound any vehicle they wished.

That area of Phoenix was somewhat familiar to Jerry. The road to which the grid led was the road to the airport – eventually. He turned onto it and pressed the accelerator with a passion. There was no thought of a game plan now, only instinct. By these instincts he'd have to survive for as many days as necessary. Putting distance between himself and Blackwell was primary, but knowing that the airport option was out of the question, Jerry felt that he had been left high and dry. Yet fate would be kind this day. Not far down the road was a sign that caught his eye. He steered the van toward the building emblazoned with flashing lights which read, "Vegas flights via Grand Canyon." That's what the billboard said. Perhaps he'd better get off the road, and investigate this as a real possibility. There would even be refuge in parking the van behind the airplane hangar. It became nearly invisible, and he was sure no one had seen him make the turnoff. Responding instinctively, he did just that.

Jerry exited the van, locking it as though he owned it. Heading toward the office in the hangar he heard a myriad of sirens wailing on the highway. No doubt the search was on. "That was fast," Jerry pondered. 'Course, Blackwell could do what he wanted with the full authority of the State department behind him. It was becoming obvious he would do what was necessary. Jerry's heart was in his throat. He was going to die!

"How in heaven's name did he find out about the flight to Phoenix. Jerry's escape plan seemed dead indeed. But like the Phoenix he had previously contemplated, he too would have to rise from the ashes of despair and find new life. The best possibility was to hope for a plane readied to take him to Las Vegas, even though this meant a detour over the Grand Canyon. He determined not to beg for a direct flight. That might cause suspicion. If any general announcements had been aired about him, an aviation company such as this would certainly be on the lookout.

"What can I do for you, sir?" the lady clerk politely asked.

"Well," Jerry said casually, "I've decided to treat myself to something very special. When are your flights over the Canyon to Vegas?"

"Whenever we can get a plane full," she answered.

"Anybody signed up for today yet?" he inquired.

"Not yet! Would you like to be our first?"

"Do you ever take passengers solo?" he continued.

"Sure, if you want to pay the flight costs. Is that what you had in mind?"

"Why not? Heck, I have the means and I wanted to make this special."

"Well, let's see," she continued, "it would be $660.00 there and back."

"No problem," Jerry said. He wasn't a very good liar, but he had noticed the Visa/MasterCard sign.

"When can I go?"

"Probably have a pilot ready to go in thirty or forty minutes at most. Let me check." Jerry's mind kept racing, but he was sure it hadn't shown in his demeanor. He had plenty of credit left on his credit line. Of course, he hadn't counted on that much money to get to Las Vegas. He hadn't even considered going to Las Vegas. But then this was a charter outfit. It also seemed the only way out of Phoenix given the time and circumstances.

Money became secondary to his mission. He began thinking of Jenny. It wasn't anywhere close to three pm yet. She should still be in Sabino Canyon. "How the heck did they find out?" The question was now academic. The Reverend Jerry Grant was in a run for his life. There was little doubt that, if Blackwell caught up, he would have him whisked away and either held incognito or simply eliminated, a euphemism used for murder.

The lady came back from the outer office. "We can have a plane ready in half an hour," she assured him. "If we get another passenger or two, do you wish to have them come along? Or would you rather go solo?"

"No matter," he replied. "Would that reduce the cost?"

"Yes sir. The trip costs $660.00 whether there's one or 6 passengers. We just divvy the cost among the passengers we book."

"Either way's fine," Jerry said. "Shall I wait to pay you just before we leave then?"

"That'll be fine sir. Are you paying by credit card?"

"Yes ma'am."

"Well, why don't you let me take an impression then and I'll just write in the correct amount for you to sign when the plane is ready?"

"Sounds good" he responded. Jerry was shown a comfortable lounge and offered a cold soft drink on the house. In a way, he hoped no one would show. Finances were hardly a matter of import at this point in his life. In addition, maybe he could get his plan of action together if he were alone; no verbal intercourse with other oohing and aahing passengers. He wasn't in a position to call the shots. So whatever transpired, he'd have to play along. Given the fact that Blackwell had come after him with such vigor, he was more convinced than ever of his need to reach Calgary. Even that had changed. Now his goal had become the

Canadian border — any border crossing would do. For there he would be given refuge and a chance to spill the beans. After Las Vegas - who knew?

If there was a God in heaven, He'd open some doors. From here on in, it was all "play as you go."

The time dragged on, but true to the clerk's word, in thirty minutes he was called to the counter. "No other passengers sir," she reported. "I guess we have only one today."

"That's fine," he said. "You only live once. Let's go for it." He signed the Visa slip. "Gambler I bet," she asked him.

"What's that?" Jerry asked.

"I said, I bet you're a gambler. Are you going to Vegas to play the games."

"Yeah, thought I'd try my luck there," he lied, not looking up. He despised this whole process of one lie after the other. It was all quite against what he believed in and stood for.

"Okay sir, this plane will remain in Las Vegas till we get customers for a flight back. We do have an airstrip in Vegas, and if you decide to stay a few days, your voucher is good for a full month." Jerry was handed a ticket with a return voucher, and summoned by the pilot who had entered from the hangar. "All ready, sir," he said. Jerry followed to the waiting plane, a twin engine Cessna.

"Your van behind the hangar?" he was asked.

"Yes, should I move it?"

"No, it's fine where it is. I just hope you left your window open a crack."

"You bet." Actually, Jerry neither knew nor cared whether he had. He was confident it would be located in short order. Someday he hoped to have an opportunity to tell his story to Gordon Woods. For now he could only imagine the kinds of lies Blackwell was telling Gordo not to mention the betrayal his dear friend must have been feeling.

He walked to the best seat in the cabin. Soon the engines roared and the plane taxied to the end of the private runway. The cockpit door was open, and he could see the pilot and the instrument panel. Turning around the pilot waved to him and said, "We've got clearance from Sky Harbor. Have the time of your life. We'll be flying at rim level over the canyon, so I'm sure you'll enjoy it. Ever seen it before? I mean from this vantage?"

"Nope, not yet," Jerry affirmed. Actually he had, but he needed to have everyone believe that he was just a rich tourist who hadn't seen the canyon, and who had charted a private flight to support a spoiled lifestyle.

`The plane began its run, and was quickly airborne. Jerry looked out the window on the left side of the plane where he was seated. Passengers were mandated to sit in the back over the Canyon. For the second time that day, he was in the skies above Phoenix. Perhaps none too soon. Just after liftoff, Jerry saw, on the highway parallel to the runway, another black limo. He couldn't see whether or not it was turning off to the hangar he had just left. He prayed that it wouldn't. Trouble is, he wouldn't know till they got to Las Vegas.

"Is that all those guys drive now is limos" he wondered? Then he shook his head, wondering why such a question would even be significant given the circumstances.

Chapter 16

Designed to cruise at about 280 mph the Cessna was a little fireball with power to spare. Jerry had been in one before as a flyer. His license had lapsed some two years earlier and it appeared a few changes, simple but easily discernable, had been made on the control panel. One Calgary parishioner had been a flight instructor and became Jerry's personal tutor at the mere cost of his own expenses. He diligently taught Jerry the craft of flying. Jerry had passed the test on the second try ("they never let you get by on one try" his tutor had told him) and for a couple of years he indulged himself and his family in a few rentals for vacations in particular. However the expense of the hobby was a little too steep to maintain for much more than a few rentals. Jerry did wish he were in the pilot's seat to give this one a try.

This aircraft was very new, but Jerry watched the pilot maneuver the controls on takeoff. Becoming a pilot was, in those days, a natural segue for Jerry's pioneer spirit. Below was rolling terrain, with hills getting ever higher as they flew northbound. The ride to Flagstaff was uneventful, even soothing. Before long they were over the San Francisco Peaks, those twin towers that land marked the city of Flagstaff and signaled that seventy miles to the north lay the Grand Canyon. In short order they were in view of it, and the pilot leveled off to just above the rim.

"Lots of air traffic down here," he said. "The EPA won't allow us to go below rim level anymore. So what you see from here is all we can give you."

Jerry glanced down. "That is a hole in the ground," he thought aloud. He had seen it before from Rim level on the ground. Nor were they alone in the air as the pilot had suggested. There were planes and helicopters in almost equal numbers, swirling around and passing each other. "Rules of the air are stay to the right," the pilot shouted back. "Anytime you want me to circle a spot you like, just holler out" he invited Jerry. "Then we circle right too."

"That's just fine, "Jerry responded. "I'll take what you give me." What an amazing sight it was. In effect they were at ground level, yet the floor of the canyon was still a mile or more beneath them. The river wound its way across the bottom, at one point narrow, and at another, wide and white with rapids. It had been a special desire of Jerry to ride the rapids of the Colorado some day. If Burt Reynolds could do it, he figured he could do it as well. Now and then the plane moved rapidly to one side or the other. Such heavy traffic mandated the quick moves, and the swift air currents tossed the crafts to and fro at the will of the wind. There were a few special regulations in effect. So navigating over the abyss was a visual matter without instrument assist. This routing was quite an endeavor for any pilot and this man was great.

With good cause there were times when Jerry was more occupied with the air traffic than the sight below. It was hard to believe that the safety record over the Canyon was as good as it was. Not that those accidents didn't happen! They were plentiful, yet few in proportion to the number of aircraft flying in that limited space.

"Come on up in the cockpit," the pilot invited.

Jerry unbuckled and accepted the invitation. He strapped himself in next to the pilot.

"Hi, Jerry Hansen."

"Jerry Grant." The two men shook hands.

"This is against the rules but since you're the only one on board you may as well have my vantage point," the pilot suggested. Jerry was glad to accommodate him. It was remarkably clearer from the front than from the passenger compartment, especially for the forward view as would be expected. Nor would the sight last as long as he had hoped. Las Vegas was but a short time away and Jerry was bent on giving thought to his real mission once again. As with the balloon ride, he wished this had been a part of his leisure life. But it just wasn't to be. "If things ever get back to normal," he thought, "I'm going to bring Jenny and the kids up here. This is something awesome."

Now there was a plane lofting aside them; very near to their aircraft. "Wonder what he's doing so close to me," the pilot queried aloud. "Idiot, he's supposed to go over top or to my extreme right to pass. There's too much traffic coming the other way."

Jerry glanced to his left and noticed the proximity of the other craft. It was close — very close. Then without any warning, the right door of the other plane swung open.

"What's going on," the pilot commented. "That guy's nuts."

Jerry looked again out the pilot's window. "That's a rifle sticking out the door," he bellowed. "That guy's going to take a shot at you. Move it out." Hansen reacted and his plane dove to the right and downward, followed expertly by the second aircraft. Then it heaved left and the now evident chase plane did the same. Jerry took a closer look. The door was still open and somebody with a gun was perched and ready to fire. Before he could shout another warning a shot rang out passing through the side window and out the front.

"Get down in your seat," the pilot advised Jerry. "We're under fire and I don't know why? That guy must be a madman or something." A second shot rang out and Jerry Hansen slumped over in the seat, leaning forward on the wheel. The aircraft began to dive into the canyon, and the bottom was coming up to meet them in a big hurry.

Jerry Grant hadn't counted on this at all. Blackwell's people had caught up to him in mid air with one resolve — to shoot down the plane in which the Reverend Grant was now the only conscious person. Jerry could only do one thing. Grabbing the pilot's slumped body he pulled him back off the wheel. Then, from the passenger side, he lifted the wheel to the level position. The plane made a violent upturn. He had pulled back too quickly. What it needed was a more gentle touch. This he remembered from the few times he had flown in a Cessna. Go easy on the controls.

There was little time to lose. With one big effort Jerry Grant unbuckled Hansen's seat belt and with another heavy heave Jerry virtually tossed the pilot, apparently dead, to the back of the cockpit. He landed in the aisle to the doorway. Jerry slid behind the wheel and tilted it backward, leveling out the aircraft. Glancing to his left he saw his attacker once more. It was like a wartime dogfight, but Jerry had no gun. He sent the plane into a rapid dive. Then he leveled it out again as Jerry sought and found the artificial horizon. "Where was he now" he wondered?

Looking around, first left and then right, he was unable to spot the attack plane. He noticed he had drifted to the left side of the canyon and straight ahead was an oncoming craft. The two planes were on a collision course. A second before a collision occurred he jerked the wheel to the right and pushed the lever forward, taking it into a dive at the same time. The approaching aircraft slithered past with a whooshing sound— much too close to appreciate. Suddenly there was a massive explosion behind him. His attackers had been right on his tail, so when he darted down and right, the approaching aircraft had smashed head-on with the attack plane. Death in mid air! What had his life become?

"Oh my God, forgive me," Jerry exclaimed in a rigid prayer. Glancing backward, he could see the fireball. Two aircraft were going down in flames and it was the fault of nobody but himself. Self-defense my foot! Jerry caused a crash.

"My Lord, what have I done?" he moaned. He was sure his pilot was dead and equally sure that some other innocent people were dead. The crash he instigated was non-survivable. Some innocent, harmless people had died! Maybe kids. All he could do was to press onward and hope that somehow he could walk away from whatever landing lay ahead. This whole thing was becoming a life or death quest. He wanted life, the instinct in all humans. Jerry certainly could not fly like he had the smaller ones years ago. But he could read, and one thing was most unmistakable. The oil gauge showed a drop in pressure. He was going down and there was nothing he could do. Now the edge of the Canyon was in sight. He glanced to both sides. "Better to get out of the Canyon now," he thought. With that, he veered the plane to the right, nearly at ground level. Jerry stabilized the craft after it pitched and yawed, but he was still dangerously close to the ground. A streak of black oil fumes was marking his tail, and the oil gauge, prominently located on the panel, showed a continued drop in pressure. The line must have been punctured by a bullet. Pure rock covered the ground at this point, some smooth, and some craggy. It was only a hundred feet below. Scanning for the throttle Jerry found it. Crash landing was not an option, but there was a simple logic to it. If you can get the plane to ground level you cut the throttle and it should eventually stop, hopefully without an assist from some immovable object.

Survival became his immediate concern. He noticed that the rocky ground was very smooth at this point. The strange canyon formations almost seemed like a sheet of ice in places but they still sported some hazardous rocks in all the wrong places for an altogether smooth landing. "Put 'er down," he determined. Slowly, he pushed the throttle forward; the engines cut back. He tilted the wheel ahead, leveled out, and tilted it some more. This would have to be the spot. No large impediments were in sight. Small ones, yes, even intimidating to the best crash-landing experts. Funny though, there was no fear; just the basic instinct to walk away - alive - from what would be a rough landing.

Pushing back on the throttle a little more, he cut the engines back again. Now he was riding but a few feet above the ground, and still descending.

"Why weren't the wheels touching down?" he thought. "The wheels! Noooo, I forgot to lower the landing gear." Mentally he slapped himself. It was too late. The plane skidded on its belly as Jerry pushed the throttle to the off position. First it went straight, then like a carousel out of control it began whirling rapidly. One of the wings smashed against a giant rock and was sheered off. Jerry was praying that he wouldn't catch fire by virtue of the impact.

Fate would be kind once more that day. The aircraft skidded to a halt with Jerry alive to see it. He moved his arms and legs, trying to determine if he was hurt. He was but he wasn't dead. He sensed a dislocated or broken shoulder. But this much was obvious; he would walk away from this one landing, though probably the worst landing in aviation history.

Jerry glanced about the area. He unfastened the seat belt and moved toward the other Jerry. He had slid down the aisle of the plane, halfway to the back. He looked at his limp body and then took his pulse. There was none. He was indeed a casualty of an episode in Jerry Grant's life over which he had no control. His head had obviously taken a shot or two, directly in the left temple. Whoever fired upon them was no amateur. He must have been a sharpshooter.

No doubt Blackwell had given instructions to kill the pilot, leaving Jerry stranded in the plane alone. Believing that Jerry would panic even though a seasoned flyer some years ago Blackwell could be reasonably sure that a crash in the canyon would terminate this pestilence called Jerry Grant.

Breathing deeply a few times the battered preacher gathered his wits. He could smell gas and oil. "Better get out of here," he thought. Instinctively, he grabbed for his backpack, but its contents had spilled all over the cockpit. His wallet! Where was his wallet? He would need that more than anything. He found it under the seat. Then it occurred to him there might be a way to buy time. If the plane did catch fire and the possibility still existed, perhaps he could convince his trackers that the dead man was himself. "What a ghoulish thought," he told himself.

There was no time for qualms of conscience now. Jerry took his credit card and cash from the wallet, but left his basic identification card and this was risky – his driver's license inside. Then, going out the bent door, he placed the emptied wallet a few feet from the downed plane. It contained only a that basic I.D. He would need the driver's license with his picture on it for car rental but he'd deal with that as was needed. His arm really hurt now, and he sensed it was indeed a dislocation. Earlier in life he had experienced this same injury twice, both in sporting events. He knew what they did in wartime and he was about to try anything to reduce the dislocation so he could move the arm a little. Taking a small but firm pillow, he curled it up, placed it under his arm and, by firmly jerking the right arm downward with the left arm, heard and felt it pop into place. For a few seconds he was in a grey out, not quite fully passed out. The pain took its toll. He had however done the right thing! Had he left the dislocation unattended the lack of blood flow to the head of the shoulder bone would have prompted serious health issues like gangrene.

Suddenly there was smoke, lots of smoke, billowing up from inside the cockpit. Something in the instrument panel had shorted out and given the heavy odor of gas and oil, Jerry figured it was about to blow. He began to hobble from the plane but felt a sharp pain shooting in his ankle. "Not this too" he groaned. He had severely sprained it and yet knew it could also be a fracture. Jerry hobbled quickly away, glancing back at the aircraft. Then it happened. A spark had ignited the fumes and the whole plane was engulfed in fire. The explosion knocked Jerry to the ground and there he laid, arms folded above his head, wondering if he had been burnt by the ruptured fuel tank explosion.

Within a minute the aircraft was virtually consumed. As for Jerry, he had no further injury. But his ankle throbbed. So did his arm and head. Jerry was a fighter, and until now, had never known how much of a fighter he was. "I've got to get to Canada," he said aloud. "I've got to get to Canada."

His mission was still on his mind. By now he realized that reaching the Canadian border and surviving had become one and the same thing. Trouble was, the Canadian border was a long way north, and he was still somewhere short of Las Vegas. Maybe, and this thought turned his stomach once again, maybe the pilot's burnt body would be considered his.

If that were to happen, perhaps once more he had bought more time to pursue his quest.

Jerry looked to and fro, front and rear. Not far off was a house in the midst of the rocky terrain that bordered the rim of the Canyon. He would walk there and seek assistance from the people in that house. 'Course he would also beg assistance in getting to Las Vegas. He couldn't let on he was badly hurt. The last thing he needed was to check into some emergency room of a hospital. He would minimize the limp, live with the pain, and only then request a little rest and some transportation. So if lady luck were with him Jerry would still have a chance. In his heart the Reverend Grant knew there was no such thing as luck, only divine guidance.

Approaching the house, he saw a man standing by the front gate gazing at the approaching limper. Two Dalmatians were barking away, but held tightly with a leash and gripped by the apparent farmer. Jerry waved as he approached and the man opened the gate to the yard as if to invite him.

"You the pilot from the crash over there?" he asked Jerry.

"Yep, that's me," Jerry said, extending his hand. "Jerry," — he paused a moment," Jerry Hansen." Guess my plane didn't fare as well as I did.

"Glad you're okay Jerry. Hurt your leg?"

"Naw, just a minor ankle sprain. Nothing serious."

"Lucky you got out before she blew. What happened?"

"Don't really know," Jerry replied. "All of a sudden I was trailing smoke. And down she came."

"Good thing you decided to get out from over the Canyon," the man said. "By the way, I'm Alan Dixon."

"You live pretty much alone out here?" Jerry queried.

"Yeah, but I love it," Alan answered. "I work over at the dam and it's not that far. We have a plane to get around in too."

"Really, what kind?"

"A little Piper Cub," he said. "That's my hobby."

"Would you consider chartering a passenger?" Jerry asked.

"Nope, but I'll freely take you where you want to go — within reason of course," Alan offered.

"That'd be great," Jerry smiled. "Much appreciated and I am most happy to pay you for your trouble."

"No way friend," he answered. "We pilots take care of one another, don't we? Where are you heading –- Vegas for some medical attention?"

"Yeah. Vegas."

"Well, come on in and freshen up. I can work up a sling for that shoulder. Looks like it's really hurting you? You can rest for a while if you want. Anybody you need to phone?"

"Don't think so," Jerry said, "if you can get me to Las Vegas I can contact my company there. We have a landing strip at the municipal airport."

"Charter company, eh?"

"Yeah. I've been with them a few years. First accident."

"Any passengers dead or hurt back there"?

"Nope," Jerry was quick to reply. "This was a solo. I'll do a report after I get checked out at a clinic of hospital in Las Vegas."

"Well that's a lucky thing for you. Nothing worse than goin' down with someone aboard. Ends your flyin' days. But take my phone and let the company know you're okay! Be sure to call your family. You've got to consider their feelings."

Both men entered the home. Alan Dixon led Jerry with phone in hand to a quiet room and then shut the door leaving Jerry to make his calls in privacy. A nice gesture on the part of his host. Jerry faked two phone conversations and then reported everything was taken care of.

Through the back window of the kitchen where he sat Jerry could see his gracious host's little plane and the small grid runway. It seemed that it was his destiny to get to Las Vegas. He hoped Blackwell would consider him done and finished. And having told Alan he was Jerry Hansen he had hopefully covered himself in the event the CIA came knocking at the door of the Dixon home.

After a bite to eat and a quick wash, they headed out to the neat little bird. Once again, Jerry was airborne. Only this time he would get to Las Vegas without incident. After all, his plane had crashed and burned. Jerry Grant had perished, had he not? How he prayed that Blackwell would receive such a report and believe it. It would expedite his trip north, not yet planned out, and most certainly extend his days in this life. His mission was still possible to fulfill, though now it was more like Mission Impossible than ever before.

Chapter 17

Alan Dixon requested and received his landing clearance. He bid Jerry good-bye. Of course he had offered to help Jerry get a cab to find a hospital or clinic, tactfully declined by the Jerry "Hansen" he was known as by this Good Samaritan. Jerry promised to get assistance after checking in to a cheap motel for rest and telephone access. Shaking hands with Dixon and bidding gratitude for his kindness he headed for the nearest payphone in the small aircraft hangar area and called a cab.

The day had taken its toll, and Jerry needed a night of rest. Still, his mind could know no rest. He was plotting his next move to get out of Las Vegas and believed he knew the answer: rent a car and drive north on the back roads — grids if necessary. Jenny had marked out both major and secondary routing, but the maps had gone up in flames. Or so he now hoped. If they had survived the fire and Jerry was presumed to be alive and driving, then all that routing could be tracked and followed. He had a pretty good memory from studying them in the weeks before he left, in the unlikely event that a quick commercial aircraft exit from Phoenix might not work. The reason it did not work was one that had never occurred to him.

Secondary routes would take him nine hundred miles to the Canadian border and prove safer than any major interstate. If he were to tackle that in one stretch it meant twenty hours of driving ahead. Okay, such was the task of the next 24 hours. He would find a road map somewhere and study it. Then, retiring as early as possible, he would rent a car at sunup and begin his trek.

Jerry Grant was on his own, and, though he had never been a great navigator of highways and byways, he would need to assume the role with immediacy. After finding a motel, Jerry bought a Nevada - Utah- - Idaho map from a vending machine. He studied the map's Interstates, State routes and grids as well.

Then it hit him like the proverbial brick against the henhouse. If his pursuers had been capable of tracing him beyond the wreckage, wouldn't they do precisely as he was planning — read his mind and concentrate their efforts and manpower searching those secondary routes? The Interstates must prove the best way to go it! Of course, a straight beeline for the Canadian border on the biggest, busiest roads in a vehicle no one knew he'd be driving. Such would be his routing all the way. Blackwell would anticipate back roads, but to this point he had no idea where Jerry was. It was a "guess what I'm going to do and I'll do the opposite" strategy.

The drive would prove trying; even more trying would be the final stretch between Coeur d'Alene, Idaho, and the Canadian border crossing, for the road was very mountainous and the going was slow. "Eastport!" That was the Canadian port of entry he marked as his target. As he lay on the bed, tired and aching, his mind kept replaying the details of the day. That had been a habit in the last two months starting in the IRS office. A bike ride, a balloon ride, a plane ride, a crash, another plane ride. All it gave him was four hundred miles and change between Tucson and Las Vegas. Not that this had been the worst aspect of the day. Innocent people had been killed. That tormented him. So did his concern for Jenny's safety.

Realizing he needed to get cleaned up, Jerry rose and went next door to a clothing store. He bought a shirt and some casual pants, along with some shaving gear and underwear. Then, dragging his weary body back to the motel, he had a bite to eat, showered and hit the pillow. It was a cheap motel, very cheap. A wake-up call for 5:00 a.m. had been ordered. The clerk had even asked him if he wanted a special treat that night reminding him that "it's legal in Nevada." Without comment, he had declined. It was not within either his power or his will to moralize at the moment. Just to rest. With the T.V. providing a soothing backdrop, Jerry Grant fell fast asleep. It was 10:00 p.m., and tomorrow was Sunday. For Jerry, his pulpit would be the driver's seat. It would prove to be the first time in his recollection that he had ever missed church barring the Calgary episode. Under the circumstances, he had a feeling the good Lord would be quite understanding.

Jerry sat straight up in bed at 3 a.m. It had been a restful night but all too short. Never mind the wakeup call. Now he wanted to move it on out. He shaved with one of those quickie Bics, took a hasty shower, put on his new clothing, and grabbed his credit card and cash. The early morning was truly beautiful. By 5:30 a.m. the sun was bright and warm. Down the street he saw a rental company which specialized in low-rate cars. Something like "Rent-a-wreck"! Fortune was still smiling upon him. A small company would serve his purpose well. If he was being trailed, and there was no doubt about it, the agents would surely interview the major car rental companies first. So this one, sporting an unfamiliar name, appealed to Jerry Grant.

The clerk walked to the counter where Jerry was standing. "Good morning sir. Early morning that is! Do you need a car today?"

"Yes, please," Jerry answered. "What do you have available."

"We specialize in a bit older models," he said. "That way we can keep our prices pretty competitive. Big or little?"

"Pardon?"

"Do you want a standard size vehicle or a compact? We have some sub-compacts too."

"How about a medium?" Jerry inquired.

"Sure, got a Plymouth Reliant for you. Will that be by the day or the week?"

"One week please," Jerry was quick to reply.

"I'll need a credit card and your driver's license sir."

"Driver's license," Jerry thought. "I don't have a driver's license."

He had left it as I.D. at the crash site. Once more, it would be necessary for him to dig into his pocket of ingenuity. He put on his most pleasant personality. "I'm sorry ma'am; my license is back at the motel. They wanted it to validate my Credit Card and I guess I left it on the counter. It'll be there. I'll just run back and get it. Only about six blocks," Jerry said, hoping to draw sympathy and showing off his limp. The pleasantry and deception worked well.

"Tell you what," the clerk continued. "You've got an honest face mister. You put down your occupation as a minister of religion. Take the car, get the license and bring it back over here before you head out. I can live with that."

Jerry wasn't fond of the option, but he'd have the vehicle and, of course, he had no intention of returning with a driver's license he didn't possess. A small price to pay. But he needed to buy a little head-start time.

"Yes ma'am. One Arizona driver's license shall be retrieved."

"What part of Arizona are you from?"

"Phoenix, actually Tempe, he was quick to add. That matter he would not need to verify since he had no intention of bringing back a driver's license that didn't exist. But playing con man was not a role with which Jerry felt comfortable. Circumstances left no option. This was grand theft—auto!

"Oh," he pondered out loud, "Do you mind if I grab a quick breakfast first?" That request was to buy a little time as well and it was granted with a firm but rapid "sure! Or you can even phone in the license number if you choose. Save you a quick trip back here." That offer was not to be refused.

The clerk drew up the necessary papers and made an impression of the credit card. Jerry signed on the dotted line, declined the insurance offer and was soon behind the wheel. The easy part was behind him and ahead of him lay nearly a thousand long miles of highway. He was alive, reasonably well, and for the first time in a while, felt a sense of security. He made his exit slowly, as though going back to his motel. The necessity of planting some false information nearly eluded him. When he was leaving the rental agency he turned and asked the customer service lady a misleading question. "So, hear anything about the weather in Los Angeles area?" he inquired.

"Not yet," the lady replied. "Hope you don't meet up with any quakes there." The seed of a false destination was now planted for whatever way it might prove worthy of assisting him. Soon he was northeast of Las Vegas on the major state route, headed for Utah and northbound from there into Idaho on the Interstate. He hoped to reach Canada without a significant stop. There could be no rush about this part of the trip.

What was least needed was any encounter with the authorities.

Perhaps there was a general alert for him by now. An APB as the police called it. If that were the case any traffic violation would result in his capture. Setting the cruise control on 70 mph in the 75 mph zones, he was determined to stay below the speed limit. The radio was reporting the national news at the moment, and he wasn't on it. So much the better. The road was good and harbored amazingly little traffic.

Okay! Take some deep breaths and pretend this is a vacation drive home to "eh" country. Relaxation began to set in and it would hardly be possible that anyone consider Jerry going this far to the West to reach Calgary or Ottawa, which of course was way in Eastern Canada.

Jerry hummed, "And the driven' is easy........." Not for long sad to say. He noticed a vehicle creeping up on him in a hurry. He hadn't gone but an hour out of Vegas yet. Could it be possible that Blackwell had found him? No, not even the CIA was that good. He terminated the pessimism, chastising himself for his paranoia. "Likely just a car in a big hurry," he reasoned. But it was no such animal. Riding on Jerry's tail, a Highway Patrol Vehicle siren blew harshly and red lights flashed. Then they quit. What to do was to be on the safe side and pull over like a faithful citizen. But had he inadvertently broken a law? Was this the end of the line? His mission might well be over so quickly after hope had smiled for a time.

The thought of trying to outrun the patrol car swiftly passed. Jerry pulled over in a casual manner, and awaited the verdict and if it was the divine will, the termination of his plan.

"Morning sir," the officer said. "Got an early start, did you?"

"Yes, officer," Jerry replied. "Did I do something wrong?"

"Not at all. You dropped a hubcap around that last bend, and we thought we'd bring it to you." A hot flush ran through his body as the adrenaline rush sank in. The officer showed Jerry the hubcap and graciously offered to put it on for him. Stepping out of the car he saw the trooper already doing so. Inside himself Jerry was now laughing. He had just been frightened half to death over a stupid hubcap. There was no violation and there wouldn't be a radio check either.

"All set, sir," the officer said, indicating the hubcap had been replaced. "Serve and protect. We really mean that."

"Guess that's what I get for renting an older car?" Jerry commented. "I do appreciate your taking the time to do this sir."

"My pleasure. Sometimes people see us as the enemy but we're really not. 'Protect and Serve.' So today I served a little; no big deal. Have a good day and drive safely now, you hear," he ordered with a genuine smile. Both had a brief laugh over a hubcap scaring the devil out of a motorist.

Jerry sat back and took a few breaths — deep ones. He had some well earned palpitations and was on the verge of serious hyperventilating. At least one thing was certain. So far, he was not known to be in the area and his belief that he had bought some quality time had been reinforced. Still, it was an incident he was not likely to forget. After all, a wanted man being stopped by the Highway Patrol to be given his hubcap wasn't exactly run-of-the-mill.

A small town was finally in sight. One cup of coffee to settle his nerves — kind of an oxymoron, but very true for some people — might be appropriate. Jerry took the time for the coffee and sandwich special and then headed toward Ely and Wells. As expected, the drive was long and tiring. Wells would be a rest stop for big time food as well as car gas and fluid checks. There were still no radio reports concerning him, but then it was difficult to know for certain. It was Sunday morning, and the stations were jammed with religious broadcasts. Sunday notwithstanding, what Jerry yearned for right now was a good long newscast. And for information on where the authorities suspected he might be.

The Idaho border was upon him, but it was midday. He began thinking about the Canadian border crossing. Not all of them were open twenty-four hours, especially those in secluded mountain terrain. Perhaps he would need to change his game plan and stay overnight somewhere. It seemed safe enough to consider.

Setting his sights on a little place called McCall, Jerry had to call it a day when he arrived there. Without incident, he reached the town, tanked up, checked the oil, found a motel and settled in. It was a tiny motel, and the clerk accepted the cash and the explanation his driver's license was missing.

Getting this far had proven a minimal risk, though this was the Interstate. But from there he could take a good secondary highway to vary his course and then the Interstate again. He'd go as the spirit moved him so to speak. The decision to call home was pressing him.

"What the heck, why not." His thoughts drifted to Jenny and the kids. "I should call home," he shuffled his thoughts around. "Jenny should be back at the house now." Jerry decided to wait till early morning.

If the CIA believed he was still alive, or even remotely suspected it, then an early a.m. call home might just catch the eavesdroppers off guard. That is, if Jenny were not in federal custody. "Of course," he decided," call Jenny in the morning; bright and early Monday morning."

The night would not be kind to Jerry. Central Idaho was hit with a boisterous thundering storm. In fits and starts he tried to sleep. Sleep would not befriend him. This would be a night to watch the very seconds tick by as they twitched on the illumined clock, two little dots between the hour and the minute digits. He began to wonder why he hadn't just continued to drive. Nightfall's cover may have been to his benefit, and especially so on such a stormy night as it had recently become. Then, submitting to the will of his mind, he gingerly lifted himself out of bed at 3:00 a.m. and prepared to depart. Perhaps he had enough rest to endure and finish the course. If not, he would need to pull over sometime during the daylight hours.

The urge to call home was now a compelling drive. So, just before departure Jerry picked up the phone and dialed direct. He heard his home phone ring, four, five times. "Come one Jenny before the answering machine kicks in he muttered."

"Hello," a sleepy voice answered.

"Jenny, it's Jerry."

"Jerry, are you okay?" she blurted.

"I'm fine, love. How about you?"

"Okay. Listen, I had to hear your voice. The mission is proceeding." The familiar clicks could still be heard.

"Where are you, Jerry?" she pleaded. "They think I know." Her tone was almost angry, not characteristic of her desire to play along.

"Can't tell you love," he continued. "Let's just say I'm a long way west." Jerry was trying any means to throw Blackwell off the trail. "I just wanted to let you know I'm okay. Has anybody contacted you?"

"They won't stop hounding me," she said, still with an angry tone. "I came home after church Sunday and you were all over the Tucson news"

"Like how?" Jerry pleaded.

"Like you're wanted by the CIA for spying and by the F.A.A. for aviation violations and maybe second degree murder. What's been going on? Didn't you get a plane out of Phoenix? Give me a hint, Jerry, for goodness sake."

"Can't tell you right now, love. But I will."

Jenny began to insist. For whatever reason she begged Jerry to tell her.

"Jenny," he said, "Don't believe any of what you hear and don't answer the phone again. When I call again I'll use the signal." They had a signal —one ring, hang up, and then call again in a moment. "

"Okay, Jerry. I love you." Jerry knew his time was up.

"And I love you too hon. Give me some idea of where you are, Jerry," she pleaded once more. I'm praying for you, remember that."

Jerry hung up the phone. He knew a trace took almost five minutes and he had talked much less than that. But if Blackwell had called in the heavy tracing equipment, a trace could be made in a few seconds. He didn't think so however. That would have cost a hundred grand. Jerry knew, at least, that his wife was safe. She knew he was okay. Whatever the consequences, this was information worth the risk he took.

He dressed and went to the motel lobby. No one was there. The last thing he needed was an unpaid motel bill, so rather than ring the night bell he made use of the rapid checkout system. His Visa Card was on record and they could add the price of a phone call to it as well. Still, a younger girl came to the desk.

"Yes, sir," she inquired.

"Just checking out the quick way," Jerry said. "I've got a long ride south and need an early start." Jerry got his receipt from the sleeping beauty he had stirred awake and headed for the car. Soon he was on Highway 95, a major State Route with whatever town or city would be a convenient pit stop.

The towns came and went rapidly. Cascade, Donnelley and others which were not especially memorable. Dawn was now approaching, and Jerry began to feel the fatigue. He forgot an old trucker's trick he once practiced when traveling to and from school, 32 hours driving without stopping to sleep. When the sun comes up, you pull over and wait for a while till it's daylight. Make sure your eyes are closed or covered. Watching the sunrise is the killer. That's what makes you sleepy. Truckers use this little body-deception all the time. You'll be fine as long as you don't actually see the sun rise or the dark change to brightness. What would be welcome were a heaping breakfast and an overdose of caffeine. Not that he was hungry. What he needed was to elevate his energy with sugar and adrenaline; this would be for the sprint finish so to speak. But wait for awhile. Keep going now.

The road was lonely and he tested his own resolve about speeding as he now nudged the limit in the lightning and thunder and rainy confusion of the night. He only had stopped for a take out coffee, and then got the urge to do what he needed to do. Move it on out! Jerry Grant went on and on and on, going till the incentive of a bigger city was in his sights. By high noon he was still burning rubber and then began rolling to a stop in Coeur d'Alene. He heard somewhere the name meant something like "devil's fork" or close to that. And the highway he met intersected his present highway and another Interstate. He needed that Interstate for the northern dash and he needed fuel big time. Finally, after more than 6 hours and a whole tank of gas, Jerry sputtered to a major truck stop. He hadn't realized how far and how fast he had gotten here. But he had in fact been holding steady at 80 mph on a dark, cold and wet night in Idaho.

It was noon, Monday. During a hefty meal at a local café, while nursing his coffee, he watched the news on a little TV perched above the lunch counter. Still nothing about him. He was not yet a national fugitive I guess. Either that or the government authorities didn't want the news about him to get Jerry's side of the story. So he concluded chances were that the search for him was of a quiet, unobtrusive style, detectives whispering to other people and showing them Jerry's picture.

Jerry leaned down to finish his coffee and got up to pay the tab. Then it happened. A scenario that could not have been any worse. His optimism had crashed like the stock market of black Friday. In a flash, his picture was on television and the news bulletin said, "If you have seen this man, please report it to the local authorities. He is armed and extremely dangerous. He was last reported in the Las Vegas area."

Jerry peered around cautiously. No one was looking at him, save a little old lady. She quickly turned aside, and Jerry knew he had been spotted. He stepped hastily outside and raced to the vehicle.

"Hang the speed limit," he thought. "Good-bye, Coeur d'Alene and hello Canada." Jerry pressed hard on the car accelerator and stayed around 80. There was a sense of urgency. He would have to put some distance between himself and the little old lady. For the most he loved sweet old gals, and he had no doubt that this one was equally sweet. But under the circumstances she had become his enemy. He knew by her body language she had recognized him.

Jerry continued northbound. The border was about a hundred and twenty miles away and the terrain was getting tougher to drive. There were mountain passes and hairpin turns and some unexpected company as well. A cavalcade of cyclists appeared to be having a race. Jerry thought about his desire to do that kind of thing some day. But not today. Curious and noticing a cyclist pulled over on the shoulder of the road ahead, he stopped the car to find out what was happening.

"Hello, young fellow," he began. "I noticed you guys along the road. What's happening?"

"It's a ride for a local charity," the young man answered. "Coeur d'Alene to Canada. We call it "Coeur to Can". It's an annual event."

"Okay, just curious. How many of you are in the pack?"

"Don't really know. I'm in about the middle of the pack, so there's a lot behind and a lot ahead."

"Hope you make it all the way," Jerry waved. And off he went.

Given the ups and downs of the highways he was riding, the young men had quite an undertaking. But since these men were young, and in great shape to do it, Jerry had no doubt most of them could finish. He himself was too old to consider such a rigorous task. Perhaps some day he could take a leisurely ride through Arizona if he ever got back in one piece. It was a biking Mecca! Even the Canadian biking teams came there for winter practice time.

Before he had finished that thought, Jerry spotted a police vehicle behind him. Then, the lights flashed and the siren wailed. He would have to run for it this time. Since he had a small car the curves could be taken at a higher speed. But on both the up slope and the straight-away the chase car would have an advantage. There was no way Jerry could win this one. So he thought he better try to out-brain rather than out-brawn the officers.

Slowing his vehicle to a crawl he pulled over to a very steep scenic lookout. The police car came in behind him, and as it did, Jerry peeled off to the left and down the road. He checked the rearview mirror. The police car had pulled out burning rubber, but with the swiftness of Jerry's departure his pursuers hadn't taken note of the guard rail. It was a railing only about five feet wide, and a car in front of it would cover it unless they had been there before. Of course it was likely they had. This time, in the excitement of catching a fugitive from justice they slammed right into it! A billow of steam rose from their radiator. Seems they looked bedraggled, not hurt, as they got out of the vehicle. Jerry had won a temporary victory but wasn't quite sure how. He had disabled a car driven by patrolmen who should have known the setting. Too much to think their radio was disabled.

That wasn't important right this minute. He had been given a renewal, a new lease on life, and he began to wonder how many of his nine lives this lucky cat had left. The larger town of Sandpoint lay straight ahead. He was low on gas, and certain he would encounter the police again. Pulling into a service station, he quickly filled his tank and emptied his bladder. Then he noticed a sight of interest down the road. A group of the marathon cyclists he spotted earlier were stopped at a park on Main Street, and they had left their bikes unattended by the side of the road.

"A bike ride to Canada" he quizzed himself? "Naw," he thought. "Too far out." Or was it? The police now knew his car, and Jerry was a marked man. Perhaps he could waltz away on a racing bike. Would that be overestimating his stamina or sanity? Jerry parked the car across from the shaded area where the cyclists were resting. They were in the center of the park, and appeared dead to the world for a rest period. He looked at the bikes and noticed the helmets were hung on the handlebars. What did he have to lose. He picked a bike, put on the helmet as though he owned it and pedaled down Main Street. It was part of the highway through town. Perhaps the disguise would work.

Canada was sixty miles north through the ups and downs and arounds of the highway. Though he was normally in mint shape, the last two days had exhausted him. His ankle still hurt, but his energy level was high. Fear and determination were keeping him going. Checking back, he noticed that no one was after him. Apparently he had taken the bike without being seen. The most Reverend Jerry Grant had just stolen a racing bike after absconding with a rental car and wrecking a highway patrol vehicle. Carnage marked his trail and his only consolation was that none of this — not one bit of it — was of his making.

As for now he was now one of the boys in the marathon, save for his civvies. But the helmet covered a multitude of sins. Like it or not, his final run for the border would be aboard this vehicle. "Lord," he prayed, "Lord, let me get to the Canadian Border Station."

Chapter 18

If he had to be a thief for a day, Jerry certainly chose the right equipment. Not that he didn't feel badly about taking it, but the old "lesser of two evils" issue was the matter which made the difference. Never had he ridden a true speed bike like this. Then again, there were sixty miles to pedal. With twenty-eight gears he could maintain what seemed like thirty-five mph on the level. The many upgrades would be slower. Maybe very slow. But the downgrades would be very fast. By the look of the map, he was heading for Kanisko National Forest, a scenic ride.

He also knew what the last dozen miles or so would offer. There would be more ups and downs and many curves to navigate. Copper Creek was the last town on the American side, and from there, after one grueling climb through mountain passes, six miles on a steep downgrade to the Canadian border town of Eastport. Gliding, ahhh! If only things were really that appealing. Jerry Grant was a fugitive, a thief, a liar by necessity, but still a liar, a man responsible for death — all because he wanted to play hero and prevent international conflict. He had a hard time justifying all that happened, well intentioned as he might be. Now his lifelong dream had become a surrealistic nightmare in his long awaited major biking expedition. He was fleeing on a bicycle. That sounded utterly stupid. No, he wasn't fleeing at all. He had a cause.

Still, Jerry found the ride a most appealing experience when he could keep his mind off the trail of death and deception. Pacing himself would be a given. A water bottle was about two-thirds full, maybe 10 ounces or less. And while on occasion he had ridden thirty miles at a stretch, he had never before attempted sixty. Certainly not across mountains.

There were times when he questioned both his sanity and his resolve. Maybe he had made a mistake. Maybe everything he had deduced was pure speculation. Maybe it wasn't Carl Blackwell's people who had tried to kill him over the Grand Canyon. There were a lot of maybes, but a lot of affirmative evidence as well. If these things were all in the realm of his imagination then why was he pursued after leaving Coeur d'Alene, and why had Jenny told him he was plastered all over the Tucson area news?

If there was any doubt in his mind, it was about to be put to rest. He had pedaled over a moderately high hill, and what he saw on the downside renewed his resolve. There they were - troops. Thousands and thousands of troops. And they sure weren't playing any games. Jeeps and trucks were slowly traversing the highway, albeit it at a snail's pace. They were going north, going to Canada. Nor could he believe this highway was the only one used for such a convoy. There must be many more along secondary routes elsewhere in Idaho and Montana. It wasn't even the end of October and they were mobilizing long before the news had indicated.

Jerry pedaled by, feigning a smile. One after the other he sped past the convoy, vehicles crawling like ants seeking the anthill. Hundreds of infantry were loaded in the trucks. He saw missile-bearing flatbacks. Perched atop of other vehicles were digging machines and graders, and with this vision, any and all doubt either about his sanity or the correctness of his conclusions vanished. The convoy was forty miles from Canada now. Chances were it would leave the highway a few miles before Eastport and cross secretly over the forty-ninth parallel. Or maybe stick around in US territory for a while until everything was ready to do the deed. The deed — taking Canadian water without asking for it. Was that really so wrong? Maybe Carl Blackwell was right in saying his heart was in saving the people of the American southwest.

Jerry picked up the pace. The hills were not high hills here, at least not on the roadway. His speed was rapid, and he felt no fatigue. But thirst was beginning to trouble him. Riding in Tucson, one didn't perspire till the ride was over. But here in Idaho, a damper climate by far, perspiration was splattering with every movement. He was going to need nourishment. Jerry slowed down some, and about ten miles further saw a small service station with a little convenience store. He wanted to save his water bottle. Besides, he had already sipped it and it was too warm to give relief. He pulled over, entered, and bought some Gatorade. That's what he needed; to replace the fluids and chemicals drained from the body with heavy perspiration. Athletes used it all the time. Jerry drank slowly but heavily, then bought another bottle for the journey. The frame of the bike had a wire holder for water containers, and, with a little effort, he fitted the bottle to the container discarding the extant bottle.

The forest ride was stunning. Once again, he was hoping that someday he could cycle there as recreation. Not as a fugitive! Slowly but surely the miles passed. On the downgrades he reached some high speeds, perhaps as high as fifty or sixty mph. Canada was coming to meet him, but in a way he had never considered possible or feasible. He puffed and pedaled, at times wanting just to stop. Now the ride was taking its toll. Jerry felt his right leg cramping, a sign he had better stop and again replenish the fluids his body had lost. It was a timely decision. The roadside was hot. He could see no shade, at least not on this stretch. The next few miles appeared to be a heavy duty ascent. This was the time to freshen up a bit; suck some oxygen which, at the present altitude, seemed to be limited in the atmosphere.

He walked around, then sat down and rubbed the cramping muscle. That ankle sprain still punished him as did the shoulder which had dislocated. His right leg had bothered him before. Knee surgery years ago had left him with a somewhat weaker leg. But Canada was now so close, and his mission so nearly accomplished, save for telling a believable tale.

Climbing back aboard the bike, he began the long upward ascent. This was a stiff gradient. In the lowest gear now, it still seemed a supreme effort. the summit was visible and not too far up. With a goal in mind Jerry would endure. Half a mile, then a quarter mile. He was dying, or at least it felt that way. He had given his best effort but there was nothing left.

Jerry dismounted and began to walk to the top summit. There he found the little town called Copper Creek. That meant two things. Canada was six miles away, and it was all downhill from here. He lay beside the roadway, and for a few moments, breathed deeply. The air was even thinner now and what he needed most was plenty of oxygen.

Whooosh, whooosh, whooosh. Jerry heard a strange sound. Maybe it was just the wind, sometimes making strangely spooky emanations at high altitudes between mountain peaks and valleys. Then he heard it again — whoosh, whoosh, whoosh. "What is that?" he thought.

His question was answered. Above him he saw an Army helicopter, a big, bulky army helicopter. Jerry watched as it flew overhead. It made a "U" turn, and headed toward him. "My gosh," he thought, "They're after me. He needed some adrenaline and it came. Jerry mounted the racing bike and headed downhill. The chopper followed, but each time there was a curve in the road, he bought a little time. Most of the curves were through little rocky spaces that concealed him from the whirlybird, if but briefly.

Ratatatata! Ratatatata! A gunner was firing at him from the aircraft. He rounded another curve, garnering a little more time and distance. Yet it was nearly impossible to lose the helicopter. Jerry weaved the bike from side to side, dodging bullets. Fear engulfed him, then resolve. Time and again he was fired upon. The strikes were all around him, but he knew none had hit. He was in a war zone. They knew who he was, what he was doing and they were going to try to assassinate him. Ratatatatat!

Straight ahead a tunnel stretched out. It was a long tunnel that wound around the mountainside, downward. It would also be protection. If he could make it through the tunnel he estimated there would be two miles of straight down gradient to Eastport and he could lay claim to safety as a Canadian national. Ratatatata! Ratatatata! The bullets bounced off the rocks and the pavement, and Jerry hit the entrance to the tunnel unscathed. There was only one problem. The sign before the tunnel had cautioned it. "VEHICLE LIGHTS MANDATORY".

Jerry was riding blind. It was pitch black and the end of the tunnel was not in sight. He had no idea where in the road his cycle was set. It would be a ride of instinct, of faith and not sight. His bike rubbed against the left side of the tunnel. Jerry felt the skin on his arm and leg peel off. It hurt. He bounced off the other side, and his right elbow took a violent blow, almost paralyzing his sensation. He was coasting now, and the bike was accelerating at the mercy of gravity.

Instinctively he kept moving to the right, extending his hand as a feeler toward the right tunnel side, and knowing that the left wall of the tunnel posed the greatest danger. Traffic did come from the other direction. Still, black is black, and once again he brushed his already battered body against the left wall. Again he bounced off, still aboard the bike and still descending. Then he saw it - the proverbial light at the end of the tunnel. It appeared first as a pinhole, then as a doorway. Bruised but clear-headed, he emerged from the black and into the light, The helicopters seemed to have given up given the danger of the narrow spacing the mountains provided for the tunnel.

Blood dripped from Jerry's left arm and leg. The right side had escaped with minor abrasions. The left side showed open flesh. The helicopter was soon on his tail again, squeezing itself with reckless abandon between the sides of the hills. Ratatatata! Ratatatata! They were firing at him in one last effort to stop this renegade. But all he could do was to shimmy and swerve. Down the hill he flew in serpentine fashion. Ratatatata! He did not know whether he had been hit, but if not he wasn't sure how the gunners could have missed.

A sign on the road read "Eastport — Canadian border: 1 mile." Jerry throbbed with pain and was racked with anxiety. His speed was so very fast and he wondered if he could make the final curve. The final speed warning sign read, "45 mph." He was going at least 55 mph.

Pulling to the outside of the road, he approached the curve on a wing and a prayer. His left foot hit the guard rail, but he made it past the curve. It was now straight downhill, and the wind-blown Canadian flag was beckoning him to home. The helicopter veered off now, probably to escape detection from the Border people. Jerry Grant would live another day. A few hundred yards away was his native country.

Yet another snafu. Brakes! There were no brakes on the bike. The tough slugging had stripped both brake cables from the wheels. He couldn't have foreseen this, nor did he need any more surprises. Now he had no choice about where he would stop. He was at the mercy of the decline. Probably he was the only rider ever to attempt biking this part of the Idaho mountains without brakes. Yet perhaps ignorance had proven to be bliss, for had he known of the failure, he would have begun worrying much sooner than needed. This way, he had but a few moments to panic.

A hundred yards from the border crossing Jerry dragged his feet. It was mostly in vain. He was high up in the seat, and only the tips of his toes touched the ground. A customs agent was standing by the crossing, ready to check this vehicle approaching Canadian territory. He began waving for Jerry to stop.

There would be no stopping. Jerry flew by the officer waving, dragging his feet and yelling "help me!" He tried to yell out that he couldn't stop, but the wind created by his speed impeded his call. He had, for all practical purposes, crashed the crossing. That, he knew, was against the law. To add insult to injury he realized the road continued downhill for another mile into Canada.

Jerry looked back over his shoulder and soon saw what he expected. A border patrol vehicle was in hot pursuit. Again he was being chased. The only advantage to this was that it was on the right side of the border. He dragged his feet some more, pushing his toes down with all his might. But to no avail. The bike would stop when it decided to stop, and no sooner. The car pulled along side of him, and over the speaker Jerry heard the warning. "Stop at once or you will be shot." He shrugged his shoulders and pointed to his dragging feet. He was trying to communicate his lack of ability to bring the bike to a stop.

The car nudged ever closer and the officer on the right extended his hand. Jerry had communicated his dilemma. He reached out and grasped the hand extended, then slipped away. A second time he reached over, and this time the officer got a good hold. Gradually, the agent slowed the car, and with it, Jerry and his bike. Soon, they were at a standstill, nearly a mile beyond Canada's Eastport border crossing. He dismounted, and as the officers approached him, he felt a sudden, strange sensation. Everything was going black, and in short order, Jerry Grant collapsed to the road.

"Where am I?" he asked the nurse standing bedside. "What's happening?"

"Take it easy, Mister Grant," she urged. "You're in a hospital bed in Creston, British Columbia."

Noticing the intravenous drip in his arm, Jerry asked the nurse, "What's this for?"

"You're seriously dehydrated, sir. You nearly died. We're trying to get some fluids back into your body. The doctor ordered a glucose solution. Just lie back and relax."

Things were starting to make sense now in terms of his present circumstances. Before long, the sense of urgency which had driven him to such limits returned. He tried to sit up in bed but was deterred by some kind of restraints. "What's this for?" Jerry asked.

"Oh those," she answered. "You were thrashing around pretty good and we didn't want you to get hurt. So the doctor ordered an arm and body restraint."

"Can I get it off now?" he asked.

"I'm afraid not, Mister Grant. I'll have to wait for doctor's orders."

"Well, go find him, please. I have an urgent matter to take care of."

"What's that?" she asked.

"I have to meet with the P. M."

"The Prime Minister - of Canada?" she said.

"Yes, the Prime Minister of Canada."

"Sir, why not lie down and rest awhile. Your body looks pretty black and blue to me. If you try to get out of bed you'll just pass out again."

"Come on, sick or not I need to get word to the government," he insisted.

"What kind of word?"

"Can't tell you. You'll just think I'm crazy. Look, Miss, can you get me a police officer — a Mountie?"

The nurse said nothing, and left the room. Jerry tried moving again, and pretty soon realized that he didn't have the strength to struggle. She had been right. His body was void of all its reserves. Resigning himself to that, recollecting what he had endured, Jerry closed his eyes and drifted back to sleep.

"Reverend Grant. Reverend Jerry Grant?" a voice now summoned. Jerry opened his eyes and saw a well dressed man standing next to his bed.

"Yes, I'm Reverend Grant," he said.

"My name is Sergeant Moser of the Creston detachment, Royal Canadian Mounted Police."

"Boy, am I glad to see you," he confessed. "I need to tell you something, and I might sound a little loony doing so. But I guarantee it's very important."

"That'll have to wait a while sir," the officer stated.

"How come?" Jerry replied.

"Because I have something I need to tell you first."

"What's that," Jerry continued. "Is it about Jenny and the kids."

"No, sir, it's about you," he retorted. "I'm placing you under arrest."

"For what?" Jerry asked. "I couldn't help crashing the border. I didn't know the bike had no brakes."

"Oh, there's no problem with that. We know the bike was out of control."

"Then what do you want to arrest me for? I've got to talk with the Prime Minister."

"Not now, Reverend Grant. You - are - under - arrest - for - suspicion - of - murdering - Richard – Green he said staccato style."

Jerry's heart sank. "I didn't kill Richard Green," he said. "But I know darn well who did."

"You'll have your day in court," the officer answered. "Right now you're being placed in custody right here in the hospital room. There'll be an officer outside the door till you're feeling better. Then we'll be taking you to the holding cell downtown."

Jerry turned his head aside. He had nearly died for his country and now no one wanted to hear him out. He wasn't getting anywhere begging and pleading. As he relegated himself to silence the officer left the room. Jerry could see a uniformed Officer stationed outside the door.

With all the effort he had expended, he now doubted the wisdom of expending more. "The heck with it," he said. "Screw everything. At times, nothing seems worth the effort. Screw everything" he mumbled. "Screw everything." And, with that profanity, he drifted into another sleep, wondering what his awakening would have to offer.

Chapter 19

There seemed to be nothing left. Drained both of strength and will, Jerry floundered in a current of torrential thoughts. He tried to remember all that happened but the fog was yet to lift. Somehow it didn't move him. He sensed that so much had resulted in so little while details eluded him. He had lost heart, for it was Tuesday morning now, and though new days normally brought him new joys, Jerry Grant felt he was a beaten man. Defeated! Would anyone believe his story when he got it back together? He wished now he had his story on one of the computer diskettes they had prepared. So whatever he would tell would have to be consistent with the facts as he had encountered them. But for now, sleep and let tomorrow come.

But not just yet! The door of his room swung open. Coming to his bedside was a man with a briefcase. "Most likely, he's an investigating officer with the R.C.M.P.," Jerry thought. But it didn't faze him. Indifferently, he rolled over with his back to the man.

"Reverend Grant," he inquired, "May I speak with you?

"No," Jerry said gruffly. That was uncharacteristic of him.

"I think you might want to sir," the man responded. "My name is Schlak, Dale Schlak."

"Is that supposed to mean something to me?" Jerry grunted.

"Not yet, but I hope it will," he answered.

"Like what?"

"Sir, I tend to believe something of what you told the police."

Jerry turned around and looked at him. "Say what? What did I tell them?"

"The police said you had to see the Prime Minister of Canada."

"Yeah, but they thought I was a Looney."

"They still do, but maybe I don't."

"Aren't you a police officer too?"

"No sir. I've been asked by the local Sergeant to represent you. I'm a lawyer."

"What are you going to do? Listen to me and then tell me I'm a Looney?"

"No sir." The gentleman was very kindly, smiling, sincerely and truly sympathetic to Jerry's plight. It was the kind of empathy Jerry needed. He sat up in bed, still tethered by the hands, but no longer by the waist.

"Tell you what," the lawyer said, "call me Dale and I'll call you Jerry. Let's put the formalities aside, okay?"

Jerry nodded his assent. "Know what" he spoke with a slur, "e-mail my wife at "JJGrant2@att.com" and ask her to send—ah—." The file name was eluding him. finally it came back; "Ask her to send a copy of "rawsmage! If they let her do it."

"I can do that if it'll help you?"

"It'll help you more" Jerry asserted.

"In the meantime sir" the lawyer continued, "I do believe some of the things you were mumbling when you were semi conscious. The reason I believe you Jerry, excuse me, Reverend Grant, is that not only am I a lawyer. I also knew Richard Green."

"In what capacity?" Jerry asked.

"I was also a Member of Parliament till last year. Then I lost the election and resumed private practice".

Jerry raised his eyebrows intently interested. "You knew Rick?" he asked.

"I knew him. I gather, since you're a preacher, that you were his minister in Calgary at one time."

Jerry's ears perked up. "Yes, for ten years. We were dear friends. I didn't kill him."

"I don't think you did either," Dale replied.

"What makes you think I'm innocent?" Jerry asked.

"Because Rick had some premonitions about his safety. The last year he'd been spouting off about the political fundamentalists in Ottawa, and how they were so terribly angry with him. He felt he was targeted for a hit; not literally, but a demotion or something like that!"

Jerry remembered Rick's nervous behavior at the golf course. "Targeted for a hit by his own people. No! It wasn't the Canadians who killed him," he affirmed.

"What makes you think so?" Dale asked. "These men were, well, fanatical protectionists. Radical nationalists I would call them."

"Got time for a bedtime story?" Jerry asked.

"Sure, fire away." Dale sat down beside him, loosened his tie, and listened with sincere intensity as the details returned to the forefront of Jerry's memory. Starting with the IRS letter, Jerry related his strange tale. He reported how he had personally seen the troops in the last fifty miles south of the Canadian border. It was an unhurried, precise report of all that had taken place. Dale Schlak got up and walked around. He rubbed his chin, and then suggested, "Would you be willing to tell your story again? I'll have a stenographer come in and tape it."

"I already told it once," he said. "I am so, so tired. Can't we wait to see if my wife's e-mail gets here?"

"Sure, but sketch it out for me while we wait. I asked the hospital if we could use the computer to reach your wife. In the meantime tell me what you can remember. It's very urgent that I know it."

"It sounds very fictional" Jerry admitted, "but I'll tell you the outline to this point." With that Jerry began his accounting. It took about fifteen minutes after which Jerry queried, "I don't think it sounds plausible sir. I have no hard feelings if you don't believe me."

"I know it's hard to fathom all that. I do believe you however, but I still have some pieces to put together. I can believe everything you said, except that the troops are actually advancing. See, we know there's military exercises going on down south, but the American government — no, make that the American military — told us they'd be staying south of Coeur d'Alene and a hundred miles south of any Canadian point."

"I can guarantee they're not," Jerry assured him.

"That's what I want to check out," Dale replied.

"How?"

"I'll go up in a helicopter and take a first hand look" Dale insisted.

Jerry's passion for his mission was now aroused. "Don't go over the border

"Well I have to!" He got up to leave and Jerry squeezed his forearm to restrain him. Dale Schlak looked askance at Jerry and yanked his arm away in anger. "No more of that" he cautioned. "Tell you what; if you'll give your story just once more to the lady I send in I'll keep you out of the slammer and in this hospital bed till I get back. Deal?"

"Deal!" Jerry and Dale shook hands.

"So when are you coming back?" Jerry asked him

"Soon as possible. I'm going on a little helicopter ride for a firsthand look."

"Be careful, "Jerry cautioned. "They've got guns to shoot you down and you're the closest thing to my friend right now."

"Oh it's a commercial chopper," he assured him. Besides, we won't get that close. I just want to fly south of Eastport and see how far down they are. Then I'll be back. I have, let's say, a rather good relationship with the R.C.M.P. We'll talk turkey. The sergeant knows I'm doing this. Says I'm going a little too far for a client. But we'll check it out"

Jerry was grateful for this small favor and his resolve to tell his tale began to return. He lay back on his pillow and waited for the secretary to come. No sooner had Dale Schlak left the room when a finely dressed lady entered. She introduced herself as Alma Payne, sat by the bedside and turned on the machine. Then Jerry made her an offer. "I can save you tons of work and typing if you get me down to a secretarial area with a phone and a computer in it."

"Let me see what I can do." Ms. Payne opened the door of the guarded room and touched the shoulder of his R.C.M.P. watchman. "Mr. Mountie," she said softly, "I need to get a story from Mr. Grant in here. But I need a new steno device or tape recorder. I got orders from my boss Mr. Schlak to take a deposition and my machine is shot. Would you find out if your detachment has one I might use? It's just a few steps down the street and I promise to keep our main man here under wraps" she avowed.

"Ah, okay ma'am. Take me about ten minutes. Are you sure he won't run out on you?"

"Oh not at all. He's is too crippled up" she blurted as she shook her head side to side.

The Mountie left, and, when the halls were quiet and clear, she led the Reverend Grant to the steno room. He was rather humbled, holding the back of his hospital gown together to keep his rump from bouncing out. It appeared Alma knew her way around the hospital. Apparently the R.C.M.P. detachment used this hospital to detain many an injured suspect. The two slipped into the office which housed all things secretarial. "What now" Alma requested?

"Let me call my wife and tell her to send an e-mil here—if you have the address. You can download the attachment and print it out. I'm sure your boss will be quite pleased with the expedient work.

Jerry looked around to be assured no one was watching, then dialed home and dictated the following. "Jenny, this is Jerry! No talking; just e-mail "rawsmage" to this address. Jerry summoned Alma Payne to tell her the address. She pleaded, "This is urgent Mrs. Grant. Your husband is alive! So just do it if all is clear. Please and double please!" With no further ado she hung up the phone.

Suddenly the phone rang. Instinctively, Alma picked it up and heard the voice of the same Jenny Grant. "Just verifying the number on my Caller ID box" she explained. "Shall do —is Jerry okay?"

"Oh yeah! His life may depend upon the careful notes I was told you placed on computer and copied to diskettes. Trust me Mrs. Grant. I am helping your husband." Again Alma Payne replaced the receiver.

The two worked their way back to Jerry's room none too soon. Jerry's appointed guardian was coming down the other entrance to this hallway with a deposition steno machine under his arm. He brought it in and gave it to Alma. She thanked him and he stationed himself outside the door on the rickety chair they provided for him.

"What now" Jerry asked.

"We'll pretend I'm taking notes for a while. Then in a couple minutes I'll go out—-I'm under no restraint to stay here — and go back down to see if the hospital computer had an e-mail entitled "rawsmage". If so I'll print the whole thing on hospital paper. No one is around there so it must be a slow day. Any problem with that?"

"No, and if Jenny gets it to us it'll be a better report than I could mumble now. Dang, I need something for my shoulder pain."

That was the perfect cue Alma used to pass by the guard at the door and go back down to the office room. It must have been a good day for the gods. There it was: "You've got mail." The download was direct to print -- 15 pages—-and then saved automatically in home drive C. She returned to Jerry's room, smiled at the officer now reading the Creston Daily Mailbox paper and entered the room of the Reverend Grant. "Got it" she said with a grin!

"My pain pill" Jerry asked?

"No, the e-mail; 'Rawsmage'! "Were you serious about the pain pill?"

"Oh yeah" Jerry retorted. Ms. Payne reached over Jerry's bed and pulled the string to call the nurse. Quite shortly she came in with a pain pill and said, "Were you going to ask for this medicine? Sorry Reverend Grant; I'm kind of alone with 8 patients today. But I knew it was long overdue for your meds. Here you go." Jerry nabbed it and swallowed the two tablets without water, then washed it down with some stale Sprite sitting by his bed on the cabinet side.

"Thank you nurse. You are an angel of mercy indeed."

The young nurse departed and Jerry took Alma's hand and told her he was grateful for her help. "I hope my wife doesn't get in trouble down in Tucson for sending this out. Those guys can't be watching 24-7-365 I'm sure."

Thanking him for his co-operation, the secretary left the room, and Jerry was alone once more. He could only hope that Dale Schlak would believe him, and, that as he had said, he had a "good relationship" with the local Mounties. Creston, B.C., was a headquarters of a large R.C.M.P. detachment, and covered a great deal of territory along the southern Rocky Mountain area. The scenery was beautiful, and Jerry could see much of it from his hospital bed. The mountains rose some 15,000 feet, splashed with pine trees. A major highway wound over and through these massive Rockies. The sight was breathtaking.

After waking up and becoming more alert he rang the nurse for some food, and was granted his request. Some hours had passed and he was beginning to wonder about his final fate. Would Alma Payne help him get an audience with Ottawa? Would the government leaders consider hearing him out at all? Would the name of

Richard Green, if used frequently enough, raise some eyebrows? Or would he be formally charged and given a preliminary hearing to ascertain whether there was enough evidence to try him for murder? After all, he was under arrest!

Sergeant Moser reappeared. "I think you're well enough to come along with us now, Reverend Grant. The nurse is going to cut the tethers and we'd like you to get dressed, please."

"Into what?" Jerry snapped. "My clothes were torn apart." Jerry restrained his temper. "I'm sorry Sergeant, I've just been through a living nightmare," he apologized.

"We've got some things for you to wear. Just casual pants and a shirt — if you don't mind."

"That's very kind of you. By the way, when will I get a chance to see the lawyer you sent me?"

"I can't be sure," the Sergeant responded. "To tell you the truth, we're a little worried about Dale."

"What do you mean worried?"

"Did he tell you his plans?"

"Yes sir, he said he was going across the line to check something out. He said he'd be back to talk to me."

"Reverend, I'm afraid his helicopter is reported overdue at the landing base."

Jerry was shocked. Had his worst fears been realized? "I told him to be careful," he continued.

"Careful of what?" the Sergeant asked.

"Careful of the troops. I saw the missile guns on the flatbeds."

"If you say so, sir," replied the Mountie.

"No, it's true. That's what Dale Schlak went to check out - to see if my story was true."

"Yes, sir, he told me some of your story."

"Well, if it's remotely possible, why isn't someone out looking for him? Or is there?"

"No sir. We can't send anyone out till we're certain he's in trouble."

"He's in trouble, believe me. Especially if he spotted the troops and they spotted him. Sergeant, I got chased by the Highway Patrol and also by a military chopper."

"You are a wanted man," was the cold response.

It was obvious to Jerry that he was getting nowhere; so it seemed best he terminate the subject for now. The secretary had his story on hardcopy from the e-mail Jenny was able to send out, so if and when Dale Schlak ever returned Jerry would be blessed with a sympathetic ear.

Sergeant Moser escorted Jerry to the waiting police car. He was so sore. Not far from the hospital was the detachment headquarters which the two men entered. Jerry had not been handcuffed, a sign, so he hoped, of the officer's readiness to hear Jerry's story, perhaps even a hint that he believed it. According to routine procedure, he was formally charged, then fingerprinted and taken into an interview room. Sergeant Moser was with him throughout the process. The two men sat face to face, across the table from one another. Jerry was asked to tell his story. At first reluctant because he had already recorded his story, he reconsidered. If he gave the same story as he had given Dale Schlak, perhaps his consistency would enhance his credibility. Or should he bid them get the printout in the hands of Alma Payne. No, he would just talk as best he could.

Starting with the certified letter, Jerry reiterated the details as precisely as before. There were no interruptions. With a ready ear, the officer heard him out, making only an occasional note. His tale was again being recorded and he was doubly careful to be as accurate as he had been earlier. After an hour, the process was completed and the sergeant began some questions.

"How do you account for the fact that the CIA knew your every move"?

"I don't know."

"I can tell you if you like."

Jerry's ears perked up. "By all means," he summoned.

"There's a central clearing house for credit card purchases. We have a line to every credit card company on earth and one especially reliable outfit for North America. Hell, we've tracked people from here to Madagascar." Jerry bent over, as if disgusted with himself. "Of course! I don't know how I could have been so stupid. I used it for the car! What with all the confusion — oh Lordie!"

"I don't know whether to believe your story, Reverend Grant," the sergeant confessed, walking around the table. "Coffee?"

"Sure." Jerry needed something. "Look sergeant, it's about as far out as you've ever heard, I'm sure. What about a polygraph?"

"Too unreliable," he admitted. "We use those things to frighten people into confessions mostly."

"Why didn't you try it with me?"

"Because there's something about your story that sounds almost — well — believable. Besides, I'm waiting to hear from Dale Schlak. He is your lawyer after all!"

"No word about him yet?"

"None."

"What's the next move?" Jerry asked.

"I have to put you in a holding cell for now Reverend. I'd rather take you to my house, but - procedure you know."

"I understand. Do what you need to do. But before you take me there, can I make one more statement. It's off the record."

"Sure, go ahead."

"This country is facing an impending invasion. The American CIA, the State Department, and I'm not positive about that, as well as the military, are planning to trench our water to the western United States. That is a fact of life. If we don't do something about it we're going to find out too late that it's true. Right now you're the only one with authority to act."

Jerry had spoken those final words in convincing fashion.

"Your solution is to talk with the Prime Minister?" the sergeant asked.

"Or some other high ranking government official. Richard Green told me a few of them had suspicions that this would happen somewhere down the line."

"That what would happen?"

"The theft of water."

"You know, Reverend, I want to believe you. I almost can. But stealing water….I don't know. Right now, I'm at the mercy of my vocation. You are a prime suspect in Richard Green's murder, and I can't change that for now!"

The cell wasn't really so bad. There was a door in the hallway leading to the main office, and the sergeant left it open so Jerry wouldn't feel too alone. This officer of the peace had proven quite friendly. Jerry believed he concurred with the story. All other cells were empty. "It must have been a slow week" he thought.

Jerry contemplated the past. The mission which he had set out to fulfill now depended upon his credibility. But he wasn't certain who would determine that. He was sure the police officer had no such authority. Certainly Dale Schlak didn't, even if he was alive. It was still Jerry's heartfelt prayer that his lawyer was alive and well. But if so, what in the world was keeping him. Jerry dozed off, still feeling the effects of his two day pursuit. How could he have been so simple minded as to forget that credit card purchases could be traced?

Suddenly his eyes popped open. "My gosh," he thought aloud, "That still doesn't answer how I was discovered leaving Tucson. Somebody had to know about it. Somebody close to me. Either it was Gordon Woods or Bert Benson. Maybe Bert found out. After all, Blackwell had hinted that Bert was a willing actor in the drama. That has to be it," he affirmed. "My head deacon found out, maybe from my colleague Reverend Woodford, and let the cat out of the bag. Probably it wasn't even intentional."

As he considered those possiblities he heard footsteps coming toward his cell. Stepping to the front of the cell, he saw a lady being escorted down the hallway. It was Dale Schlak's secretary, Alma Payne. The Sergeant unlocked the door of the cell and motioned for Miss Payne to enter. "Ten minutes," he said. Then he left the two alone and Alma Payne began to speak.

"Good to see you again Reverend Grant. Sorry it has to be in this cold cell and not that cozy hospital room. I know you're going to think I'm a terrible person but there's something you need to know. See, I believe everything you said when I read this e-mail printout. And truthfully, Dale or I can likely get you off."

"Go ahead," Jerry offered. "I won't think you're a terrible person, Ms. Payne. That's a promise."

"Please call me Alma."

"I'll call you Alma if you call me Jerry, okay?"

The soft-spoken secretary agreed, and began her stunning confession. "It's no coincidence that I work for Dale Schlak," she began. "I knew him as a friend in Ottawa."

"You lived in Ottawa?"

"Yes sir. I worked for the Department of the Interior as confidential secretary to Richard Green. And Richard and Dale are — were good friends."

"Go ahead."

"Well, this is the part I feel so ashamed about," she submitted, "I was also Rick's lover. His murder was a horrible shock to me." She paused for some heavy crying, expressing her remorse in heaving sighs. Then Jerry compassionately placed his arms around her. She seemed genuinely touched.

"I was also the reason he got divorced," Alma continued. Now she was looking down in shame and grief. Once again Jerry reached out to her.

"Alma," he said softly, "I'm glad you came in. That took a lot of courage for you, and believes me, I have great respect for your honesty. Do you feel like going on?"

"Okay," she said, still sobbing, but more subdued.

"Can you pull any strings in Ottawa?"

"Yes, I think so," she said sobbing. Something still troubled her she had not yet blurted out.

"What is it Alma," Jerry offered with a most compassionate plea.

"Well, back to the murder. I......I was there. I was living with Richard and I had moved into the guest house — you know, the one down the path toward the tennis courts? Anyway, I saw the men shoot Richard." She cried!

"My gosh, that must have been some kind of hell to witness." Jerry extended an arm to her and she took it as a gesture of consolation.

"But I just shut up about it because I was too stupid and too afraid. I let you take the blame, but I'll make sure they know I was an eye witness."

"Thank you Alma, but look; what's past is past. I am not a judging person. Nobody has the right to be. I'm just one imperfect human talking to another imperfect human, okay?"

Alma wiped her eyes and blew her nose. "What kind of strings do you want me to pull?"

"How about the Attorney General?" he questioned. "Or the minister of foreign affairs? Can you get through to either of them?"

"Yes I can. I have the Attorney General's number. I'm afraid I have a lot of numbers of Ottawa politicians." Once more she hung her head in an honest display of shame and regret.

"Alma, there's so much at stake. Remember that story you read? Well, it's all true. If you can set aside your guilt and your pride right now, maybe we can do this country a giant favor."

"What is it you want me to tell the Attorney General?"

"Tell him you know for a fact that the man arrested for Rick's murder has some information of national importance. And that I need to speak with him. Is he in Ottawa now?"

"No, better yet! In Vancouver. That's his home constituency."

"Will you try it, Alma? Please."

"I'll try it," she promised. With that she stood up. Jerry embraced her, expressing both his forgiveness and their single minded purpose. "Everybody can be forgiven," he said. "So let's get this show on the road and remember the stakes."

"Thank you Reverend Grant," she sobbed. "Jerry, I mean. I'll get back to you as soon as I find out anything. And if Dale gets back, tell him what's happening, will you?"

"Sure. Thank you for coming in. My neck's on the line too," he said.

Alma Payne summoned the sergeant. He came down and opened the cell, and, as he left he said, "I'm going to leave the gate open Reverend. You have no plans to walk out, do you?"

"None whatsoever," he pledged. "Thank you. I appreciate the gesture." The sergeant and the mistress left the hallway through the door to the office. Once more, Jerry was alone. Unlike previously, he now felt like at least like the fans in Mudville when Casey first stepped up to bat. He had "the hope which springs eternal in the human breast." For that hope he had a political mistress to thank. "I know the Lord works in mysterious ways," he whispered. "But if this works out, it's the most mysterious way I've ever seen."

Sergeant Moser came back half way down the hallway as Jerry peeked out of his cell, now open for his convenience to feel a little less confined. "Reverend" he called out, "I got a radio dispatch just now. Dale's craft is down somewhere. The beacon is sending out the automatic signals. That does mean impact I'm afraid. Sorry to have to blurt it out!"

"I — I tried to caution him the flight may be construed as an enemy approaching. Remember I told you that the military thinks the border of Canada and our own waterways are being guarded with reconnaissance missions, some of them simple helicopters. Dang, I wish I could have stopped him from going to look the situation over himself."

"Don't get too down on yourself Reverend Grant. He was trying to verify your story for your sake; he told me he was going to prove you were telling the truth and not some international conspiracy fable. He paid the price in pursuit of justice for you Reverend; if in fact he is dead in a crash."

"Well too many people have died for me" Jerry bellered." Backing into his cell sobbing, Jerry Grant slammed shut the cell gate with a potent swing, then, sitting on the little cot, just cried his heart out. If God works in mysterious ways, he no longer wanted a god who worked this way.

Chapter 20

Jerry admired the courageous confession of Alma Payne, though stunned that Richard Green would have fallen so far. Still he refused to judge either. This mistress had looked beyond herself both to Jerry's and Canada's best interest. Given the moral superiority style and downright insolence of many preachers she had taken a big risk in confessing as much as she did. Then again, she had gotten to know Jerry in their time at the Creston hospital. By now, Jerry also realized the truth about her relationship with Dale Schlak. More than being his secretary she and Dale lived together. Yet he would not pass judgment on her because he sensed the deep love Alma had in her heart for Richard Green, and her desire to see that true justice be done. Fate had served up a menu of strange offerings: A lady of ill repute now became Jerry's partner in an effort to avoid a possible conflict. That one person at least believed him was some kind of morale booster.

Feeling safe in R.C.M.P. custody, Jerry determined to phone home. "Sergeant Moser," he shouted. "Can I talk to you a moment?" There was no answer! Jerry swung open the door of his cell a little further and peered into the hallway. Once more he called, "Sergeant Moser, are you out there?" Still no answer! He sat back on the bed, then, boldly strode down the hallway to the open door. The office was vacant and a phone was on the desk. Glancing around, Jerry saw no one. So picking up the phone he quickly dialed home. Just as quickly, he heard the ring. "Yeah" some man answered. Stunned by the voice on the other end, Jerry slammed the receiver down, and rushed back to his cell. "Who the heck was that?" he thought. "Lord, don't let Jenny be in custody." He tried to rationalize. "Maybe I got a wrong number." But try as he might, the feeling wouldn't go away — Jenny had company. He would have to trust her to her own resources. That was an agreement they had. Both would have to fend for themselves in this corporate mission. The pastor roamed back to his cell. He had, as such, been given freedom to roam the area when Sergeant Moser had left the door to his holding cell unlocked and slightly ajar.

The station door was opened. Jerry felt a breeze come down the hallway. The desk sergeant had obviously returned. Should he tell Sergeant Moser about the phone call? No, that might be taken as a matter of deceit. Jerry would keep that issue bottled inside him for now. Momentarily, the sergeant came down the hall calling for Jerry. "Yes sir," Jerry replied. "What's happening?"

"I guess you're going on a little trip with me," he said.

"To where?"

"Vancouver. We'll be flying in the R.C.M.P. craft. Do you mind?"

"Not at all. Who are we going to see in Vancouver?" Jerry believed he knew the answer already, but wanted the good sergeant to seem in charge and call the shots.

"The Attorney General of Canada has asked for an interview," he said.

A deep, oozing, feel-good "whew" came from Jerry. "Will I get a chance to tell him my story?" he requested.

"Guess so," Moser answered.

"When do we leave?" Jerry asked.

"Yesterday," was the reply. "Somebody wants to hear you out Reverend. I'll be escorting you as a prisoner, remember that."

"I certainly will," he answered the sergeant. "How long does the flight take?"

"About ninety minutes from here. Not quite as fast as a commercial jetliner." As the crow flies, they were looking at five hundred miles to Vancouver over some of the most rugged and astonishing terrain on earth. At the end of the flight Jerry hoped he would be confronted with the most important opportunity of his life.

"What's his name?" Jerry asked.

"Who, the attorney general?"

"Yes sir."

"Macmillan. Stuart Macmillan. Best we've had in a long time."

Meanwhile, brief paragraphs about Canadian politics appeared periodically in the newspapers of Tucson. The U.S. was numero uno in the world. As a result, Jerry had not kept up to date on political happenings in Canada. He was just happy that his mission might succeed. He worried about succeeding in time. The last thing he wanted was the proverbial success of the operation and the death of the patient, the Dominion of Canada.

They were not long in leaving. The plane climbed quickly to rise above the mountains. Jerry had driven through these mountains a few times during his Calgary stay, an eye opener indeed. Equally beautiful was the trip through the Fraser River Canyon. By car the road overlooked the canyon. By train, the tracks ran along the bottom of the canyon. Jerry had seen it from both perspectives, but never from the air. Now he could look down and see what British Columbia was all about.

Mountains and pines and rivers were sprawling. Timber was cut here. Much of the world's timber in fact. One other resource came to mind as they ascended in the police aircraft. The river snaking through the canyon called to mind another resource. Water! There was so much of it. It was so clear and pure and he wondered how long it would belong to Canada. Then again, he considered whether Canada should willingly share it with a dear neighbor.

Brian R. Dill

Time passed swiftly and the plane landed softly in Vancouver. "I've got to handcuff you now," Moser said, apologetically. "Appearances. They won't be tight."

"I understand quite well," Jerry smiled. "Be my guest." He extended his arms for the Sergeant and was slapped with the cuffs. Then, escorted from the airplane by the good officer, Jerry Grant was led to a waiting police vehicle and whisked away for his private meeting. The car's siren wailed and the lights flashed. Someone considered this to be an urgent meeting. Either that or the police couldn't be bothered with city traffic.

The interview was to take place in the Vancouver detachment, R.C.M.P. From the airport, the trip had taken twenty minutes, and before long, Jerry and Sergeant Moser walked into the interview room. Sergeant Moser motioned for him to sit in an easy chair, and then sat himself down next to him. The office door swung open, and a man dressed in a jogging suit entered.

"Reverend Grant," he said. "My name is Stuart Macmillan, the Attorney General of Canada." Jerry stood up to acknowledge him.

"I appreciate your seeing me," he said politely.

"Well, sounds as if we might have some international problems, eh?"

"Yes sir, we surely do."

"The sergeant gave me this printout of your wife's e-mail you and Alma Payne salvaged somehow when you were in Creston hospital. "I'll read it and we'll listen to it together, and if I have further questions I'll stop and ask them along the way."

Jerry was relieved that the hard copy had indeed been confiscated or re-copied from the hospital steno room. "Sure," Jerry said. "My objective is to be heard, so whatever way you can accommodate me will be much appreciated."

Sergeant Moser began to read rapidly and clearly at that. The three men listened attentively to what Jerry had earlier related.

There was utter silence throughout, and when the paper was read Stuart Macmillan rose to his feet. "Wait here," he demanded. "I'll be back shortly. Get the hospital to send us another copy of the e-mail. Tell them they may not know it but there's a system document titled "rawsmage" on their hard drive. Find it, send it, and we'll copy it and take some floppy disks with us. And do it yesterday."

Macmillan left the room and Jerry made small talk with the sergeant. They discussed recent happenings in Canada, and the why and wherefore of Jerry's move to Arizona. Moser was a warm man, not the typical overbearing police officer. His interest in what Jerry was saying was genuine, and Jerry reciprocated by listening to the sergeant.

The Attorney General was taking more than a few minutes. An hour later, almost to the second, he reappeared and sat down next to Jerry. "Reverend Grant, your story seems quite genuine. I've also been informed that your court appointed lawyer has been arrested south of Eastport by United States Immigration Officers."

"What are they holding him on?" Jerry inquired as he thanked God Almighty that Dale Schlak was not dead in the crash he was told about.

"Illegal entry into the United States. The government's been informed. Apparently, they forced down his chopper with a military helicopter and then booked him. He's back at an undisclosed location."

"Have you spoken with him?"

"Nope. The I.N.S. says no talk. We'll have to use diplomatic channels."

"Sure," Jerry snickered sarcastically. "They don't want him to confirm my report."

"Could be," Macmillan nodded. "Guess we are into something big! He paused, deep in thought. "Well, there goes my big trip to Tahiti." Macmillan paced the floor, deep in thought, contemplating his next move. He again asked the two men to wait while he went to check out some thing. This time, the wait was short. Momentarily he was back in the room.

"We're going to visit the P.M., he said. "You and me Reverend."

Jerry pondered another airplane ride. "My gosh" he said. "I've been in the air half my life this week. Now we go to Ottawa."

"Nope, not Ottawa, Washington."

"Washington," Jerry reacted. "Why Washington?"

"'Cause there's a bilateral conference going on there for three days. Prime Minister Gervais and the President of the United States."

"I'm a marked man" said Jerry. "How can I get to see the Prime Minister in Washington?"

"We have a private jet sir, and there's no security or customs clearance. Nice thing about this job. It's called diplomatic immunity. You'll be going as my press secretarial aide, okay."

"That's just fine with me, Jerry said. "What's our game plan?"

"We're going to request an interview with the P.M. and the President together," he affirmed. "And we'll confront the two of them with your story. That's going to make it or break it. The floppy disk is so well worded and so believable—well—that's why I want to use it as a basis for discussion."

"I understand the risk," Jerry admitted. "Pretty high one at that isn't it?"

"Not really. The story will be ready for release in a Vancouver paper and in a Seattle paper. But it will only be printed if we don't get out of this alive. Versteh?"

Jerry was growing more confident. Macmillan had the bases covered. The strategy seemed ideal. This whole matter was now going the route of diplomacy, and if that didn't work, then nothing in the world would work.

"We're going shopping first," Macmillan said. "My aides will take you and dress you up to look like a press agent. You'll have to change roles, Reverend. Preacher to press man, how does that sound?"

"Better than war," he exclaimed. "Better than war." Two aides then entered the room and took Jerry to a very exclusive clothing store right downtown.

"Take your pick," the men said. "The tab's on us." Jerry was set loose to buy all the clothes he wanted, and the suits bottomed out at five hundred dollars. Since ordered to do so he fitted himself with the best there was for the occasion. He picked out a gray vested suit. When he had done his shopping he was taken to a hotel room to clean up and shave. Slipping into his new assignment, he dressed the part, and from stem to stern, Jerry looked more like a press agent than a press agent himself.

Nightfall had arrived. The ride to Washington would be the red-eye special. There would be a pilot, Stuart Macmillan, and Jerry. For the sake of security there would, by law, be one bodyguard assigned to take care of the Attorney General and his "press agent." Jerry did not look forward to another emotional drain, but now knew it was necessary and the best possible plan of action. From here on in they would be proactive and not reactive. After learning they would be picked up at the hotel near midnight, Jerry and the two aides relaxed in the posh room, watching television and sipping soda. Television was the last thing Jerry wanted. For the time being however, it would have to fill the minutes of waiting for what he hoped would be his last plane trip for quite some time.

Stuart Macmillan arrived at their suite with his bodyguard and picked up Jerry for the drive to the airport. The Learjet was ready for takeoff, and so, with no further delay, the sleek aircraft was en route to the American capital.

Press Agent Grant was seated next to Stuart Macmillan so they could replay some of the events that had made Jerry a significant personality in the life of Canada's chief law enforcement officer.

"Do you fly?" Macmillan asked Jerry.

"Oh a little sir. Nothing major till the Grand Canyon episode," he recalled. "I'm not sure why I walked away from that one either."

"Well, you did. And we're grateful for your perseverance. And you actually cycled the last sixty miles just to get here; is that what you're saying and sticking to?"

"I'm not a martyr," he replied. "Any loyal citizen would have done the same or died trying. By the way, what made you believe me?"

"Several things." Macmillan stroked his chin. "We checked your background and found out that you had never owned so much as a hunting rifle. Besides, Rick's murder was professionally done. We had to find you to get to the bottom of it though. Actually, the press did you a real disservice. Made you look guilty before we found you."

"As long as we get to the Prime Minister it'll all be forgotten, believe me," Macmillan said. "Your name will be cleared. So don't worry about it, okay."

"A little hard to do right now, but if you say so, sir."

They were about an hour out of Vancouver now. The cabin lights had been dimmed to allow them to sleep, but neither Jerry nor Attorney Macmillan thought about sleeping. The bodyguard was dead to the world, and snoring at that.

Opening the cockpit door, the pilot came back to chat. "Who's flying this thing?" Jerry quipped.

"Otto, "Macmillan answered. "Automatic pilot. We call him Otto for short."

Jerry heard a click. He looked toward the pilot. A black pistol was aimed at the two men. Both sat erect, quite stunned by what they were seeing.

"What's happening, Nick?" Macmillan asked the pilot. "Why the gun?"

"Sorry, boss. You know the saying. They made me an offer I couldn't refuse. Hey, I'm set for life if I land this thing in Atlanta with three bodies. So everyone up and move to the back."

Jerry looked at Macmillan and the two men instinctively raised their hands. Then, with the turncoat waving this pistol, the pilot ordered them toward the back of the cabin where the bodyguard was asleep. Snoring!

"So close and yet so far," Jerry moaned, glancing at Macmillan.

"I tried," he said. "God knows I tried."

"I know you tried, Reverend. And believe me, whatever happens, your country will be eternally grateful. If we die, this thing will hit the Canadian and American press in a big way. If I fail to phone my office in five hours after departure, the press gets the story on both sides of the border. But I never expected Nick here to play traitor. You, Nick? How long's it been? Four years? How did you find all this out?"

"Shut up and move back, sir. This is the one big chance of my lifetime."

"Just out of curiosity, what are they paying you?"

"A quarter million," he smiled. The men were walking down the aisle, gun still brushing the back of their heads, first Stuart and then Jerry, always with a little push of the barrel.

"You know you'll never live to collect it," Macmillan told him. "The CIA is going to wipe you out too."

"Just shut up," Nick ordered. "They told me the money was in an Atlanta bank. I just have to go walk in to collect it. Then I've got their protection for life."

"Boy, have you got a surprise," Jerry piped up. "I can tell you all about the CIA. I suppose it was a man named Blackwell? How did he find out the plans?"

"Never mind. Shut up and get in the seat behind sleeping beauty and say your prayers."

Jerry and Stuart slid nervously into the seat behind the bodyguard. Just as quickly a shot rang out and instinctively both men covered their heads. There was no blood! Then they looked at each other. Neither was hit, but Nick was. He lay in the aisle of the plane, dead or so it seemed. Behind him stood the bodyguard.

"It's what I get paid for," he said with a smile. "He's just wounded. I always play the 'sleeping beauty' game."

Jerry and his new compatriot embraced. Then they hugged the man who had saved their life.

"Easy boys," he said. "You're going to ruin my renowned reputation as a tough guy."

"Who's going to fly this thing?" Jerry asked in a quandary.

"Be cool, friend," Macmillan answered. "I'm a flier. Just thought it would be more restful if Nick took us. Guess I'll have to do double duty now. Wonder how they got to him?"

"I've stopped asking those questions a long time ago! They can do whatever they set out to do" Jerry affirmed.

"By the way, what's your name," Macmillan asked the bodyguard. "I'm sorry I didn't stop to ask earlier. We had a lot on our minds."

"I can see why," the man answered. Fred. Freddy Ford."

"Fred, you'll get your reward. I don't know how to thank you, but by heaven you're going to get a promotion if I have my way."

"No thanks, sir. This is what I was cut out to do in life. First time I ever had to shoot anybody. I'm just glad I could be of service."

"Service," Jerry said. "There's got to be a better word than that. Thanks, Fred. I'm sure glad you're the bodyguard. Stuart Macmillan took the pilot's seat and deftly navigated the plane toward Washington, DC.

"Two hours," he said. "Sit back and take it easy."

"Take it easy!" Jerry responded. "This is the first time in my life I really wanted some chemical assistance to relax. No, make that the second time" he spoke recalling the flight from Tucson when he caved in to a C.C. Rye whiskey."

"Will a couple shots of Canadian Whiskey do?" Macmillan offered.

"Sure, right now this tee-totaller will take anything."

"Right back of the cockpit," Macmillan pointed assigning Jerry the role of bartender. "Make mine a double. I could use a little chemical assistance about now too. On second thought, hold off on mine. I want to fly this thing by the book and the book says no booze."

Chapter 21

The Canadian embassy was a beehive of activity. A.G. Stuart Macmillan had promised Jerry freedom from security and customs and the promise held fast. The Attorney General had landed the plane like a pro and seemed most comfortable with the diplomatic protocol. Canadian embassy personnel had sent a car for official transfer. Jerry admired the style of Stuart Macmillan. He was definitely in charge but not bossy. Both men were fatigued from the flight and the stresses which the assassination attempt engendered. As for Fred, the bodyguard, if he was tired he didn't show it.

The two men were seated in the embassy lounge awaiting someone to respond to their request for an appointment with the Prime Minister of Canada. Jerry hoped that now he could relate his story with the same consistency as he had before. That might bring the Prime Minister of Canada to a reasonable belief that there was a crisis — a crisis of international proportions.

"Do you think we have a chance" Jerry asked the attorney general? I mean a chance to ever meet the U.S. President?"

"We'll have a better chance if we set the dinner up for our embassy," Macmillan replied.

"Can you convince Prime Minister Gervais?"

"Oh yes. See, normally, the minister of foreign affairs would handle something like this. But Alma and I — well, you've guessed by now she was a fixture around Ottawa. So when she called me and pleaded with me to take on the job I decided I'd have as good a chance as anybody. Poor Alma! The only guy she really loved was Richard Green. The rest of us, well, we were just playthings."

"Do you know the Prime Minister personally?"

"Gervais? My best friend! Heck we grew up together in Manitoba. A little French town five miles from a little German settlement. Not a bad combo, eh? So when we get together, he talks to me in French and I talk back in German. And we don't understand squat?-all — 'oops, 'scuse me Reverend — what we're telling each other. But we fake it and love every minute of it."

"Macmillan? That's hardly a German name."

"Nope. However, when you're smack in the middle of little Germany, the lingo rubs off."

"Bet that proved a bit of a family feud — I mean a French settlement next to a German settlement."

"Oh, we had our days. Mostly though, it was the religion thing. French people are Catholic and Germans are Protestant — mostly Lutherans."

"How about yourself?"

"I'm just a religious semi-agnostic," Macmillan answered.

"That's one I've never heard before," Jerry laughed. "A religious semi-agnostic. I'll have to use that in a sermon some day. Can I quote you?"

"Sure, why not? I must confess, though, that it's people like you that restore my faith in religion a little bit. Who else would have made it through what you said you did?"

Jerry wondered if he should read between the lines of that last statement. ".......through what you said you did."

"So what's going to happen," Jerry asked.

"We're waiting for a call from Gervais. It's a priority from signals."

"What's that?" Jerry questioned.

"It means he'll receive a communication from his office that he needs to contact the embassy. It is the most urgent way of getting his attention. Something of personal or national importance has happened."

"And then…?"

"Then I'm going to beg him to get down here. When he comes, we lay out our plan."

"Which is…?"

"Which is to set up a dinner here at the embassy for the President of the United States and his wife after I have told him your story."

"How're chances that the P.M. will agree?"

"Pretty good, it seems to me," Macmillan nodded in the affirmative. "According to our information he has a free evening tomorrow night as does the President."

"Then what happens?"

"I ask him point blank," Macmillan said. "The President that is! 'What are your troops doing by our border? Were they not supposed to staying 100 miles south?'"

"Do I talk?" Jerry asked.

"Not unless I tell you. I want you to be incognito. If the President's behind the plan your name will be mud."

"But he might not be in on this."

"Perhaps not. Ever read 'Seven days in May'?"

"Yes, I have," Jerry said. "That was about a U.S. military coup attempt, wasn't it? If I recall it starred Burt Lancaster and Kirk Douglas".

"Precisely. And we've noticed all along how much weight the military carries. It's been growing steadily. The chiefs of staff really run this country. So we're risking everything on the hunch that the President is out to lunch on this one."

"When did you formulate this plan by the way?"

"Oh, I guess when you were at the Vancouver detachment with Sergeant Moser. And then while you were waiting at the hotel. I spent my time on the phone and in conference with a few fellows, guests at my home."

"The big boys?"

"Those are the ones. I even had the leader of the opposition over."

"The enemy dines together," Jerry replied.

"The enemy?" Macmillan answered. "Nobody could ever imagine how much government planning is done with the members of the opposition party. Some of them have top secret clearance status."

Jerry was learning some new things about the way his government worked. The party in power and the opposition party could even work together, and hastily so in matters of urgent concern. It was becoming obvious that, in Jerry's case, a well orchestrated symphony of ideas had been assembled into a finely tuned piece of musical action danced to a political twist.

"Do you people actually believe me, or is this just another headliner for future elections?" Jerry was fishing for a definitive response.

"Yes, Reverend, we do believe you. Our weather satellite confirmed the presence of troop movements. They're ten miles south now, and still moving toward the 49th."

"You got that off a satellite? Then why didn't you detect it sooner?"

"We weren't looking for it sooner. You know the saying. You see what you expect to see. Heck yes, that little trailblazer sends us lots of stuff. The Americans are even more sophisticated with theirs. They can read an Iraqi license plate from up there. They've looked down the smoke stack of every factory and every missile-building outfit there is in the old Soviet

Union. You don't think those satellites are for weather forecasting?"

"Well, I guess I did up until about now." Jerry shook his head, concerned about the naiveté of the general public, including himself in matters of government. "Maybe it's a good thing we know as little as we do," he suggested.

"That's the attitude," Macmillan countered. "Leave it to the boys upstairs."

"I guess I've never appreciated the responsibility my government has" Jerry confessed.

"Not many people do," Macmillan affirmed. "Not in Canada or the U.S. or most any country on God's green earth. We're just a bunch of corrupt politicians as far as John Doe is concerned. Not that we're above reproach. You've found that out already. But as in your business, there are lots of burdens to bear. So, if something goes wrong on our watch, we get the boot in the next election. It's called democracy."

A page boy came into the lounge. "Telephone call Mister Attorney General."

"Excuse me, Jerry, I'll be right back. Listen, if you want to walk around the embassy feel free to do so. But don't take a step outside our property. That's an order. You're still in my custody even if you are my press agent."

Jerry nodded in agreement. He left the lounge, looked around the embassy and then stepped outside. A colorful flower garden bounded by precisely trimmed shrubs greeted him. Iron gates secured the embassy entrance, and stationed at each gate were uniformed

Mounties, sporting their Red Surges. This was the formal wear of the R.C.M.P., used only for show and diplomatic relations. And "must-wear" garb if a Mountie got married since it was his best and most formal dress ware. They were the counterpart to the Marine guards at the American embassies around the world.

Jerry breathed the warm fall air. Indian summer had stormed the Capitol. And now it was mid-morning. Though they had flown five hours, the crossing of time zones had landed them at 8 a.m. A beautiful day was shaping up for D.C. What would make it truly beautiful would be the ultimate resolution of the brewing conflict. That was foremost on the mind of Jerry Grant.

Stuart Macmillan came out to find Jerry. "Good news," he said, "Gervais will be here over the noon-hour. We'll be having lunch with him. But I want thirty minutes alone before he meets you."

"You're calling the shots," Jerry noted. "Whatever I can do, I will. But not till you say so." Jerry wondered if he could restrain himself from blurting out his saga at the first sign of the Prime Minister. Macmillan was a persuasive personality however, and if he could get Jerry an audience with Gervais, then it would be for the better to wait.

Shortly, the main gates of the embassy swung open. Jerry easily recognized the man in the limousine as the Prime Minister of Canada, so he went back to the embassy lounge to await further instruction. True to his word, Macmillan came in and escorted Jerry to lunch.

"This is Reverend Jerry Grant, Mister Prime Minister. He's the man I was telling you about."

"Reverend Grant," the Prime Minister said, "Thank you for joining us."

"I really didn't have much choice sir," he countered. "Mister Macmillan insisted I come along. I must add it was my desire to do so, sir."

"Let's order first," Gervais suggested." Then I want to hear your account Jerry. May I call you Jerry?"

"Oh, of course, sir," he replied. "That's how I'd like it to be."

The menus were placed before them minus only the prices. "This is lunch?" Jerry thought to himself. The selections were out of his class. They ranged from filet mignon to Cajun Salmon steak, his all time favorite, and everything between. As the wine was being poured, Prime Minister Gervais toasted the occasion, "Vive Le Canada."

"Dankeschoen," Macmillan retorted with a friendly smile at Gervais. The three men drank, and afterwards the Prime Minister leaned forward, "Let me hear your story, Jerry."

"Yes, sir," Jerry replied. Then he washed his mouth clearly and cleanly with a final sip of wine. Setting his wine glass on the table, he dabbed his mouth with the linen napkin as he had been so instructed by the embassy protocol officer, and spoke his piece articulately and concisely. For this singular moment he had chosen to defy hell and high water, and he wasn't about to lose his chance by delivering a deranged report.

The Prime Minister listened attentively. His eyes were glued to him, intent on reading his body language. At key points he squinted in near disbelief. He scribbled notes prolifically on the linen napkin. For thirty minutes Jerry briefed him, offering both the concrete and circumstantial evidence he claimed he had encountered. At the end, he simply said, "That's where it stands right now, honorable sir."

"Tell me again, Jerry," Gervais requested, "What was the first and last name of the CIA agent you had your dealings with.

"Blackwell, sir. Carl Blackwell."

"And the auditor who interviewed you with the IRS?"

"Andrew Clinton."

"How about the name of the man who flew you to Vegas after your crash landing?"

Jerry had to think about that for a moment. The pause was longer than he wanted. Then it came to mind. "Alan Dixon, sir."

"Well," the Prime Minister said, "You're certainly consistent. Tell me, Stuart, do you have any problems at all with this man's credibility?"

Macmillan looked Jerry in the eye then glanced back to Gervais. "None at all sir. He's most credible."

"You know your opinion has always meant a lot to me," the Prime Minister responded.

"Yes, I know Jacques. And maybe at this point it's going to pay off."

"Let's hope so," Gervais said. "Let me make a phone call to the White House. If I can arrange a dinner tomorrow night we might get lucky. The President's schedule fills up in a hurry."

Canada's chief executive left the dining room, and, breaking the silence, Macmillan offered, "He believes us. Now it's up to him."

"Does he have much pull down here?" Jerry asked.

"Right now he does." "They're discussing the timber tariff and all the trouble that's caused between countries. Right now we have the upper hand."

"With timber! How do you figure that?" Jerry asked.

"Because for every tariff they slap on our timber, we counter with all the magazines and books published in the U.S. and a threat to place a levy on American produced television shows. That one really hit a sore spot. And we still have some aces up our sleeve."

"Such as ——?"

"Such as stricter quotas on Americans coming to Canada. I tell you, if we bring that up we can have them eating out of our hands."

"Why is that such a big deal?"

"Americans have always been attracted to Canada. The major investments are in oil, uranium, real estate and potash. And they need to be involved in our nickel production in a very significant way."

"Why nickel?"

"Armaments! Because of weaponry production. They have very little nickel. And if it becomes an all-Canadian industry it's going to cost the U.S. an arm and a leg. Especially given the anti-American sentiment in terms of weapons around the world. I'm afraid your countrymen have been very vocal about that in the last few years, mostly since Vietnam."

"Is that good or bad?"

"Well, it's not really good. I mean, Canada's defense is the United States' military. That's a given. But they're not half as worried about Canada as they are about their own country. Pretty natural too. Charity begins at home. But right now, it could be a big bargaining chip if we have to use it for the present crisis: Especially if the President doesn't choose to believe us."

"How can he choose not to believe us?" Jerry wondered aloud.

"If he's not in on it, it might take some friendly persuasion to get him to check up on the military. But Gervais is a gem at doing that kind of thing."

The two men rose as the Prime Minister reentered the room. He motioned for them to be seated, and as they were, their meals were brought on silver trays. It had taken quite some time for their dinner orders to arrive, given the fact they were specialized entrees. "Dig in," he said. Jerry

And Stuart Macmillan glanced at each other waiting for more information from Gervais. The Prime Minister noticed them doing so. "Oh, sorry dear sirs," he apologized. "Yes, it's all set. Tomorrow we'll be having an embassy dinner for the President and his wife."

Jerry nodded at Macmillan and both men expressed their pleasure with the prospect of dining with the

President of the United States. "How do we handle it"? Gervais asked Macmillan.

"Well sir, I believe I should question him straight forward. 'What are the troops doing ten miles from Canada.' If he pleads ignorance, then Jerry tells his story."

"Again," Jerry laughed.

"Once more," Macmillan assured him. "And if need be, it'll be the most important 'once more' of your life and maybe in Canada's history."

"But if he's in on the plot," Jerry interrupted, "then we're in deep trouble, right?"

"Not at all," Gervais replied. "This is Canadian soil we're sitting on. At the very most he can up and leave. But then, that would be an admission of guilt. If he does leave, we'll release the story to the press. Then we'll get our own air force to the border areas and start buzzing the troops. Outnumbered or not, if this gets to the fighting stage, we're going down kicking and screaming."

"Sounds scary," Jerry admitted.

"Listen, Reverend," the Prime Minister admonished him, "I just don't believe there's going to be a conflict. And as long as we're talking we won't be fighting."

"Let's hope not," Jerry added. "My wife's in Tucson. And my kids- good Lord, they'll be home a week or so." I'm counting on the diplomatic corps."

"Vive le Canada, libre," the Prime Minister said, raising his wine glass again.

"Und Canada, mein heim! Ich liebe dich," Macmillan countered.

Jerry raised his glass too, but found no words to contribute. With the seeming levity between the other two, Jerry suddenly felt a surge of guilt that perhaps he may have taken everything too seriously. But then, neither Macmillan nor Gervais had encountered what he had just lived through. Tomorrow night would make or break the lifetime friendship of the two countries.

Deep within, Jerry hoped that this international affair would all come out in the wash. But he wasn't sure at all. Such doubt he found difficult to handle. "It's all small stuff," he pondered. And then he tried to convince himself this was really the case. This was not small stuff. This was an international case of national survival. And maybe the fittest were those most capable of doing whatever needed doing to keep their country going and to keep their people alive. Like it or not, whatever Jerry had been through, the U.S. had an obligation to provide security for its own people. If the price of such security was a century of friendship and mutual respect, so be it.

Chapter 22

The Attorney General had strongly urged Jerry to refrain from calling home. "One more day," he pleaded. "Just go on faith for one more day." Jerry would have been ill advised to ignore the caution. Were Jenny in Blackwell's custody, any tip-off that Jerry was perched in Washington may well incite Blackwell to drastic action, and especially so if this invasion had been planned without the blessing of the Executive branch. That was now the burning question.

"Who planned and initiated the action?" The P.M. would not speculate and nor would Macmillan, though he had hinted at a purely military endeavor. There would be big trouble in the U.S.A. if such were the case. Could Jerry and his family count on government protection? It was not easy to trust anyone at this point. The Canadian

Embassy, though technically on American territory, gave him a security he hadn't felt since the days prior to the audit. An embassy is the exclusive property of the country to which it is designated. Embassy officials had summoned a physician to examine Jerry, and aside from some moderate hypertension and obvious fatigue, he proclaimed him hale and hearty. At the doctor's strong urging, Jerry had taken a sleeping pill, and as another morning dawned, he was grateful for the blessing of a night's sleep.

Glancing at his watch, he noted the lateness of the morning. Jerry had slept a dozen hours, almost noontime in Washington. Hearing a knock at his door Jerry ambled over and opened it. A member of the embassy staff stood there, clean towels in hand, and an invitation that, if he chose to, he was invited to brunch in half an hour. After thanking the young man, Jerry cleaned up and headed downstairs to the reception area. Macmillan, conferring with the catering staff, noticed Jerry at the foot of the stairs, and summoned him to join. "Just making some final arrangements for tonight," he informed Jerry. In a moment the staff was dismissed and Jerry followed Macmillan to the outside patio where a tasty brunch was laid out. "How are you feeling, Reverend?" Macmillan inquired.

"Just fine, sir," he answered. "Nervous!"

"I think we've covered all the bases," Macmillan continued. If you would like to you're free to go out for a while. Downtown maybe. But only with an embassy chauffeur and Fred Ford."

"Thank you," Jerry said. "Perhaps I will. I'm not sure what to do until this evening."

"Okay," Macmillan nodded. "We'll have a driver ready when you are. Just go to the front driveway and let him know when you want to go. He'd be happy to take you on a little tour of the Capitol."

"I could enjoy that," Jerry nodded. "I never had a chance to be here before; under normal circumstances that is."

The two men finished their bounteous breakfast and Jerry bid the Attorney General farewell in the only German he knew. "Auf Wiedersehen," he waved. And with that, he looked for his driver.

"Where to" the driver requested?

"Oh, how about dealer's choice," Jerry suggested. "Take me where you think I ought to be taken. By the way, I'm Jerry Grant."

"Bill Haskin," the driver announced. "From good old Calgary."

"Calgary," Jerry perked up, "That was my home for ten years."

"Nice town," Haskin affirmed. "I hear it's the fastest growing city in Canada."

"How did you get down here?" Jerry requested.

"Oh, lots of politicians from Alberta knew me. I chauffeured several of them in the Calgary area and they got me a job in Ottawa. Before I knew it, they sent me down here to work."

"Do you enjoy it here?"

"No, not especially. But it is a promotion. And I get to meet a lot of important people. No offense, sir. I mean big politicians from around the world. Last year I drove a big shot Russian on a tour of Washington. Spoke pretty fair English. "Not a bad fellow for a Russky either. I think we sometimes used to feel that all Russians want America wiped out. Hell, they're just ordinary folks like us. They want a serene life too."

Haskin rattled on a great deal, but with the expertise of a tour guide. He was good at what he did, and well accustomed to the traffic of D.C. With a car marked "Canadian Embassy," he was able to nudge the speed limit without checking for police cars. The tour took about two hours, and Haskin suggested a break. "Want to go downtown, sir?"

"Sure, can you let me loose for a time?"

"Not without Fred here." The bodyguard had been a quiet companion from the time they left the embassy. Haskin dropped the two men off in city center and suggested he wait with the car. "Take your time, sir," he urged Jerry. "I'll be right here when you get back." With that Jerry Grant and Fred Ford got out of the car.

"Go where you wish, Reverend," the bodyguard said. "I'll be two steps behind wherever you are."

"I appreciate the offer," was the response.

"It's my job," Ford reminded him. "Do your thing sir, and pretend I'm not around."

Jerry chose to tour some buildings. There were department stores, boutiques, and gift shops. He walked and walked, and finally ended up near a small park in the tourist area. He bought some popcorn and a soda. Then, sitting on a park bench, he began to feed the pigeons. He felt matters were beginning to work in favor of a resolution to his dilemma.

"Always wondered what it was like to do this," he said to Ford. "Fred, Fred are you here" he shouted? "Must have lagged behind somewhere," Jerry thought. "Anyway he said he'd be close by."

The park had few people in it, some resting, some jogging, and some cuddling with sweethearts. The pigeons outnumbered the people ten to one. Jerry felt serenity in tossing the popcorn to the awkward little beggars.

"Reverend Grant," the voice called out.

"Yes Fred, right here," he called, continuing to feed the birds.

"Nope, not your bodyguard," the voice countered. "He's asleep on the grass back a bit!" Carl Blackwell sat down next to Jerry Grant. "Don't worry," he said, "I'm just here for a talk. You've given me quite a run for the money, Reverend."

Jerry was shocked, but unafraid. He felt no anger at this point, only disdain and some real pity for Blackwell. Gazing around for Ford he still could not spot him. Then he made up his mind to test the waters of his relationship with Carl Blackwell.

Pointing to a policeman across the park, he said, "I'm going to get up from this bench and walk straight toward that police officer. There's nothing I have to say to you right now. Later. Believe me; I'll talk to you later."

"Do what you want," Blackwell offered. "But I'll tell you this. You're too late. Your date with the President is twenty-four hours late."

"I don't believe you, Blackwell," Jerry said, walking toward the policeman.

"Quite a wife you have there," Blackwell sneered. "Nice body."

Jerry turned to him. Without visibly reacting to Blackwell's newest obscenity, he spoke softly, "Jenny wouldn't look twice at you."

"Ask her" Blackwell taunted. "Just ask her. Nice ass and bosom."

"Look Blackwell or whoever you are. We've had our game of cat and mouse. You lost; I won, so forget it."

"I must say, you're taking this very well, dear Reverend. I thought you'd shoot me first chance you got."

"You're not worth the price of the bullet."

"You don't believe your wife had the hots for me, do you? Ask her." Jerry was feeling more incensed but kept on walking. Right now, he couldn't afford the luxury of breaking Blackwell's face. He disliked the disdain he felt. Looking for the bodyguard, he still couldn't see him. Perhaps now he needed a bodyguard to restrain his own boiling temperament.

"Hey, Reverend, "Blackwell shouted. "How do you think we knew your plan to get out of Tucson? I got it by — let's say — being intimate with your wife."

Jerry still didn't react, not knowing what to expect yet.

He neared the police officer. Just then, Fred Ford came running up behind him. "Reverend Grant, you okay?"

"Yeah, I'm okay. I guess this wasn't entirely a surprise. How about you? You all right?"

"They nabbed me off guard, sir. No rough stuff. Said they'd hold me just long enough for the big boss to talk with you. What did he say? Did he threaten you?"

"He had nothing to say. He just wanted to antagonize me."

"Who was he?"

"A CIA agent from Tucson."

"Look," Ford suggested, "let's get back to the limousine and take you home to the embassy. Forget that guy. You've got more important things to do."

Jerry glanced back at Blackwell who had gone back and was seated on the bench, smirking at Jerry. Somehow, it suited him. Jerry was troubled by the references to Jenny. If Blackwell had made a pass at her at all, Jerry was determined to follow him all the way to hell's doorway. There on a park bench sat a man who knew no scruples. Whatever his role in life, his was a conscience 'seared with a hot iron', as the saying goes." He would say and do anything to advance his cause. For the first time in his life, Jerry Grant knew what it meant to despise — to hate with all his heart. Much as he tried he could no longer label it disdain. He knew it would take a long time to heal this bitter wound, if ever it would heal. Jerry pondered that this man and all the grief he had created that would dominate his mind, soul and heart for life - and maybe longer.

The two men found the limousine where they had left it. Faithful to his word, Haskin was waiting patiently, engrossed in a newspaper. Fred and Jerry had agreed to say nothing till they met Macmillan, so the drive back to the embassy was a quiet time. Haskin kept up his chatter apparently accustomed to pointing out every detail in the Washington area. When they got back, Jerry shook Haskin's hand and walked indoors. Dinner with the President was only two hours away. Jerry walked up to his quarters, closed the door, and began to contemplate the next few hours of his life. The dinner call finally came. Everyone went to the prescribed area.

A press agent always took a lesser seat. Such was the protocol. Jerry had been introduced as Brian Becker, and was seated down line from the Prime Minister and President. Macmillan sat to the right of the P.M. and the first lady to the left of the President. The affair was professionally catered, something the embassy personnel had done many times before. This was how the other half lived. With style, but garnished with an air of overkill. There was just too much politeness, or so it seemed to Jerry Grant. Things were said that had to be said, such as the usual compliments concerning the arrangements and the dress of the President's wife. Everyone was supposed to compliment the first lady. That too was protocol of which he had been briefed.

One other facet intrigued Jerry. Both the Prime Minister and the President heaped garlands of praise on one another for their expert leadership of their respective nations. Those words were well rehearsed. They came from the lips, but — or at least it seemed to Jerry — not from the heart. So the stage was set for an official dinner and the plan was to eat and drink, then retire to the lounge. At that point, when the brandy was being poured, Macmillan was assigned to initiate conversation concerning the true purpose for the assembly. Jerry Grant just couldn't wait. Macmillan had been informed of the brief encounter with Carl Blackwell Jerry had experienced. This would be discussed only if ammunition was needed.

The hour had come. Retiring to the lounge, the entourage took their assigned places. It seemed that everyone knew where to sit. Except Jerry of course! Sensing that bit of confusion Macmillan motioned unseen to others, indicating where Jerry should take his place. Gervais lit his pipe and the servers brought the brandy.

"Mister President," Gervais began. "Mister Macmillan has a matter he wishes to discuss with you — off the record, of course."

"Go ahead, Stuart," the President invited.

"Thank you, sir. It's in regard to the military exercises in northern Montana and Idaho. You're familiar with them of course?"

"I have been so informed. My understanding this is a routine exercise."

"Well sir, reliable sources inform us that their real purpose is to cross the forty-ninth parallel and trench water from Canada. Is that your understanding of their function?"

"Good heavens no," the President replied indignantly. "Your sources have misrepresented our maneuvers. They're war games."

"But sir," Macmillan continued. "A Canadian national was recently blackmailed by the CIA into seeking information about Canada's water supplies. He did so because of threats to his family — and some other details we won't get into at this time. Just after he received the information from a Member of Parliament in Calgary the M.P. was shot and killed, apparently by CIA agents."

The President listened, apparently astonished. Macmillan then continued presenting his side of the story. "We now have information that the troops up in the northwest have advanced to within five miles of the Canadian border and that they are carrying anti-aircraft weaponry as well as trenching machinery and what seemed like tactical nuclear underground bombs. We do believe that either with your consent, or without it, the American troops plan to invade – uh, move into Western Canada for the purpose of siphoning the fresh water supply of the many waterways. And sir, we believe that the intent is to shoot down the chopper reconnaissance we maintain."

"Is that why I'm here?" the President asked, setting down his brandy glass.

"Yes sir. We would appreciate your response concerning the matter."

"Response?" the President added. "Well, for one thing, I sure haven't given any input to the military or to the CIA. What sources are you talking about?"

Macmillan stared at Jerry Grant and with a single hand motioned for him to rise and speak. Jerry stood up and began his tale of woe.

"Mister President, my name is really Jerry Grant. I am actually a parish pastor from Tucson, Arizona, and a resident alien in your country. May I speak my piece to you frankly and precisely?"

"Please do, Mister Grant. Our countries have coexisted without incident for many years. If anything is impeding that relationship, I would be most interested to know. I must know!"

For what he prayed would be the final time, Jerry Grant recounted his story. He came across as a sane individual, truly convinced of what he was relating. His expressions of concern for his wife moved him to tears, and when all was said, he thanked the President for his ready ear, and sat down in his place. For a brief time, only a few seconds but what seemed all eternity, the room was deathly silent. The statement ended and a very awkward pause ensued.

"That's a tough one to swallow, Reverend Grant."

"Yes sir," Jerry replied. "But it is still the truth. Today in a downtown park, the principal agent found me and told me that I was twenty four hours late in meeting with you."

"Can you give me names and dates?" the President asked.

"Yes sir, right from here," Jerry said, pointing to his head.

The President summoned Jerry to sit next to him, a risky move for any head of state. Prime Minister Gervais moved one seat down and Jerry wrote down the names and places and dates that were part of his story. Handing them to the President, he reaffirmed his earlier statement.

"Sir, all of this is the truth."

"You will check it out, Mister President?" the Prime Minister requested.

"Of course, Jacques," he pledged. "This is no small matter. But if it is true, then believe me this did not come either from me, or from the Pentagon or State Department. I am in charge. Or at least, I think so."

"I have one immediate concern, Mister President," Jerry asked. "Would it be possible for you to send F.B.I. people to my home and check on my wife?"

"Right away, Reverend. Where's the phone?" he asked an attendant.

"I'll bring it right to you, sir," the attendant promised.

"I thank you for dinner, Jacques and Stuart. I'm going to phone my aides from here and ask them to contact the Tucson bureau of the F.B.I. Then I'll take my leave and investigate the matter soon."

"Pardon me," Jerry interrupted. "Perhaps you didn't hear me out. Soon is not good enough, Mister President. We want action now." Jerry was speaking louder now, and far more assertively as well.

"Shut up, Jerry," Macmillan ordered in a loud whisper.

"No, I won't shut up. You officials sit here and treat this thing like a tiny molehill. It's a mountain, and it needs moving now."

"The President said he would attend to it soon, Reverend Grant," Gervais admonished with a somewhat terse tone of voice.

"That's not good enough," Jerry said. He got up and walked toward the President. Standing next to him, he pleaded once more. "Sir, with all due respect, there's going to be an invasion unless you do something to change it. Do you want war with Canada?"

"Of course not, son. Now take it easy. I said I'd act on it soon, and I mean soon."

Jerry sensed an end run. "What does soon mean?" he inquired.

"Tomorrow morning," the President answered.

"Sit down, Jerry," Gervais ordered him. "Now!"

"No sir. I believe this matter should be handled tonight. Right here and now. How many phone calls would the President need to make to find out the truth if he doesn't know the truth? You've got the phone here, Mister President. Why not use it?" Jerry was becoming angered. His face reddened and he inched closer to the President.

A Secret Service agent quickly stepped between Jerry and the President, arms folded, prohibiting Jerry from further advance.

The President rose to his feet a second time and threw his napkin on the table. "Nobody tells me what to do and when to do it," he affirmed, looking at Gervais and Macmillan, then toward Jerry. Seems you have a madman on your hands. The President of the most powerful country on earth was visibly angry and shaking.

Jerry was not about to be hushed. His rhetoric became all the more turgid. He tried moving around the bodyguard, but with each move, the secret service man moved with him.

"What in heaven's name am I dealing with here?" he shouted. "I bring you facts about a plot that nearly cost me my life. I get blackmailed and followed and shot at in the air and on the ground and you treat the whole blasted thing as though it were something that can be handled 'soon'."

"Jerry, just calm down and be seated, will you?" Gervais ordered. Macmillan echoed the Prime Minister. Both Canadian leaders were utterly flabbergasted.

"Calm down?" Jerry was ordered.

"Calm down? There's a bloody war in the making and you're acting like a bunch of ladies in a sewing circle discussing tomorrow's luncheon. No I will not calm down."

Jerry pointed a finger toward the President. Now he was livid with anger and his emotions were nearly out of control. Fred Ford came and placed his hand on Jerry's shoulders in a token effort to restrain him. Jerry grabbed the hand and pushed it off.

An embarrassing hush came over the room. The principals eyed one another. Macmillan tried to bring Jerry to his senses but Jerry was beyond reasoning now.

It was going to be his say and the others were going to listen. The Secret Service men were flanking the President, edging both him and the First Lady toward the doorway to the dining area. Jerry followed, shaking his finger at the President and continuing his tirade. "I thought I had the protection of this government when I moved here," he hollered. "Do you need to see my Green card Mister President"? There was sarcasm in that statement. "Or do you want to wait till morning and find out the whole army's engaging Canadian troops that are trying to protect the waterways of Canada. What do you want, Mister President? What do you want?"

He continued pressing in upon them, and the more he pressed the harder S.S. agents pulled the President and his wife toward the exit. They were nearing the doorway when Jerry made a sudden move to block the entrance by attempting to skirt around them.

Gervais motioned to Ford. Ford jumped Jerry with such force that he knocked him to the floor. He restrained the normally placid pastor, now turned Mr. Hyde, though Jerry was still protesting the President's lack of action. Seeing he was finally safe from Jerry's wrath, the President grabbed the First Lady by the hand, and, following the lead of his own secret service men, made a rapid exit from the embassy.

"You'll see," Jerry hollered after him. "You'll see."

Gervais and Macmillan surrounded Jerry, still pinned to the floor by Ford.

"I thought we agreed to use diplomatic channels," Macmillan chastised Jerry. Jerry had no rebuttal. Suddenly he became silent, trembling with a great passionate anger. Gervais and Macmillan were fighting off a state of shock and they too were greatly unnerved by what had happened.

"Do you know what you've done?" Macmillan asked. "You blew it."

Jerry said nothing. He put his hands to his forehead, distraught with himself.

"I don't know just what's going to happen now, "Macmillan told him. "But I have a feeling you're in trouble, Reverend. You're grounded in this embassy. If the President prefers charges you'll be turned over to his people."

Jerry turned from Gervais to Macmillan. He spoke now in a subdued tone, but in defense of his actions. "There's only so much one man can take," he said. "I guess I went off the deep end."

"No crap" Macmillan concurred. "Believe me Reverend, you sounded like a maniacal fool. And in this business, when there are any implied or direct threats, it doesn't take long before the compost hits the ventilating system."

Ford was ordered to escort Jerry to his room. He was pushed rudely into the quarters, and the door slammed and locked behind him. Jerry kicked the inside of the door in disgust, frustrated both with the President's response and his own reaction. "I've often wondered what it felt like to die," he thought aloud. "Now I know. I'm drowning in political bullbull"."

Chapter 23

In the aftermath of Jerry's desperate but futile attempt to provoke action, a matter others most deeply regretted, gloom and solitude had settled throughout the Canadian Embassy. Stu Macmillan spoke few words to him. Gervais said nothing. While not totally confined to his quarters, Jerry was nevertheless to consider himself under house arrest until further notice. Fred Ford had been his shadow since the incident and even he had little to say to Jerry Grant.

Yet Reverend Grant was now becoming increasingly certain as to the appropriate nature of what he had done. The American President had promised that action would be taken soon. If Blackwell had been right in suggesting Jerry was too late, then soon certainly wasn't soon enough. If Blackwell had lied, then soon had to be right away because of the proximity of the troops to the border.

Should it be that even if the American troops were on Canadian soil, something might be worked out to designate this as a simple error in calculation and terminate the incursion with a formal state apology to the Canadian government? Perhaps he hadn't been at all wrong in his desperation. And perhaps the President would perceive it as such, if indeed he had been induced by Jerry's outburst to begin immediate investigations. The only hope Jerry had left was that the latter would be the case. If it were, there was a remote possibility the President would forget the incident and not consider it an implied or overt threat to his person. That is, if he were not the instigator of the military invasion. With that consideration, Jerry sought out a brief talk with Macmillan. Reluctantly, Macmillan agreed to "five minutes."

"Reverend, I'm not sure there's anything left to say," Macmillan began. "But go ahead anyway."

"Sir, do you consider me a madman?"

"I hadn't," Macmillan answered. "But after last night I'm not so sure."

"Have you heard anything at all from the President?"

"No! But it shouldn't be long. Threats toward a President do not go unaddressed."

Jerry shook his head in dissent. "There was no threat." Macmillan suggested it was implied in Jerry's voice." During the silence which followed a pageboy entered the office and presented a written message to the Attorney General. He read it, then, looking at Jerry, said, "Reverend Grant, the President has made a formal request for you to be brought to the White House. Get ready, please."

"Are you coming with me?" Jerry asked.

"Nope. You're on your own. You'll be driven there by our chauffeur. But once you get outside the gates of this embassy, an F.B.I. agent will join you in the car. Then it's up to the American government. Good luck."

"Will you follow through on my report" Jerry pleaded?

"Why not wait and see what the President has to say," Stuart suggested. "There's a chance he's looked into it. If we don't hear from you within a few days, we'll look into it."

Now Jerry felt suddenly forsaken, solaced only by the one hope he had — his sincerity and therefore credibility in the eyes of the President in spite of the outburst of the previous evening. Of course the other alternative was an arrest for uttering or implying a threat, or whatever terms would be used in a court.

Jerry clung to the only hope which kept him sane. "He's got to believe me," he thought aloud. "He's got to believe me."

The vehicle left the compound. As Macmillan predicted, two F.B.I. and two Secret Service agents stopped the car outside the embassy gates, climbed in with Jerry, and tightly flanked him. This would be a silent ride, a blessing in disguise. Jerry could debate the merits of begging forgiveness as opposed to persisting with vehemence that action is taken forthwith. He would have to decide whether determined begging or a humble spirit would reap the greatest benefits. His ingrained habit of kindly words had proven efficacious all throughout his life. Now, even that was in doubt. Twenty minutes later he had made a firm decision.

Jerry was led by the agents and several other personnel into the Oval office. In itself, such a gesture was a positive sign. This was the office where the most powerful man in the world conversed with people, not where people were detained and arrested. He hoped his decision would be the right one, even though he might still have to suffer consequences for the actions of the previous night. For now, he was disregarding his personal future and concentrating on stopping the pending disaster of a continental conflict. His actions would not be on his own behalf, but on behalf of the two nations he loved. His native land and his adopted land, regardless of recent events.

Seated in the corner of the office, Jerry was told to await the arrival of the President. Still flanked by the SS agents, he sat — meditating, praying and thinking; thinking and praying. For a man who was acknowledged to have all the right words at all the right times he felt totally inadequate. Even more so as the President entered the office.

Seated at his desk, the smiling C.E.O.requested that Jerry be brought to stand before him. The time of accounting had come and the President motioned for Jerry to initiate the conversation.

"Sir, I have a great love for this country," he began. "And I have a great love for the land I call my native land. My actions last evening cannot be justified, except if you can believe they were prompted by my desire to maintain peace between our countries. I do not seek reprieve from the consequences of what I did, but I do plead and beg that you investigate what I told you. I stand solely at your mercy and I'm prepared to face the results of my folly. Personally, it is important that I have your forgiveness. But even more important Mister President, is my need to persuade you that everything I related was the truth, so help me God. I have one further request, and I realize I do not merit it at all. But I make it nonetheless. That is to ask your aid in ascertaining the status of my wife Jenny, and my two children, Kenton and Kerry. Thank you for permitting me these words."

"Sit down, Jerry. May I call you Jerry" the President asked, once again most kindly?

"Yes sir, please do."

"You gave me quite a start last night you know."

"I believe so, sir."

"But you're right."

"What?" Jerry asked, his face brightening.

"You're right that I needed to investigate it. So I stayed up the entire night piecing it together. And yes, I do have some answers."

Jerry sat even more erect, wondering what he would hear. The President continued. "Let me put your mind at rest concerning your family. Your wife is fine. She has F.B.I. protection now. Your children are both safely en route from their outposts—I know all about their fine work!

"Sir," Jerry interrupted! "The fact that Jenny is watched by the F.B.I. provides me little consolation. Let me explain; I mean Mister Blackwell is with the CIA. Aren't they all organized together? He's the one who orchestrated this thing and tried to kill me."

Glancing at his aide, the President ordered, "Bring in Blackwell and Gatz. "Reverend" the President continued, "Mister Blackwell is here with me together with the director of the Central Intelligence Agency. They have something to tell you about this whole matter. In the interim, I'm afraid our military has indeed inadvertently crossed the forty-ninth parallel. They're deep in the interior of British Columbia, and they've been ordered to stay there and advance no further. My secretary of defense has been directed to go there and terminate the war games."

"Were they just war games, Mister President?"

"I'll let Gatz tell you," he answered, as he saw the CIA men enter.

"Mister Gatz," the President motioned. You have the floor."

"Thank you, Mister President," he said politely. He then sat in a chair aside the President's desk and Mr. Gatz turned toward Jerry.

"Won't you sit back down, Reverend Grant?" he motioned. "Reverend Grant, you have done your country and ours a most outstanding service. You have uncovered a strategic error on the part of our military forces and some workers in our CIA"

"Error," Jerry replied. "With all due respect, Mister Gatz, I would consider it a plot."

"No, no, it wasn't a plot," Gatz answered with nervous laughter, raising his eyes to the ceiling. "It was a lack of communication."

"In what way?"

"Mister Blackwell here was ordered by the D.O.D. - Department of Defense — to recruit you for assisting in an effort to find out if the Canadian government was willing to reconsider the matter of NAWAP. The recruitment was to be in the form of a request. As you now know he was a bit too zealous, however, and understood it as an order to incriminate you if you did not cooperate. I might add, a very honest error at that."

Jerry didn't believe any of what he was hearing, but he believed he had somehow succeeded in foiling the plot. "But the military is in Canada."

"True enough! I stress as the President did, quite inadvertently. The secretary of defense is on his way to personally order a withdrawal. Then he's going to meet with the Canadian minister of defense and offer a formal apology for advancing across the border by mistake."

"I'm sure it will be accepted," Jerry suggested.

"Now there will be consequences that Carl Blackwell here must pay for his lack of restraint. You'll have to take our word for that."

"I will, Mister Gatz," Jerry said. "But there's one thing I don't understand. How did the military and the CIA get in this together?"

"As I said," Gatz replied, "lack of communication. You see, Carl Blackwell is a regional director of our agency. In his eagerness to do the job he fabricated a top secret memo in my name and wired it to the military bases of the northwest."

"Any chance I might see those memos?" Jerry asked.

"I'm afraid not, Reverend. Such memos are destroyed upon reaching their destination. But all the memos said was to begin war games close to the Canadian border - and that the Canadian government had granted permission for the troops to use whatever territory they chose, including entering Canadian territory if they deemed it expedient. But not to use live ammunition in the playing out of the War games if it was on Canadian soil."

"And the military acted upon those memos — without a direct order from the defense secretary?"

"That's how it's going to show up in the press releases."

Jerry was biting his lower lip. The death of Richard Green hadn't been mentioned. Was he to be a mere casualty of this affair? While he knew the story the CIA director gave was full of holes, mere drivel, he wasn't about to question it further. The troops were going to be withdrawn and the defense secretary was going on a friendly visit to Ottawa. Suddenly Jerry was content. Regardless of the veracity of the story his mission was accomplished. The troop movement was terminated, and what he had set out to do was now done.

Gatz shook Jerry's hand. Blackwell wouldn't make eye contact. The two men begged their leave, and were excused by the President.

"I hope you will remain in our country," the President offered", shaking Jerry's hand?

Somehow Jerry felt sorry for Carl Blackwell. He had been a real jerk, and at times Jerry wished he were dead. But he was also going to be the fall guy for what was a poorly and rapidly contrived story to put an innocent end to a foiled plot, a plot set in motion not by the executive branch of government, but by lesser powers. Or so the story would say.

"Mister President," Jerry asked. "We were told the State Department was in on this as well. Could you comment on that?"

"There's no truth to that, Reverend Grant. This was a matter which neither the State Department nor I had any knowledge about—real knowledge— until last evening. As far as the shouting incident last evening, well, perhaps we could strike a bargain on that matter."

"Please, sir," Jerry hastened to add, "What can I do?"

"Maybe you could plead with your Canadian leadership to reconsider our request to participate in talks concerning continental water supplies? I mean, even if you put a word in for us — as a Canadian living in a part of the United States which needs desperately to consider long range plans for water. It's my understanding that this is what prompted the whole misunderstanding. Would you do that for us, or at least try?"

"Yes, sir," Jerry promised. "I'll do my very best. I beg you, please do forgive me for my bitter words last evening."

"That's between us, friend," the President advised. "No repercussions on that. I not only forgive you. I understand why it came to that. As for the military incursion into Canada, well, there's to be a small press release on that. The Prime Minister and Attorney General have received copies of it. So has your defense minister. There'll be a story in the Tucson papers about your heroic efforts to avoid a conflict. Of course, we will emphasize the error happened on Blackwell's watch." (That was a naval term he was using) But you'll be totally vindicated and reimbursed for every single expense, as well as paid for a two month leave of absence from your work should you desire it."

"And cleared of all charges? Vindicated as a victim?" Jerry asked.

"Yes, of course. But I can't guarantee how your church people will take it."

"A small press release," Jerry thought to himself. "A war had just been averted, and a small press release would be used to cover up a military plot to steal water. If that would be the necessary price, then so be it." In his heart Jerry was certain the President believed what was told him. He saw it in his eyes and heard it in his voice. There was an integrity about him that struck Jerry as genuine, and, even though the President should have known the strategy, he didn't. For that, Jerry could readily forgive the chief executive officer of the United States of America. He should have known, but now Jerry believed that even the United States C.E.O. could sometimes be caught up in a 'clerical error.' But how? Wasn't he in charge?"

"My men will take you back to your embassy," the President said. "But first, you're welcome to call home. Then if you'll do your best to put a bug in the ears of the P.M. and Mister Macmillan about the water talks we'll fly you back to Tucson in a government jet thirty minutes after your people call us."

"Jerry rose, and, thanking the President, walked out of the Oval office. He called Jenny expressing great relief she was fine and telling her his approximate time of arrival; he also assured her that he was well. They would discuss the details when he returned. His heart pounded with excitement, not just because the conflict had ceased, but especially because he would soon embrace the one person who meant more to him than anyone else on earth. In a few hours, Jerry and Jenny would be reunited.

Outside the presidential mansion stood a car, ready and waiting. Behind it was a second vehicle, with Carl Blackwell seated inside. He rolled the window down, and in a scornful tone yelled out to Jerry, "Just ask her, Reverend. Just ask her."

Jerry shook his head at Blackwell, as if in pity, and, entering the official Canadian embassy car, readied himself for a serious meeting with Gervais and Macmillan. There was a happy reception awaiting him. The entire embassy staff stood ready to greet him as a hero. Chief among them were Gervais and Macmillan.

"Thank you, Jerry," the Prime Minister said. Macmillan offered a grateful handshake. "Anything you need" Gervais requested?

"Yes, there is, Mister Prime Minister. I would simply plead and beg, if necessary, that you reconsider including the Americans in the water talks again. I live in Arizona, and we know the trouble we're facing. And if this hasn't been a lesson to all of us in the need for international cooperation then we're pretty slow learners."

"I'm certain it will come to pass, don't you agree, Stuart?" the Prime Minister replied.

"Without a doubt Jacques."

Jerry gathered his few belongings, and after the embassy secretary had called the White House, he left in the staff car for Dulles International. A private plane was waiting. Farewells were exchanged, and thanks were again heaped on Jerry. He boarded the plane, waived farewell to his countrymen and was soon flying southwest bound for Arizona. The outcome was gratifying, even considering all that Jerry had endured. He was headed home now; a thought so becoming it brought a smile to his face.

"Jenny, Jenny," he said to himself. "I love you, Jenny." As happy as he was, some unknown matter was gnawing at his gut. There were still some loose ends dangling. "Did I achieve a victory? Got some loose ends to ponder. Perhaps they'll come to me en route to Tucson. Perhaps!"

Chapter 24

Whether the experiences of the past week would affect Jerry's life forever was a troubling unknown. How could he forget it-ever? Would he be asked to repeat the episode countless times? Would his relationship to his beloved church terminate or, if it remained, could he garner the same trust from the members of his parish? Much as they loved him, he knew some members of any congregation were fickle — down to the best person, and troubling gossip had foreshadowed the demise of many churches or parish pastors. His name had been in the paper and once that occurs, in a negative fashion, it's guilty till proven innocent. Period!

Then again, the main problems would ultimately lie not with the people, but with Jerry. His meeting with the President hardly enhanced his faith in American political leadership, though it was ostensibly true — so it seemed — that the plot really was unknown to the President. The escapades which had hardened him were firmly embedded in his mind. He had evolved from a caring and personable human being into a suspicious, name-calling, angry and vindictive man.

The emotional wounds kept goading him to an inward bitterness. Carl Blackwell had once told him, "When it's all over it's life as usual," or words to that effect. Jerry was not one to consider lawsuits as an option to get justice or revenge, but he knew he had an ostensibly potent case against the American government. Especially so the CIA. There was a temptation to pursue it. For the first time ever, this confident man felt he didn't really know himself. All that was evil about the human psyche was part of his feelings. Worst of all was the desire to curse. These and other feelings kept coming and going. That they should remain hidden was his honest desire. Even more desirable was that they would disappear completely.

The government jet soared across the land of the free. Jerry now thought of a line in the pledge of allegiance, "And justice for all." It was a noble theme, but in his case, it would never happen. After all, the only repercussion for the whole mess would be a slap on the wrist to the CIA. The press release would vindicate Jerry, but press releases could never change the feelings people might have garnered during the time he was a fugitive. Maybe he would have to leave Arizona, or the United States itself. Could his own heart be so hardened that his call to the ministry would be in question? Or his very own religious convictions?

These were the thoughts that traveled with him. Yet awaiting his arrival was the love of his life. To be with her once more was worth all the heartache. Now only three hours separated him from a welcome homecoming. Jerry laid back his head and stretched out in the roomy seats of the Learjet. He fell asleep but kept jerking awake, like something was prodding him to keep on thinking negatively. When he did sleep there were frightening dreams usurping his rest, each of which would waken him with another start. "Would these nightmares continue?" he wondered. "Will they ever go away?"

Especially terrorizing were his visions of Richard Green lying dead by that front door. For his murder, there would be no justice done; no accountability demanded; nothing! No price would be paid by anyone for a precious human life. His friend was the victim of an "error." At be it was an onerous thought.

It would be futile to attempt reading or writing, given his recent history. Not that he had anything to read or to write with. Thinking was his only entertainment, and he was wearied with that as well. Fatigue enveloped him, body, soul and spirit.

"Please fasten your seat belts," the voice came over the intercom. Jerry had remained buckled up, so he moved his seat to the upright position and glanced out the window. The plane was going to the west of Tucson, and would turn back to land into the southeast wind. It would take another five minutes for the circle approach. His heart gladdened as the jet descended. After a safe and easy landing Jerry felt a new surge of life. "I'm home, Jenny," he thought. "I'm home to stay."

The aircraft taxied to the gate and Jerry was permitted a rapid departure. He bolted down the stairs heading to his beloved and expecting her to be leaping toward him like the proverbial gazelle. Then again, she may be a little laid back. This must have taken its toll on her more so than Jerry could ever imagine. Not so! Talking could come later. As for now, what was important was the assurance they were physically and emotionally together. They hugged and hugged some more.

"Let's go home, love," Jerry suggested. Holding hands, they walked to a waiting government vehicle parked on the airport tarmac.

"Are you okay, love?" Jerry asked her.

"Yes, I am," she assured him. It sounded a bit matter-of-fact and quite terse if not angry.

"Did they hurt you - in any way?"

"No, they were around a lot," Jenny began to explain. "But for the most part it was threats and intimidation. They kept telling me the kind of things you were doing and what would happen when you got caught."

"Did you know what was happening during my 'fugitive days'?"

"I read between the lines," she said. "But I'd like to get the real story from you. You look pretty tired out, hon."

"It's taken its toll. Believe me, you and the kids were on my mind all the time. God, did I pray! When are they due back?"

"About three days! They'll be driven to our house by these agents."

"F.B.I. I hope?"

"Yes, dear, F.B.I."

"What do the kids know?"

"Not a thing!"

"They must have read about me in the papers. I was a wanted man in Calgary. 'Course down where they were news was not a major facet of life."

Jenny began crying, remembering how Jerry had related to her the horrors of Rick's murder. "You never did say whether you had spoken to Betty at all?" she inquired.

"I guess I didn't mention her, did I? I'm sorry about this, honey, but Betty and Rick divorced last Christmas. It came as a real shock to me too, love."

Jenny shook her head, not yet understanding what her husband had just said. She held him tightly as they approached the house, a sign to Jerry she never wanted to let him go. The driver pulled into their roadway, stopped the car, got out and opened the door for them. Then he bade them farewell and assured them the kids would be joining them in a few days.

"What are you going to tell Kenton and Kerry?" she probed.

"Everything," he said. "They need to know it all. Their friends will be talking and they'll see the press release on me in the paper. I have to tell them all there is to tell."

"I've been thinking, Jerry. What about taking them to court? The whole U.S. government, that is. We could gain a pretty big settlement, don't you think?"

Jerry was at a loss for words. That's the matter which he had given scant consideration on the plane, but just as quickly abandoned it. It was hard to fathom Jenny contemplating a civil suit. She seemed deadly serious. Perhaps it was understandable though. Jerry couldn't hope to know the agony she must have endured — just how she too had suffered. "Look, hon," he admonished her gently. "Let's just thank God we're alive, together, and vindicated."

"Oh, speaking of that," she said. "There was a registered letter from the IRS that came yesterday. In fact, it came special delivery."

"What did it say?" Jerry asked.

"That the problem we had with them was solved. They called it a 'clerical error' and blamed it on some computer snafu."

"I was hoping I'd never hear that phrase again," Jerry replied. "Clerical error my a- -; he stopped himself after the 'a' in ass.

"I think you'd better start from scratch," Jenny said. "I still haven't pieced this whole thing together, especially from the time you left the canyon in Gord's balloon. You told me something about this clerical error thing, but I don't remember what it meant."

Jerry was confused. He had, in fact, related every detail to Jenny. She just didn't seem to be paying much attention now.

"There'll be time for that, love," Jerry promised, still wondering why the details had forsaken her. "Right now, let's have some cold lemonade and just sit in the back patio, okay?"

"Sounds good to me," Jenny agreed. "Want to put some shorts on."

"Sure thing," Jerry concurred. "It'll just take me a minute."

The two lovers sat on their favorite swing, holding hands and talking, reminiscing, not about the bad things but about previously gracious memories. It had been agreed that Jerry would wait until tomorrow to relate his adventure to the entire family.

As for now his mind needed a rest. Even more so, his soul. Jenny respected that. She was content to sit with him, and whether they spoke or not didn't matter. Not today, and maybe never.

"When the kids get in let's have a pizza," Jerry suggested. "I could use some junk food in my repertoire."

"Anything you want, hon. I guess that's the most practical," he said. "I was advised to stay around the house till the morning papers hit the street. The press release explaining the issue will appear then."

"The whole truth?" Jenny asked. She seemed stunned by the news.

"Nope," Jerry grinned. "Just what's necessary to clear my name and to slough off the whole matter as a tactical error by the military. Doesn't really seem fair, does it?"

"Nothing's fair in this world," Jenny replied, slamming her empty glass to the table. Now she seemed deeply disturbed.

Jerry peered into her soul through her eyes. "Easy hon" he admonished. "It's all over and done." Then he remembered what Blackwell had said. In a most gentle tone he asked, "Jenny, did Carl Blackwell make any passes at you?"

Jenny hesitated, and then turning to Jerry said, "He tried. I mean, he did talk about getting you off the hook if I did him some special favors."

"Did he force himself on you?"

"No way," she protested. "I wouldn't let that little creep get within ten feet of me." Jenny got up and walked around the patio, her arms folded across her breasts as if she were shivering. The topic disturbed her deeply. It seemed a good time to change the subject.

"Listen Jenny, there is one thing I'd like to do - tomorrow if possible. I'd like to have Bert Benson and Gordon Woods over if you don't mind. Just for coffee."

"What for" Jenny frowned, stymied by the request?

"I want to tell my deacon and my friend about the matter."

"What's there to tell them? Can't you just let it die?"

"Well, for one thing," Jerry began to explain. "I stole Gordon's van. For another, I want to make sure

Bert Benson knows all the facts before I get back into the church pulpit."

"Can't that stuff wait" Jenny huffed? "You just get back from God knows where, and you want to have somebody over."

"I'd rather not wait hon. Besides, I hope to find out who tipped off Carl Blackwell that I was leaving by balloon."

Nervously she responded, "what good is that going to do you?"

"Nothing, most likely. It's not really for my sake. Whoever it was did it thinking they were serving their country. I just want to let them know that."

"Well if you must," Jenny agreed reluctantly. "Why can't we just be alone for a while though? Why not let it die?"

Once more the desert night had been made for star gazing, talking, and contemplation. Jerry and Jenny assumed their familiar positions on the patio swing. The tranquility wouldn't last long however. Jerry dozed off quickly, and, after awakening him, Jenny led him to bed, tucked him in, and kissed him. There would be no further intimacy this night.

Chapter 25

Desert dawns were every bit as special as desert sunsets to the Grant family. Jerry was refreshed and glad to be home. Though still troubled by some unanswered questions he now determined to set the past behind him and chart a new course for himself and his family.

This was a day of another reunion. The children were coming home. Kenton and Kerry with their tales of joyful and loving service rendered to the unfortunate, all of whom proved so thankful they could never say enough to express their feelings. So, as scheduled, the kids arrived from the airport driven in a special vehicle and accorded VIP status. They would be asking about that and Mom and Dad would have plenty to tell them.

The embraces were long and tearful; the kids older and wiser, mature and in good health. Kenton was the spit and image of Dad — tall, strong and handsome. His soul, as with Kerry, was always peaceful and firmly founded in faith and good will.

As planned, the whole gang assembled for brunch. The questions were asked and the story was told; all the chilling, spellbinding parts. There were tears and laughter, oohs and aahs. The exchange was extraordinary as families go. Jerry advised them the computer would tell them the story in minute detail. Wrinkles were rather regular on the foreheads of the kids.

It was while they conversed that the morning paper arrived. Excusing himself, Jerry rushed out to get it. He wanted to show the kids the article that would be in it. Nor was he disappointed. Not only was there an admission of a military error, but Blackwell's overzealous part was laid out as well. The Reverend Jerry Grant was named as the innocent victim of one man's plan, a plan not to invade Canada, by any means. Rather a plan to perform massive military war games and even intrude on Canadian soil if the military felt a need. The article informed the readers that Canada had given conditional permission. The intent was good but the facts were too generalized, just as he suspected they would be.

It was stated, "Carl Blackwell has been downgraded to an office staff man and stripped of his regional directorate because he failed to inform the proper authorities of the War games and to use proper channels in initiating them."

"Look, Jenny," he pointed out. "Look at the article next to it. Then give it to the kids. They'll understand it better when they read the computer file.

Jenny glanced at the article Jerry was pointing to. "North American Water and Power project planned jointly by Canadian and American officials." That was fast. The leaders must have met right after Jerry left and quickly decided they had better cooperate. Or was it the truth? After all, the Canadian officials were not entirely blameless in this whole matter. Had they not been so defensive about the U.S. participating in the Water Resources project this whole plot might never have been necessitated. Canada had become nationalistic in a very bad sense of the word. Protectionism had become a way of governing.

Jenny took but a scant moment to review the article, then gazed off as if reflecting about something else. The chatter continued between Jerry and the kids, but Jenny had dropped out. She excused herself, cleared off the table and began to wash the dishes. How distant she seemed. As for the kids, they had already started tying up the phone lines to local friends and planning a confab of some kind. They were invited to use the house or even the church Activity Center for their gathering. The church had always been supportive of their humanitarian efforts.

"Anything special troubling you, Jenny" asked Jerry?"

"No, just bored," she said.

"Bored! What do you want to do?"

"Nothing special. I guess this whole mess just finished me."

"Are you feeling ill, love?"

"No, just blah."

"Do you want me to postpone the visit by Gordon and Bert?" he asked her.

Jenny brightened up. "Well, you've seen my side at last." It came out a little sarcastic, but Jerry shrugged it off as an emotional release.

"I'll tell you what, Jenny. Let me do the dishes. You get changed and we'll take a drive out to the monument — by car I mean."

"Whatever you want," Jenny said softly.

Jerry turned to the kids. "Your mom has been through a hard time, kids. Would you mind if the two of us just took a little ride into the desert."

"Go ahead, Dad," Kerry urged on behalf of both. She took the dish rag from his hand.

"I'll finish up. Take mom out while it's not too hot yet."

———

"Make me or break me hill." That's where they decided to stop in the loop drive. They went to the spot where they had made the original plans for Jerry's escape. What breathtaking scenery. Fall was beginning to be real. The end of October was a beautiful time of the year, perhaps the most spectacular. Once again the two lovers reveled in its natural beauty. It was so untouched by the world, such a haven for the weary and a second home to the Grants and others who wished to exit the escapades of the city sounds.

"Want to talk about anything?" Jerry asked again, sensing Jenny was shattered.

"I guess so," Jenny agreed. "I want to know why you need to have Bert and Gordon over at all. I mean, can't we leave this whole thing alone." She sounded adamant, almost as though she had initiated something.

Jerry considered her request, then paused for another moment. "Maybe it would be better if we didn't bother at all," he concurred. "Yeah, I guess it isn't necessary."

"Do you mean it?" she pressed him.

"Sure. Besides, I know how the information was passed anyway."

Jenny had no response. She looked out over the panorama of the cactus forest as if she were counting the saguaros one by one, those ever present sentinels directing the eyeballs of onlookers.

The time was right! It was Jerry who prompted the confessional. "Judas got paid thirty pieces of silver. Remember? What did they offer you, Jenny?" he asked as gently as possible. He was really trying to give her the benefit of the doubt.

Slowly, she turned, and her eyes met his. Then she looked down again. Her feet scuffed the sand beneath her. Her eyes simply could not raise to meet his.

"When did you figure it out?" she asked humbly.

"I don't really know," Jerry said. There were tears in his eyes. "I thought I had it figured out on the plane yesterday. Then I discarded the idea. I knew how Blackwell followed me all along except for one minor detail. He just trailed my credit card purchases. So how did he know I was in that balloon? Then there was the call when you were all confused Jenny. I mean, you didn't remember the 'clerical error' gimmick I told you they used in the auditing office." Jerry took a deep breath, so he could finish his explanation. "Then I remembered something I saw when I was leaving the canyon in the balloon." He paused, waiting for her to ask what he had seen, but she said nothing. "I remembered seeing you get on your bike, and we had agreed you'd stay put till mid afternoon. I remember asking myself, 'what's she doing?' and then forgetting about it. Till last night that is. Then again this morning when you got so bent out of shape about meeting with Gordon and Bert. You were worried I'd believe they had nothing to do with it, weren't you Jenny? So the only one left would be you?"

She turned her back to him. "What did they pay you, Jenny?"

"A hell of a lot more than you'll ever make as a preacher," she admitted. Jenny had never before used even a mild curse word like "hell". "Jerry, I wasn't going to do it. But there's so much I want to get in life, and so many places I want to travel to. They paid me a half-million dollars. I was saving it for the two of us. It's in the house now in the form of a U.S. bearer bond, locked away for the two of us."

"Sure it is," Jerry said in disbelief. "When did you plan it all?"

Jenny paused to compose herself. "Right after you left in Gordon's balloon. I rode back up to the top of the hill, nearly heading to the main station. Blackwell was there with his men."

"Did you go over to them right away? I mean, whose idea was the money?"

"Mine! I saw a chance and went for it. After you sailed out of sight I went right over to them in the hope they'd make me an offer. But I guess you weren't really out of sight, were you? Jerry, I even offered Carl Blackwell my body to ensure your safety. Not that I would've given it to him!"

"They made you an offer you couldn't refuse?" Jerry asked. "Does this mean our marriage has been a lie? Jenny, I thought we had it together. I thought we were really in love."

"We were," Jenny said. "There's still no reason we still can't have it all. I haven't fallen out of love with you."

Jerry looked at her, showing the pain of the moment. "It's like you've murdered me, Jenny! Half of me is gone. You're a total stranger." He began to cry as he had never cried before. Jenny walked toward the car.

"I never intended for you to get killed," she protested. "You can believe that if you want. I just wanted you to get caught, released, and then we'd live in comfort. I planned to let it all cool down for a few months and then spring the money on you as a surprise.

Lord knows you've spent you're life helping others for a — a — a preacher's wage."

"A surprise. You thought I'd consider blood money a surprise? What were you thinking? You knew the consequences if I got caught. No Jenny, you were counting on me not coming back at all. Why not admit it?"

To that, Jenny took umbrage. She was really hurt! Jerry wondered if he had really meant it.

"I wasn't counting on you never coming back" Jenny swore. "I guess I hoped all along it was just a little matter and they really intended to let you go. You did get them all that information. My God Jerry, I saw a way to make them pay for what they put you through; what they put us all through."

"Yeah, I got the information. Then we decided our country might be worth saving. Or did you conveniently forget about that too? You're a traitor, Jenny. You're a Judas to me and your country."

She was crying now in very heavy heaves, sorry for her wrongs or for getting caught: "Which was it"? But she was not asking Jerry to forgive her. Jerry wouldn't have known what to do if she did. He looked at her, turned away, and looked at her once more. His mind was whirling with uneasy options.

Finally he broke the silence. "I don't think I can live with this," Jerry confessed. "I want you to leave, Jenny. I mean, I don't want you to leave but there's no other way. I'm not sure I love you as I did."

"If that's what you want, I'm ready," she admitted. "Just take me home and I'll move on out." Jerry concurred dramatically fast!

It was a somber drive home. Sadder still was watching her pack. The kids were ill at ease, unused to the sobriety of the house, not knowing what had happened. They would be told very little in a while, not now.

"Why don't you take a motel down the east side in a safe area?" Jerry suggested. "You can use the Toyota. I'll walk you to it." He took her suitcase and accompanied her to the car.

"I'll come back at another time and get the rest of the stuff," she sniffled.

"Jenny," he said to her," I need some time. I don't know."

"You don't need to apologize," Jenny responded. "If you'd have done that to me I think I'd have divorced you on the spot."

"I just have one more question, Jenny. Was it really the money? Just a matter of getting something back? I need to know."

"Yes, it was. No it wasn't," she vacillated. "But I thought we'd get to enjoy it together. Jerry, it's true." She sounded nearly believable.

"Okay, what about Carl Blackwell? Did he mean anything to you?"

"I already told you that," she said, "and I'm not about to defend myself any more. Blackwell was a means to an end."

The kids were standing at the entrance to the house, absolutely confused, trying to hear the conversation. Jerry opened the car door for his wife. She entered and started the engine. Then glancing once more at Jerry she pleaded, "For what it's worth," she said, "I do love you Jerry. I'm happy you're not hurt — I mean, physically."

Jenny drove away. Tears streamed down Jerry's cheeks as he watched the car round the bend. He wiped his eyes, then went and embraced the kids.

"Dad, what's going on? Has Mom been seeing someone else?"

"No," he told them. "Not another man."

"Then why is she leaving Dad? What happened?"

"Your mother made a mistake, kids. It seems we won't be together any more. I'm sorry." Jerry turned away from his children and walked aimlessly around the house. He went into the bedroom, slammed the door and paced some more. There had been a death in the family, the death of a marriage; if not that, a most critical wound! It seemed unlikely that a resurrection would occur. Jerry was so hurt. "Surely not that woman. Maybe God will just damn the whole world." He took a chair and threw it against the mirror, smashing the glass into a thousand pieces. The kids were ill at ease. Then he laid face down on the bed and cried himself to sleep.

Kenton and Kerry heard the commotion. Now they were crying as well, embracing each other for consolation. Dad hadn't told them the problem and he appeared to be going schizoid before their eyes. This just wasn't Dad. They didn't yet know that their father felt betrayed by a modern day Judas named Jenny, his loving wife. They may never know, in fact. He had been blackmailed by his adopted country. Of the two hurts, the one which cut the deepest was the pain his wife of many years had inflicted. But the biggest question of all was her heart — what was in her heart when she did the deed? Perhaps their whole future would depend on Jerry's judgment of Jenny's motive. For now, let it ride.

Chapter 26

Kipling said, "If you can meet with triumph and disaster, and treat these two impostors just the same… you'll be a man, my son." By those standards Jerry was not a man. He had so often met triumph with dignity. But never in all his life, had he truly been tested in the waters of personal tragedy. Not even in his flight to Canada. That was survival instinct. So whether he would sink or swim in the present cesspool was unknown. Already he was questioning his worth as a man, a husband, a preacher, and everything for which his values stood. Deliberating this final blow in his long fight for peace and justice, Jerry was tempted to take the easy course and wallow in despair. Depression, he knew, was often a self-made affliction. He had counseled many couples in marriage crises. Scores of

troubled humans had come to him for advice. Most of
them too late, but seeking a miracle to salvage their
marriage. Now it was Jerry who needed a miracle. To
whom would the counselor turn for counsel?

Had he been hasty in his reprimand of Jenny?
Was it action or reaction in telling Jenny he couldn't
live with this betrayal? Was the pot calling the kettle
black? And she too, he discerned, in being as hasty in
volunteering to leave? For two people so much in love
it was an ignoble ending to a relationship that others
envied. Jerry knew that now. But for the betrayed,
forgiving and forgetting didn't happen in the same
breath. Forgiving was the place to start. That was the
matter Jerry would have to work on. His feelings were
the impediment now; his pride, the beast of burden.

"Till death us do part!" As for Jenny, she said she
was still in love. Whether that was spoken only by her
lips or from her heart was another haunting unknown.
Reconciliation seemed a distant hope, dashed by the
gravity of the offense. Or was it the depth of self-pity?
Jerry lay on his bed now, alone by his volition. Kenton
and Kerry were broken hearted, their parent's future
in doubt, as well as their own. They had hoped for a
joyous furlough because family was right up there with
devotion to God in their values. And now all that they
were and had always been as a family seemed lost. It
was worse than death, because it was a death in the
midst of life. Four people, once so close, were now
distant and speechless.

Jenny had checked into a hotel not far to the west
of their home. She had called the kids to leave her

number, requesting them to advise her of a convenient time to come get the remainder of her personal belongings. She wanted Jerry to be elsewhere when she did, believing he would condemn her over again, a condemnation she admittedly deserved. Kenton and Kerry had both spoken to her when she phoned, but Jerry had no such desire. Nor were the kids especially warm toward her. They spoke words; and only words that needed saying.

As for his parish ministry, that decision was still pending. He was being paid for a two month leave. The government had informed his church about that, acknowledging he had been the innocent victim of a bureaucratic error. He would take the two months and then decide his future. The options were simple; remain where he was but not remain there alone. His effectiveness as a parish pastor rested so much upon his own life's example. Especially so in his present location. People moved with frequency, a most transient town. They came to the desert southwest seeking a new location for a new beginning, especially in marriage crises. Or, he could seek a parish far away.

Starting out as a separated or divorced pastor would at least give him an honest beginning. Complicating both decisions were the lives of his kids. He wanted to be near them, but near them in a setting they desired. Though still angry at Jenny he wanted her to have access to the children she bore for them both. And he wanted his children to have a mother near by. There would be time to talk with them and to make a mutual decision. The church members were not aware of the separation of their pastor and his wife, and Jerry would keep it that way till a decision had been reached. If there were some way, any way, that he could take her back and be able to live as though the past week had never happened, Jerry prayed to God to let it come to pass. Nor did he know if his anger at her closed the door to Jenny's desire to come back.

Still troubling him was the death of Richard Green. How he despised the fact that this man's demise would not be avenged. One life meant nothing when it came to international politics — at least nothing to those in high positions of leadership. Richard Green had become a forgotten man, his name never mentioned either at the Canadian embassy or at the White House, except in Jerry's story. There had been no indication that anyone would face neither the consequences of Rick's murder, nor the death of those innocent people over the Grand Canyon chase area.

The separation, the injustice, the kids, the future, lives in tumult; all these matters were driving Jerry to the brink of mental collapse. He knew it but didn't know how to handle it. At least not yet.

A week passed, and then two. Jenny had returned to gather her belongings but did so when Jerry was out. His days still began with biking. "Make me or break me hill" was his think tank. Communication with his children was at an all time low. They too sensed his emptiness. Frequently they advised him to seek counsel, but Jerry believed the physician should heal himself. He knew that to be terrible advice.

Perhaps it was with a trip to the bank that the process of recovery began. Jerry and Jenny maintained joint accounts, one for checking and one for savings. Needless to say, the savings account was always teetering on the brink of emptiness. It was a modest amount, set aside for emergencies like major auto repairs. Jerry had received notification that the government deposited his first month's leave of absence check into his savings account, an amount totaling a meager three thousand dollars. It was an okay amount, better than his salary from church. The CIA had also sent notices via the treasury department that payment was made for all charges he incurred on his Visa card.

Feeling an obligation to evaluate his finances, Jerry asked the teller to write down the account balance from savings. She punched the information into her computer, noted the amount and wrote it down for a most valued customer. It startled him. Four thousand dollars over a half million! Jenny had obviously made the Bearer Bond deposit into their joint account. Perhaps now he might believe her professed intent. Jerry asked the teller for the date of the largest deposit.

"The day prior to his bank visit." That would confirm Jenny's claim she had the Bond at home.

"The road to hell is paved with good intentions," Jerry thought. He was still unable to put the best construction on anything his wife had said or done. He kept on trying. Jenny was not naive. Could she possibly have believed that the CIA was less than serious, and that her husband's flight to Canada was an overblown adventure? Maybe so! Not that this would excuse her treachery. Perhaps though, it could make it easier to understand why she had done it.

As Jerry thought further, one other possibility came to mind. If Jenny believed that Jerry could achieve his objective even though she ratted on him, then it was rather courageous on her part to approach Blackwell with a negotiable offer. As a matter of fact, she had obviously stretched out the talks and deliberations, because Blackwell barely had made it to Phoenix in time to pursue Jerry. Had she been so incensed at the CIA and the IRS that she took it upon herself to formulate a separate plan of retaliation? If it was true she had offered sex to Blackwell for Jerry's personal safety, this would be a sacrifice unprecedented — save for fiction.

He started from scratch. Jerry remembered well her disgust when the certified letter first arrived; her dismay in the office of the IRS. Then, she had also been lied to in a grievous way, told that her husband was on a mission beneficial to both countries, when in reality he was sent to spy. Even if all these conjectures were true it would be difficult to comprehend this gentle lady attempting such a fiendish plot on her own initiative; not impossible by any means. She was intelligent, sometimes calculating in an affirmative way. When she knew she was right she could be very single minded.

If she contrived all of this with good intent, and it went awry, then it would be difficult for her to defend what she had done on the basis of the outcome. Perhaps, just perhaps, that is why she didn't try to protest her innocence except to say she never wanted Jerry hurt or killed.

"Excuse me sir," the teller said. "Is anything wrong?" Jerry had been doing his thinking in front of the teller's station.

"Oh, no ma'am, sorry. Just got lost in thought here," Jerry replied. He left the bank, got in the car, and began to think even more intensely. Perhaps if he initiated a quiet conversation with Jenny she would be willing to confirm what he was now beginning to conjecture. And if she couldn't, then it was a clear signal that everything he had conjectured was his own last effort to justify Jenny's deed.

Quickly, Jerry drove home. He phoned the hotel where his wife was staying. A glimmer of hope was shining, like that pinhole of light when he was biking downhill through a dark tunnel; something to answer what till now was not capable of rational response. Whatever it boiled down to, Jenny hadn't touched the money. So maybe betrayal wasn't her motive. Nor greed! Maybe it was just her way of fighting back. That was understandable. Even Jerry wanted Blackwell dead at times, preferably by Jerry's own hand. Had he been too quickly a judge of another's heart?

Jenny was surprised by his call, but cheerful. "It's good to hear from you Jerry. How have you been?"

"Pretty lousy," Jerry admitted. "How have you been?"

"Pretty lousy too," she said.

"Are you okay for money?"

"Yes, there's a Wells Fargo bank branch near here. I'll be taking out just what I need to get by."

"Listen, Jenny," Jerry asked, "Would you like to go out for dinner and a drive? Just to do a little talking?"

"Sure," she said. "Where to?"

"How about if we drive up Mount Lemmon, then come back down and order a Prime Rib dinner at Paulos?"

"I'd enjoy that," she answered. "Shall I come there?"

Jerry thought about her request. He knew the kids would enjoy seeing her at home. But he couldn't find it in his heart to accede just yet. Besides, the kids had already seen her at the hotel on more than one occasion.

"No, I'll come and get you Jenny. About noon?"

"I'll be ready, Jerry. See you later." Jenny accepted Jerry's initiative, though going home would have been a most delightful offer.

Jerry hung up the phone. He was perspiring, and a bit confused at what he had done. "Kids," he hollered, "come in here a minute, will you."

Kenton and Kerry came running from the den, leaving the stereo blaring. Their father hadn't called for them in two weeks. They were happy to heed him.

"Listen, I'm going to take your mother out for the afternoon and evening. We have some things to talk about. So can you get by with dinner on your own tonight?"

"Sure," Kerry said. "I'll make some spaghetti."

"Oh yuck," Kenton answered. "Dad, I'll probably be dead when you get back." For the first time in weeks, they laughed together. After he had embraced his kids, Jerry left to get his wife. She had picked a modest place, certainly not something anyone who had a mini fortune would choose. It was characteristic of her to be modest in most everything. She shut off the TV, checked the door behind her and walked to the waiting car. High noon brought another soaring temperature, even in Fall. They would drive and talk first, then eat without bantering. By driving up the local mountain, they could leave thirty or more degrees down in the desert valley where Tucson snuggled. Their brains were scorched quite enough with emotional heat.

The first few miles were in heavier traffic. Then came milepost one, signaling they were now on the road to the top of Mount Lemmon. Jerry broke the silence.

"Have you seen the kids a few times?" he asked.

"Just a few. Mostly when you were out biking."

"That early? Did you have to drag them out of bed?"

"Not really," she answered. "Just if they'd been up late the night before." What a shame they had to take a time out from their schooling? I guess they'll get over it as soon was we decide their future."

What an astounding revelation. "As soon as we decide their future." It was true. Two kids were waiting for their life to resume based on their parents' commitment or lack thereof. Or was it deep love for Mom and Dad?

"What have you told them?" Jenny asked Jerry.

"Nothing," he said, looking at her with compassion. "All they know for now was that you and I have had some differences. And I think that's all they'll ever have to know."

"You mean you're not going to tell them what I did to you?"

"I don't think so, Jenny. I feel pretty destroyed. But it's not necessary to make them feel any bitterness toward you."

"That's a rather generous offer," she replied.

Jerry couldn't respond. Judgments and repercussions had been plentiful. There was a time for peace and a time for war. The conflict must terminate.

At milepost sixteen they pulled the car over to the parking area for Windy Point. It gave a beautiful view of the city, and of the road that snaked its way up and through the Catalina Mountains. They stood side by side, looking at their city, neither knowing whether to say anything. This place was so familiar to them. It harbored sweet memories. Whenever company came to visit them, they would take them atop the mountain to show them the desert wasn't just sand. Already, at 6600 feet, the temperature felt cooler.

A pleasant breeze wafted across Windy Point. Jerry reached out his hand to Jenny who was looking in another direction. Then he pulled it back. "Too soon," he thought. "We need to talk more first." His feelings of unconditional love for Jenny seemed to be returning. He wasn't even sure why they had left. Just being alone with her after a two week's absence lifted his spirit. The fact that she was willing to come said something of her desire to communicate with him.

"Let's talk," Jerry suggested. Jenny turned to face him.

"Who starts and what do we say?" she asked.

"Good question," Jerry replied. "I guess whoever thinks of something to say." There was an uneasy silence. Neither wanted to begin what each knew had to be said. Jerry believed the initiative belonged to him. After all, he had been judging or at best conjecturing her reasons for doing what she did.

"Tell me, Jenny, why didn't you spend some of the money? Why didn't you put it into a secret account of your own?"

"It's ours," she said with a strong emphasis on 'ours'.

"You really believe that, don't you?"

"I say things once. You should know that, Jerry." Jenny was right. She never protested her correctness. She had a habit of saying something one time and, if someone failed to believe her, that was their problem.

"What time did you actually tell Blackwell I had escaped in the balloon?"

"Two p.m.," she answered directly.

"What did he do then?"

"He promised me the money Bond would be in the bank Monday but I asked that it be given to me instead. Monday he was at the door—-just handed me this envelope and left! All he said was 'have fun'! Then he raced away. Jerry, I didn't see the helicopter he had there at the parking lot in the Canyon, so help me. I tried delaying the whole process of telling him as long as possible. I wanted you to make your connection at Phoenix. Geez, if I had known he'd get into a helicopter and make a bee line for Phoenix, I'd have drawn it out another hour." Jenny was gesturing with her hands, more so than she normally did. She desperately wanted Jerry to believe her.

"What gave you the idea of asking for money?"

"I gave me the idea," she said firmly. "After what they did to us, I thought they could at least pay us for the embarrassment."

"So your motive was revenge? Payment for what they did."

"Yes, it was revenge. No, no it wasn't! It was just a measure of justice. Nothing more, nothing less."

"And you intended to hide that from me till everything cooled down and life was back to normal?"

"That was the idea. Of course, I still didn't know how you'd react to it. But then when everything went wrong, I thought I'd die. When you came back that night and told me the whole story I wasn't about to volunteer the information."

"What were you planning to do, Jenny?"

"I was planning to wait till we could discuss if what I did was right or wrong; whether we should even keep the stuff. I even considered taking it out in cash and dumping it back on their desk - all in pennies."

"The way Judas threw back the thirty pieces of silver?"

"That really hurt Jerry."

"Oh crap," Jerry uttered, "that came out all wrong Jenny." He thought he was still testing the waters but the boundary of vilification had been crossed. He couldn't take it back, but surely wished it hadn't been spoken.

"Would you still be willing to do that?" he asked. "Take the money back?"

"I'll do anything you say," Jerry. "I happen to be in love with you in case you forgot" He hadn't, not really. He couldn't justify it, but he had put on the back burner of his mind that her love was tried and tested.

Jerry walked around the area, mulling over Jenny's account. The way she conversed and answered the questions made it plausible. She was even prepared to return the money she had taken to rat on Jerry. Jerry had judged her harshly, but now he was having second thoughts. He was glad they had taken the ride.

"Let's go down for dinner," he suggested. "Then maybe we can figure out a way of taking the money back. Are you with me?"

Jenny smiled, the first smile in a long time. "I'm with you," she said. "I've always been with you. I just hope you can someday forgive my stupidity."

"I'm trying very hard," Jerry told her. "You can't imagine how hard." He took her hand and gave it a light squeeze. Then he led her back to the car.

Both were glad they had come up the mountain. Now they had to go back down to the valley, where the toughest decision of their life was awaiting. How did the song of his teen years go? "Two sleepy lovers, by dawn's early light; but too much in love to say good night."

Jerry and Jenny would rather have stayed aloft from life, but life didn't work that way. It needed to be lived in a real world. The peaks were precious and refreshing, but the valley was where the renewal must be lived out.

Chapter 27

Jenny consented to return to the house with Jerry after the meal, but not to spend the night. Both partners wanted the kids to know they were at least on speaking terms again. The origin of their disquietude however was not revealed. Paulo's was a quiet, older restaurant, settled in a backdrop of shrubs and bushes barely visible from the street. As Jerry had earlier hinted, Prime Rib was the specialty of the house, and both Jerry and Jenny savored it.

The conversation was pleasant though somewhat subdued. Both were resigned to a lifetime of memories less than pleasant. It if was true that love conquers all, then it would have to conquer the lingering bitterness which the human heart cannot by nature accomplish. Over a glass of wine customarily used by them to toast their love, they discussed some ideas about returning the money.

"Jenny" asked Jerry, "I have an idea. Would you mind if I lay it out? The money thing that is?"

"It's your call Jerry. I did the wrong thing and if you want to help me get it right more power to you honey."

The bank would need a few days notice and both signers of the account would have to be present to withdraw such a large amount in cash. They knew they would have to sign a voucher as to why so much cash was needed, or at least to the effect this did not involve dabbling in drug trafficking. They would call the local branch of the CIA and arrange to meet the new director in a public place, just in case the agents had in mind to react to the move in any threatening fashion.

It was not the couple's intention to advise the CIA why they wanted the meeting. Only to request that it was of great importance that they do meet. Jerry would make the arrangements with the CIA and Jenny would take care of informing the bank of the pending withdrawal.

Nothing would be done ostentatiously. They would simply place the briefcase full of money in front of the regional director and advise him they had no desire to keep it. What Jenny didn't know was that Jerry had a few <u>modifications</u> to the plan prepared; to that end, some last minute details would need to be tended to come Monday morning. Jerry was glad at heart that Jenny was so willing to take this step. His belief now was that she was guilty of little more than a serious error in judgment. Yet he determined that unless she herself felt vindicated and that Jerry would not dangle this albatross over her head the rest of her life, she would not find it possible to remain married to the good Reverend. Actually, Jerry wanted Jenny to be rid of guilt. This and the injustice done them proved the motivation for the forthcoming activities.

Homecoming was a triumph of sorts. There was a free exchange of love between Jenny and the kids. Then the kids turned to their dad and told him they understood what he had said. He had called from the restaurant explaining that mom was coming home for a while, but maybe not yet for good. Jerry suggested they all sit on the patio and enjoy the summer night. It was reminiscent of the hundreds of times they had done so before, talking and sharing as good families ought.

The hour grew late, and at Jenny's suggestion, Jerry took her back to the motel. As much as he wanted to, he didn't enter the room. But he did embrace her. "Thank you, Jenny," he said. "I'll be talking with you in the morning." Then he left, wishing in his heart he could share moments of intimacy with her.

Morning would bring with it a hot day in Tucson. At 8:00 a.m. Jerry dialed the number of the Central Intelligence Agency, Tucson region.

"Hello, CIA," the receptionist answered. "May I help you?"

"Yes, please," he returned, "May I please speak with the regional agent, preferably the director."

"I'm sorry sir," she said, "Mister Blackwell isn't in at the moment. I expect him in about 11:00 a.m."

Mister Blackwell? Had he heard correctly? Jerry was quite taken aback. "Mister Blackwell," he replied. "Does this office not have a new regional director?"

"Oh no, sir," she said. "Mister Blackwell is still very much in charge."

A rush of anger surged through his body. Once more he had been told a lie. Carl Blackwell never did and never would lose his position. That infuriated Jerry. "Maybe it's just taking a little longer," he tried to convince himself.

"Is there a message for Mister Blackwell?" the receptionist asked.

"Yes, there is," Jerry affirmed. "Do you have a pen handy?"

"Go ahead, sir."

"Please tell him that Reverend Jerry Grant called. I need to meet him the day after tomorrow in front of the Federal Building. Right on the front steps," he informed her.

"I'll give him the message, Reverend Grant. But I'm not sure if he'll be available."

"Oh, yes he will," Jerry affirmed. "Tell him it's concerning a whole bunch of money and Jerry Grant."

"Would you explain further?" the girl asked.

"No, that's it. The day after tomorrow at 9 a.m. If he's interested, he'll be there. Good day."

Jerry hung up the phone. Light bulbs were flashing in his head. He picked up the telephone and quickly dialed Jenny's motel.

"Jenny, this is Jerry."

"What's the matter, Jerry? You sound hyper!"

"Can I come and get you Jenny. I want to talk to you about something, and I want to go to the bank with you as well."

"What's happening?"

"I can't tell you on the phone. I think it still might be bugged."

"Okay, when will you be here?"

"Twenty minutes. We'll have breakfast."

Jenny consented and Jerry was quickly on his way. He picked her up, took her to a local diner, and ordered a light breakfast.

"Jenny, the reason I needed to see you is that Carl Blackwell's still in town — I mean as CIA director."

"What?" Jenny exclaimed.

"It's true. I just talked to his receptionist. I told her to let him know we were going to meet him the day after tomorrow at 9:00 a.m. in front of his very own Federal building."

"Jerry, what for? You want to see Blackwell face to face. I thought you wished the little creep was dead."

"Ah, but my dear," Jerry smiled, "I have prepared for him a fate worse than death. Are you in?"

Jenny paused. Jerry awaited a response, trusting it would be a positive one. Blackwell had hinted he had an encounter with Jenny. Jenny had said no but declined to defend herself by saying more. "I like the look in your eyes," she noted.

"Whatever you're planning, I'll go along with it."

They waited for the opening hour and proceeded to the bank. After a brief interview with the manager of the branch they were promised the money in cash, placed in a briefcase, by noon the following day. The only catch was that they were obliged to sign a form to ascertain that this money was not for illegal usage — like drugs, etc. Jerry thanked the manager, and left with his wife.

"Do you want to come home tonight?" he asked Jenny.

"Yes," she said in an urgent tone. "You have no idea how badly."

"Let's go get your things. It's time we started to get to know one another again."

They went to the motel, packed up, and returned home. Kenton and Kerry were preparing reports for local churches and community organizations about their own humanitarian work results—touching reports. They also sought church and community financial aid. When they got home they would be told that mom and dad were back together on a day by day basis. Not a trial marriage, by any means. But that they had reconciled enough to begin trusting each other once again. They would spend the night together, and, if all went well, they would spend another day together as well as the remainder of their lives. Their love was not to be radically extinguished.

The metal from which kids are molded is very tough indeed. Kenton and Kerry heard their parents out and concurred with their arrangement. "I'm just glad Mom and you are together, even on a day by day basis," Kenton confessed. Kerry reiterated the sentiment.

The Grants would tell their children nothing of the money however. They were facing a difficult task in taking that money back. Jenny would hand it over in a display of regret for what she had done — feigned of course. She would do so with utter contempt for Carl Blackwell. Jerry would be there holding her hand. But the final wording would come from Jerry.

Together they walked slowly to the bedroom. She looked around, shut the door, and sat on the bed. "Are we sleeping together tonight?" she asked, "or shall I sleep on the cot?"

Jerry looked at her, passionately desiring her. Yet he was not about to be intimate for his own self indulgence. Everything had to be settled.

"Let's wait till after the money's returned," he suggested. "I'll pull out the cot, you take the bed, and we'll get some rest. I have some serious errands to run tomorrow, so I'll be up and out early. Then I'll pick you up before noon and we'll go get the money."

"What kind of errands?" Jenny asked.

"Trust me," he said. "I can't tell you."

Jenny looked bewildered, then assured Jerry, "I do trust you, Jerry. Do what needs doing."

The two sweethearts lay on separate beds. Jerry was awake and Jenny was awake. Neither could sleep, though it was late evening now. They dozed and soon awoke to deepest nightfall. Each was aware of the other's thoughts.

"What's the matter, Jerry? You're wrestling around like a bearcat."

"Just can't get to sleep."

"Me neither," she said. "Want a cold drink?"

"Sure. Allow me."

Jerry arose and felt his way into the kitchen. He had a habit of leaving the lights off so he wouldn't disturb anyone. Most of the time he managed to stub his toes. A moment later he was back, a diet coke for Jenny and a real coke for himself. He couldn't stand the diet stuff. Jerry complained it always gave him a sore stomach.

But now something changed! The full moon was framed by the window, encircling Jenny in a virtual golden halo. She looked so beautiful, so properly seductive to her husband. Jerry sat his glass down beside his cot and walked toward Jenny.

"What do you feel for me?" he asked her.

"Love," she said. "Compassion for all you've been through."

"Were you sincere when you told me it was all for us; that it was an impulse for retaliation?"

"I said it once, didn't I," she smiled. Jerry knew she was telling the truth. There wasn't any doubt; none at all!

"I love you Jenny Grant," he said. "I love you so very much."

"And I love you."

"How would you like to be ravaged by a raving sex maniac?" he asked.

"Is there one around somewhere?" she countered.

"You can count on it," he replied.

"I don't think I'd scream for help," she whispered.

Jerry walked to her bedside and Jenny rose to meet him. They embraced and held each other tightly. Her nipples stood firmly, the nightgown unable to obscure the beauty. Slowly he removed her gown, gently slipping it around and off her shoulders. Her graceful body basked more fully in the lunar glow. Lying beside her on the bed, he soothed her with his gentle touch. His lips met hers. Then, caressing her breasts and thighs, he kissed her once more with all the passion of a young lover. Jenny reciprocated. Slowly, she pulled Jerry on top of herself and the two lovers came together, their bodies joined together like the stars in the sky. It was a long, enduring sexual expression of what they truly felt for each other.

"Let's never be apart again," Jenny moaned. "Never again."

"I can handle that," Jerry replied. "Thank you for the wonderful time we are about to experience," he said.

"Thank you," Jenny answered. "I won't exactly find it painful."

Her hands reached down and rubbed Jerry all over. Passion overtook them as they rolled and moaned; then they shared their bodies. How long it had been! It didn't take long. Together they met their needs, each erupting with their personal style of pleasure. Nothing was held back. Such was the normal passion they had developed and always shared most unabashedly.

The sweethearts embraced one more time, and, holding each other closely, fell peacefully asleep.

Chapter 28

Before 7:00 a.m. Jerry was up and out. Jenny didn't ask where he was going. She didn't feel the need to know. Before noon he returned and the two went to the bank to pick up the cash. The briefcase wasn't opened. It was an amazingly light load for all that money.

Jenny asked, "Is that all the money? How's it feel carrying around a half million" she smiled?

"Try it." He handed her the briefcase.

"Oh, Jerry, she laughed. "You take it. I feel silly carrying all that money."

"Who knows it's money" Jerry asked?

"Well just hang on to it," she admonished him. "What's the difference if I were to lose it?" Jerry asked.

"None, except your plan wouldn't work then."

"What do you know about my plan?" Jerry asked. "Come on hon, what do you know?"

"Just a hunch," she said. "I'll tell you tomorrow if I was right."

"Ah, tell me now," Jerry teased."

"What's on the agenda for today?" she asked.

"Waiting for tomorrow."

It turned out that what Jerry said in jest happened in practice. The day moved slowly as if tomorrow offered a reward and somebody was trying to stop time from moving on. They went for a swim in a neighbor's pool, sunbathed a brief time, and swam some more. Then they returned home, made love again and Jenny prepared lasagna. It was Jerry's favorite. Dinner was sumptuous and the time came for a final review of tomorrow's agenda.

"Ride at 6:00?" Jerry asked. "Sure," Jenny perked up. "It's been a while. May as well start getting back in shape."

"We'll leave here about 8:30," Jerry reviewed. "That should put us downtown with a few minutes to spare. Then we walk to the Federal building, briefcase and all, and hope Blackwell shows up."

"I'm kind of hoping he doesn't," Jenny confessed. "I'm not up to seeing that man. I just might kill him?"

"I have a feeling it'll be the last time," he told her.

"Jerry, you don't plan to ….?"

"No, no. I don't plan to eliminate him. Or punch him out. But I do have something in mind I think you'll enjoy; even more than if we kept the money."

At 6:00 a.m. the routine began: the bike path, then the loop, then the ride home. Jerry and Jenny cooled off and prepared for their surreptitious meeting with Carl Blackwell. It still bothered Jerry very deeply that this man was on the loose, let alone regional director in Tucson. But just perhaps justice would be done this day.

The hour came, and the Grants drove downtown. Jerry found his familiar parking space, two blocks from the federal building. It was the same building of course, where they had first become involved in the events that changed their lives. The clerical error was about to be erased. Arriving at the steps of the federal building they sat down on a bench and awaited the arrival of Blackwell. At nine sharp he came out the door, a worried look on his face. Then he tried to goad them with his now patented evil grin.

"Well, well," he smirked. "Look who we have here. The vindicated preacher. As you see, Reverend, I still have my job."

Jerry smiled back, big time, then gave Blackwell the silent treatment. It made Carl look nervous. "Okay already, what do you people want? Thought we saw the last of you in Washington"?

"We have something to give you," Jerry said.

Jenny reached over, extending the briefcase toward Blackwell.

"Whatcha got there sweetheart?" he asked.

"Just a little gift," she said.

"Wait a minute," Jerry interrupted. "You're not going to give the money back yet, are you, Jenny?"

Jenny looked stunned.

"Money, "Blackwell said, "What money?"

"A half million dollars," Jerry shouted. Then he said it louder for onlookers to hear. "Five hundred thousand bucks." Jenny, give Mister Blackwell the money he offered you to tell him where I had gone so he could find me and murder me."

She offered him the briefcase, but he was reluctant to take it. Jerry grabbed the case from Jenny, then, taking Blackwell's hand, he wrapped it around the handle of the case.

"You can come out now with the cameras rolling," Jerry hollered loudly. "Smile Carl, you're on candid camera. Network coverage."

What Jerry had done was take the disks with his entire story, and the ending to which it had come, then passed them on to every local television station and newspaper reporter. He had readied three dozen diskettes in copy.

Blackwell had the case firmly in hand and a stunning look on his face. A battery of reporters with video cameras moved in.

"All the local TV stations are here Jenny. They have the whole conversation and transaction on tape. I think Mister Blackwell will have a hard time explaining this one."

"Any comment?" a newsman asked Jerry shoving a mike in his face.

"Just one," he said. I am Reverend Jerry Grant. You've all read about me in the papers in the last couple months. My wife and I are returning a pile of money to Mister Carl Blackwell of the C.I.A. here. It had been offered to my wife as a bribe to frame me for those things you read about! It belongs to the treasury department, but this government agent or gentleman had no intention of returning it to the proper department at all. Your tax money folks!" Now the cameras and microphones moved in even more closely.

"And how did you come to get it in the first place," he was asked. "Carl Blackwell tried to bribe my wife" he began. The cameras were rolling full steam ahead. "But she decided she'd steer him in the wrong direction and then return the money to him. 'Course, <u>he</u> never intended to return it to the treasury. You'll find half the money here in his briefcase and all the rest of the money in the Wells Fargo Bank right across the street. The account number is 2377909 — in the name of Personal Money Market account of Carl Blackwell."

"He's lying," Blackwell protested. "He's lying, that pious fool! Liar, liar, liar" he kept bellowing like a guilty child caught with his hand in the cookie jar.

"No lie, Blackwell. No lie at all," Jerry shouted for all to hear. "Try the clerical error routine. Maybe you can get off with that excuse. Good-bye, Mister Blackwell. After thirty years or so, well, it'll be life as usual."

The police had gathered because of the confusion. They heard Jerry's last statement. An officer snatched at the brown briefcase and Carl Blackwell tried instinctively to pull back. The policeman prevailed, took the case and looked inside.

"Holy hell," he bellowed, "look at all the money." Quickly they had the cuffs on Blackwell and were leading him to a waiting car. The officer replied, "This kind of money usually means drug involvement."

"You framed me, you bast...." A policeman put his hand over Blackwell's mouth. "Get in the car and shut up," he ordered him. "You can say your piece in interrogation!"

The Miranda routine began, "You have the right to remain silent," the officer began.

Jerry couldn't resist the urge: :Blackwell, maybe this is a clerical error?"

Jerry and Jenny looked at each other with sweet delight. Blackwell was protesting and cursing, but nothing could be heard because of the press of reporters.

"Sir, could you tell us what this is all about?"

"No further comment, Jerry replied. "I'm sure you'll find the CIA most helpful in this matter. Maybe even the IRS. The Tucson Citizen and Arizona Daily Star have the whole story. It'll be in tomorrow's editions. Oh by the way, here's a copy of a floppy disk with a little story on it. The papers have the same copies." Jerry began tossing out like Frisbees the exact copies of the floppy disks to those who presented credentials as reporters.

He turned over the primary diskette they had made as contingency for their safety to the police department's head man at the scene. The police department headquarters for Tucson was one block to the south. Now it would be used for meting out justice.

———————————

Jerry and Jenny sauntered away, sharing a happy glance with each other. "I guess there is a little bit of justice in the world," Jerry said. Then he thought about Rick and the innocent people in the airplanes and the enduring conflict between himself and Jenny and how he could now explain virtually everything to Kenton and Kerry. They would be so proud of their parents!

"You set him up, Jerry. I told you I had a hunch, and I was right. You set him up. I wasn't sure how you'd do it, but I knew it would be a big scene."

"Of course I set him up. He might even get off, but I guarantee you the whole business is going to shake up the C.I.A. What I wanted is a lot of red faces. I think you'll find I'm going to get my wish. We're cleared of anything and everything Jenny. It's all over."

"Is it right, Jerry? Is it really right?"

"Is it right that we got blackmailed? Is it right that Rick got killed? It's a matter of making somebody take the responsibility, Jenny. I grant you, the story I gave the paper is slightly slanted. In your favor, I might add. It's all the justice we're going to get for what happened. But I can live with it and that counts for a whole lot. Blackwell is in trouble, at least for now. So is the CIA. By God and His justice the whole party of perverts that planned this terrifying episode in our lives is going to be in such massive confusion. Nobody will dare touch us and I'll bet anything we'll never have an audit again."

"If we can handle living here the rest of our lives."

"If you can live with it, so can I," Jenny affirmed. "Now what?"

"Our future," Jerry said, "is what we decide it's going to be. I have a feeling it can be here where we enjoy life."

"If you say so, Jerry."

"I say so!"

"I'm glad you took me back, she said joyfully.

"I never let you go Jenny." Jerry cried.

"You're a tricky devil," Jenny said as they walked toward the car. "So that's what all your secret errands were about yesterday. You set up a bank account in Blackwell's name and forged his signature; you took the time to make a deposit of half the money we had withdrawn; and then you went and made more copies of the escapade! Then you called the whole slew of media. Quite a day! What did you tell them?"

"I told them there'd be something very worthwhile to check out by the federal building this morning. I gave them my name and that lit a fuse. Then I saw the editor of the Citizen and Star, gave them my story, somewhat edited of course, and asked if they would print it. They said they would if they saw Blackwell take the briefcase and if the bank verified there was an account in his name."

"Jerry, you're a devil. Any other surprises for me?"

"Oh indeed," Jerry nodded. "But dear, not downtown in public."

The End

Afterword

Some years ago, a project was in the working which dealt with Water and Power resources for three nations: Canada, the United States and Mexico. It was known as NAWAPA — North American Water And Power Alliance. Its absence from the International News sources remains a mystery. The seeming dissolution of NAWAPA, together with the diminishing aquifer of the American Southwest, prompted the writing of "Clerical Error" simply as *shock value* to bring to the surface a terrifying truth: little drinkable water remains, especially in Southern Arizona.

The early to mid 1980's saw the building of an expensive, above ground Aqueduct known as the Central Arizona Project. It runs across hundreds of miles along Arizona's hot, sandy surface, subject to the evaporating rays of the blazing sun. Therefore, much of this water is lost en route. When the first water from this Colorado River source became available in the Tucson area, it needed high resolutions of chemicals, remaining difficult to drink due to the taste. Citizens were initially advised that, while it was safe to drink this water, a caution was issued that fish would not thrive within this same water. Nor, were we advised, would it be wise to use this water alone for swimming pools. At present, and by Voter initiative in Southern Arizona, it is now being pumped into the ever depleting aquifer and, in time, filters to the surface as naturally cleansed water.

It still remains necessary to treat this water chemically. Many citizens are installing their own water filters, or purchasing water by delivery or at drive up Water Stations. Apparently, the aqueduct water, by virtue of the natural filtration up through the sandy desert soil, as well as chemical treatment, has not satisfied much of the population.

The above fictional novel was borne not only of imagination. It is one scenario of what a desperate nation may be forced to do in fulfilling her obligation toward the American citizenry, unless the authorities begin acting responsibly, in consort with Canada, to come to an amicable agreement for the well being of all North Americans. It is not known whether Canadian officials are now willing, or are in the process, of cooperating with the United States, about this life or death issue. As a citizen of both countries, yours truly hopes and prays there is sensitive concern. This dual citizen feels it is incumbent upon the country of his birthright, Canada, to offer to its foremost trading partner and longtime peaceful neighboring nation, that substance which is more precious and plenteous in Canada than any other commodity since water is the essence of life.

Consider, if you will, these excerpts, copied from the public domain of the Arizona Daily Star Internet Website. This is copied from the public domain of the Arizona Daily Star Newspaper Website.

AZ DAILY STAR—APRIL 12/04

By Scott Sonner , THE ASSOCIATED PRESS

RENO, Nev. - From the brittle hillsides of Southern California to the drying fields of Idaho, from Montana to New Mexico, a relentless drought is worsening across most of the West, water supplies are dwindling, and the threat of wildfires is rising. "Most of the West is headed into six years of drought, and some areas are looking at seven years of drought," said Rick Ochoa, weather program manager at the National Interagency Fire Center in Boise, Idaho. Arizona is facing its worst drought on record. Two enormous reservoirs on the Colorado River are only half full, and some farmers in southern Idaho might not get any irrigation water this summer.................

The National Interagency Fire Center identified three areas with the greatest fire risks - Southern California; the Four Corners region of Arizona,

New Mexico, Colorado and southern Utah; and the Intermountain region east of the Cascade Mountains through Idaho and into western Montana. Parts of Nevada, Southern California and Arizona are dependent on the Colorado River and its two largest reservoirs, Lake Mead and Lake Powell, which together can hold about 50 million acre-feet. This year, however, Mead and Powell are only about half full…………….. "Pray for rain," Larsen said. "That's about all we can do."

Brian R. Dill, Pastor Emeritus
Proud Citizen of Canada and the United States of America

About the Author

Brian Dill, dual citizen of Canada and the U.S., achieved a Masters Degree in Theology. He served as Parish Pastor in both countries. The quality of his sermons prompted Concordia Publishing House to recruit him for publication of sermon resources for clergy, and booklets for teens. His poem, in the International Poetry Book, testifies to his versatility. Currently, he is writing an autobiography about his battle with pain. Personal research and knowledge about water issues in both nations adds to his credentials for "Clerical Error." This fact-based fiction provides clever concepts in weaving highly unusual escape and chase scenes among the many thrills in the International Suspense Genre. Each page summons another, posing some terrifying possibilities.